T0246074

A
PROMISE
TO
DIE FOR

A PROMISE TO DIE FOR

STEPHEN HOLGATE

CamCat Books

CamCat Publishing, LLC
Fort Collins, Colorado 80524
camcatpublishing.com

Hardcover ISBN 9780744311693
Paperback ISBN 9780744311709
eBook ISBN 9780744311716
Audiobook ISBN 9780744311730

Library of Congress Control Number: 2024938793

Book and cover design by Maryann Appel
Interior artwork by Debela

5   3   1   2   4

For Felicia,

who has always believed in me

more than I have.

CHAPTER ONE

A SUMMONS

I HADN'T REALIZED I'd fallen asleep until the cab driver said, "We've arrived, sir."

Struggling with the cobwebs clouding my mind after the all-night flight from Portland, I blinked vacantly at the quiet residential street, bleak and drained of color in the early morning light, trying to recall where I was and what I was doing here, feeling that I had come so far so fast that I'd left some important part of myself behind and needed to wait for it to catch up.

Yes, Arlington, Virginia. Curt Hansen was dying. And he said he needed to see me.

His call had caught me raking leaves at the back end of my property outside Eugene, Oregon. At first I didn't recognize the thin and weary voice.

Cancer, he told me, leaving him no more than a few weeks.

"Curt, I'm sorry."

He grunted to deflect the inadequacy of my words.

"Sam, I need to ask a favor."

"Of course, Curt, anything."

"It's not something I can explain over the phone. I know it's asking a lot, but could you come out and see me?"

There are some requests you can't turn down.

"I can catch a flight to DC out of Portland. When do you need me?"

"How soon can you come?"

Taken aback by his urgency, I said, "What's today, Friday . . .?"

Curt chuckled faintly. "It's funny how we lose track of the days when we retire."

"I can catch a red-eye tomorrow night, be there Sunday morning."

"There's something I've left too late, Sam. Something important."

"I'll book the flight today and can—"

"Sam, you don't understand what I'm asking of you. You'll need to bring your passport. You may be gone for a while."

———◦◦◦◦◦— —◦◦◦◦◦———

Despite all my years in the foreign service, with its eight-, ten-, twelve-hour flights, I've never learned to sleep on a plane. I'm too tall for the seats, and at fifty-three I don't curl up as well as I used to. So, while my fellow passengers dozed in the darkened cabin, I had a lot of time to think about my friendship with Curt Hansen, and to wonder what it was he had left too late—and why it might require me to travel overseas.

We had served together for three years in Pakistan, not a long time in the course of a normal life, but life in an embassy doesn't follow a normal course. Deep friendships are forged with a speed and intensity unknown to those who don't live and work in a small, close community far from home.

I'd served in Islamabad as the embassy's public affairs officer, in charge of press relations and cultural programs. Curt headed up the Admin section.

With the many small grants my office awarded to universities, and the needed repairs to our aging library, we had worked together often, adapting to each other's contrasting natures.

Within the service I had a reputation as a straight arrow, something I found both flattering and a little embarrassing, as if it spoke less to virtue than to a failure of imagination, a certain naiveté. Curt was what a scientist might call a free radical, doing whatever he thought needed doing and however he wanted to do it.

The truth was I envied guys like Curt, who treated the rules as mere suggestions drafted by a bunch of constipated desk jockeys back in Washington. While the rest of us toed lines as straight as those on our pin-striped suits, Curt approached his work like a pirate approaching a wallowing merchant ship. He would cut a corner here, ignore a reg there, bend rules that hindered his intent. The rest of us gasped. We tsked. We loved it.

In fact we were all complicit in his buccaneering ways. If we agreed not to look too closely, Curt would get us larger budgets, better housing, and cheaper contracts than we deserved. "All for the greater good," he'd say with a wolfish smile.

Still, while I took a guilty pleasure in watching Curt's unorthodox approach, and happily benefited from his rules-be-damned style, his practices made me uneasy, and I kept him at a little bit of a distance.

We served in Islamabad at a dangerous time. The war next door in Afghanistan stirred fierce psychic winds among the Pakistanis, engendering deep but conflicting emotions of horror, religious pride, and a fear of—or yearning for—instability.

With security tight and knowing that Washington might any day issue orders to evacuate family members, I received a call from a man representing, he said, a small delegation visiting from Peshawar that wanted to open an American library and study center in their city.

Peshawar lies on Pakistan's border with Afghanistan at the edge of the Hindu Kush, which means "Killer of Hindus." It's a tough neighborhood. The region had for centuries defied whatever central government might lay claim to it. I'd visited the city a couple of times, briefly and nervously. An air of the Wild West hung over the place. Soldiers and tribesmen walked its dusty streets, assault rifles slung over their shoulders as casually as an American might carry a laptop to work—and more necessary to their professions. An office worker isn't going to die for lack of a laptop.

Wanting to set up an American center in the middle of this scene was an odd notion, but if it worked out, I'd earn professional favor for establishing an outpost of American influence in a sensitive region. So I told my caller to stop by my office on Monday morning.

He said that, unfortunately, his group would only be in Islamabad for two days, and their schedule was already crowded. He asked if I could meet them at our library on Sunday afternoon.

The American Library in Islamabad was located nearly a mile from my office in the main part of the embassy. To encourage walk-ins, the library kept security loose, posting only two unarmed local guards, a mockery of the main embassy's Fort Knox-style security with Marines, soaring concrete walls, and armed checkpoints. The embassy security officer hated our light hand, but with the ambassador on our side he could only mutter and let us have our way. On a Sunday afternoon the place would be deserted, even our rudimentary security reduced to a single guard.

Thinking we'd be discussing budget, staffing, and rental of a building in Peshawar, I asked Curt to join me.

"On a Sunday afternoon? This is too weird, Sam. You're sure you want to do this?"

When I told him it was important, he laughed and said, "Okay, I'll be there."

———◦◦◦◦◦—— ——◦◦◦◦◦———

Curt and I met at the library a few minutes early. I unlocked the door, turned on some lights and waited for our visitors to arrive. We didn't have to wait long.

We heard the chanting first. I couldn't make out the words, but it didn't sound friendly. Moments later they appeared on the street in front of the building, not four men as promised, but a couple hundred, young and angry, their rage leavened only by their delight in suckering two American diplomats into a trap.

This didn't seem like the moment to remind Curt that you're more likely to die in the foreign service than in the military.

For a moment we felt more abashed at our foolishness than actually frightened, though the balance would quickly shift.

Our security guard had already made like a shooting star and disappeared over the horizon. I didn't blame him. The few dollars we paid him wasn't enough to get killed protecting a couple of infidels from an angry mob.

I rushed to the front door just in time to bolt it shut and keep the mob from simply walking in and killing us. By the time we thought to run out the back door, they had curled around the building, blocking any attempt to flee.

Momentarily checked by the locked doors, some of them began to throw rocks at the reinforced windows. A few of the biggest men put their shoulders to the heavy security door, trying to bash it in. Someone threw a Molotov cocktail at Curt's car and it quickly went up in flames. A moment later mine joined it, the two cars putting out billows of black smoke. Another of the homemade bombs shattered against a window in a starburst of yellow and blue.

I grabbed a phone and tried to call the Marine at Post One, the main entrance to the embassy, to tell him we were under attack, but the line had gone dead. Curt and I both tried our cell phones, but reception at the center, always iffy, failed.

With no way to get the embassy's attention we could do little but watch our attackers through the spiderweb cracks appearing in the windows and wonder how long it would take them to break in.

Curt said, "I'll bet they're not even from Peshawar," a remark that doesn't sound so funny now, but actually got a laugh out of me at the time.

The young men who made up the mob had probably thought they would get in easily. A few rocks at the windows and presto. Frustrated that their assault might take some unexpected effort, they tossed a couple of homemade fire bombs onto the roof. We soon heard the crackle of a spreading fire over our heads. A few wisps of smoke seeped downward, carrying the smell of gasoline and burning tar.

As we began to cough from the smoke, I recalled that the building had been issued one of the embassy's two-way radios, kept in the head librarian's office. Working to control my panic, I turned it on and tried again to tell the Marine at Post One that we had an angry mob breaking in, the place was on fire, and we needed help, fast. But the fire on the roof must have taken down the antenna and I got nothing but static.

Over the shouting of the mob we heard more stones crash against the windows, saw the cracks growing deeper. The men attacking the front door had scavenged a wooden beam from a construction site across the street and were using it as a battering ram, the front door shaking in its frame with every blow. Behind us, we could hear others trying to break through the back door.

Though he might have justifiably lit into me for dragging him into this ambush, Curt took it in with as little complaint as Captain Kidd resigning himself to a final downturn in the play of odds. His remarkable calm helped steady my own nerves. I don't think I could have held myself together without him.

Perhaps twenty minutes had gone by since the mob appeared. We could feel the heat from the fire on the roof, and the smoke curling through the room burned our lungs. Our phone calls and radio message had failed to get through. We could expect no rescue.

Without a word, we solemnly shook hands, a gesture that would raise a cynical hoot if you put it in a movie but affirmed a solidarity and, yes, a sense of honor we could not have put into words. It calmed us both as we prepared to die. I thought of my wife, Janet, and our son, Tom, and how hard this would be on them.

We took the first spatter of gunfire as an escalation of the attack, the mob resorting to Kalashnikovs to finish breaking through the windows. Instinctively, we dropped to the floor.

The gunshots continued. The cries of the mob rose to a climactic pitch. I pressed my face against the carpet, tried to control my ragged breath and racing heart.

The unexpected tramping of many feet brought our heads up, both of us thinking the door had given in and we had only moments to live.

As we raised our eyes, though, the howling voices outside were descending into knots of confused shouting and cries of alarm. The popping of gunfire grew closer. Through the cracks in the windows, the forms of our attackers fractured into rapidly shifting shards of color and then vanished, replaced seconds later by slowly moving blocks of khaki.

It was the Molotov cocktails that had saved us. The Marine at Post One saw the black smoke rising into the sky, put that together with the puzzling attempts to contact him, and called for help. His intuition saved our lives. And from that day on I've never said a bad word about the Pakistani army, which quickly responded to the Marine's call and drove the mob away, saving our unworthy behinds.

As the burning roof began to cave in, Curt and I scrambled to our feet, unlocked the door, and tumbled outside, hardly able to grasp the fact that we were still alive.

Over the next few days Curt and I received an outpouring of affection and thankfulness from the embassy community at our escape. People were kind enough to ignore the fact that my folly in agreeing to walk into a trap was the only reason we'd needed to escape.

Everyone wanted to hear our description of the attack and of our rescue, and we both developed narratives rich with hair-raising detail and self-deprecating humor.

Yet, when we were around each other—and with so many administrative matters to take care of in the wake of the library's destruction, we spent a lot of time together after the attack—we never spoke of it. Perhaps we had no need. More likely, we knew that, despite the tales we shared with others, there was no way to put into words what had happened to us. Only we knew.

A few weeks later we both got medals for valor from the Department. Though awarded with no apparent irony, I felt embarrassed, as the whole mess had been due to my poor judgment. On the other hand, I thought Curt's medal well-deserved. He had sensed the risk and agreed to come anyway.

———◦◦◦◦◦◦— —◦◦◦◦◦◦———

Whatever the trauma of our shared experience, its terrors didn't so much change us as make us more deeply who we had been before. Curt, feeling indestructible now, became even less bound by regulations clearly meant for lesser beings, while I turned perhaps more cautious and rule-bound—in short, an even bigger bore. Curt and his wife, Taylor, started spending almost every weekend with Janet and me, sometimes at their house, sometimes at ours. Our wives understood we were still working through what had happened that day.

Though a good sport about all of it, Janet didn't much care for Curt. "He's a charming man," she said. "Women know not to trust charming men."

In fact, Curt already had one divorce behind him, and we hoped, a little forlornly, that our own stability might help keep him and Taylor together, or at least reduce their constant bickering.

By contrast, ours was an extraordinarily happy marriage. Though Janet never loved foreign service life, we loved each other, and that love grew deeper every year. We dreamed often of retirement, of going home to Oregon and leading a quiet life, free of the stresses, dangers, and constant uprootings of the foreign service.

Diplomatic careers often work out as a long exercise in irony. The fallout from our misadventure at the library in Islamabad propelled me to quick advancement within the service, while Curt did little but tread water. Fairness would have demanded the opposite. After a tour as head of public affairs in Cairo, I landed the plum post of Deputy Chief of Mission in Tunis, the number-two position in the embassy.

Despite the imbalance of our professional rewards, the bond we'd forged with Curt and Taylor remained strong even after we'd moved on to new posts, sustained by frequent emails and occasional phone calls.

Other, more treasured, bonds proved far too fragile. Four years after we'd left Islamabad, while we were posted to Tunis, Janet was killed in a traffic accident. To lose her was like losing my own life.

Our son, Tom, was riding with her. He escaped serious injury but fell into a deep depression that took months to overcome—if one can ever overcome something like that.

An embassy community is an extraordinarily close one, and my colleagues, American and Tunisian, shared our grief. Curt heard about Janet's death and called from Riyadh, offering to come out on the next flight if he could be of any help. I was deeply touched but told him I was heading out the next day, back to Oregon and a cemetery outside Salem, Janet's hometown.

After the funeral, Tom and I returned to Tunis. While Tom finished high school, I went through the motions of work, but living in the place we'd shared with Janet made me feel like the last ghost in a haunted house.

I was only fifty, but my twenty-five years of service allowed me to take retirement. I bought a couple of acres outside a small town less than thirty minutes from Eugene and put Tom into the University of Oregon. My three years back home had healed the worst of the wounds. I'd made some friends, got recruited for the local library board, and become active in environmental issues. The foreign service gradually became a memory, something I used to do.

Then Curt's call came, and I was once again on a plane heading toward Washington.

———

While the taxi idled outside Curt's place, I paid the cabbie, giving him, in my muddled state, a huge tip.

"Shall I wait?" he asked hopefully, no doubt figuring he might get the chance to drive me somewhere else before I came to my senses.

"Yeah. But I may be a while."

He beamed with pleasure. "That's not a problem, sir."

Leaving my suitcase in the car, I made my way up the walk and rang the bell. A young woman in nurse's scrubs answered the door.

"Sam Hough," I told her. "I'm here to see Curt."

"Come in," she said. "He's been awake for hours, waiting for you."

CHAPTER TWO

"AN ADDRESS IS ALL I NEED"

T HE CURTAINS WERE still drawn, lending Curt's sickroom a gloom only slightly eased by a lamp that shared a nightstand with pill bottles, a glass of water and other odds and ends, its disorder somehow a measure of his illness.

Curt lay in a hospital bed, the head cranked so he could sit up. His sandy hair had thinned, and his face, always heavily lined, looked older than his years. He smiled as I came in.

"Sam, it's good of you to come."

Given the long flight and my lack of sleep, I felt pretty wan. Curt joked that I looked worse than he did. In fact, the glow from the light gave his features a deceptive rosiness. I wanted to tell him that cancer seemed to agree with him.

He waved me into a chair at his bedside.

We spoke awkwardly at first, skipping over the present, avoiding the future, and speaking only of the past, of our days in Islamabad and people we'd known there, rehashing stories of life overseas. I reminded him of how he had once managed to hide from visiting inspectors a small slush fund used for irregular purchases.

Curt smiled. "You disapproved of that particular shenanigan, as I recall."

I had to chuckle at the vision of my buttondown self. "The truth is I always envied your ability to ignore the rules. You were like one of those great chefs who don't bother with recipes anymore."

"Maybe the envy went both ways. You played it straight and excelled. I couldn't have done that. The Department favors guys like you. You'd have made ambassador in a few years."

I shrugged off the compliment. "I couldn't stay after Janet . . ."

"Yeah."

He winced as he shifted position, waving me back into my seat when I rose to help him. When he'd settled back into his pillows, he took a deep breath and said, "I've been a rogue, Sam. Bigger than you realize. I've got a lot of regrets."

Knowing I had to be thinking of his failed marriages, he shook his head. "No. It's not what you suppose—not directly anyway." He paused, putting his thoughts together. "I have to admit I grew bitter after Islamabad. Despite everything I did, I wasn't moving up the ladder. The front office always loved the way I got things done. But after I'd delivered what they wanted, the ambassadors felt they had to spread a bunch of 'tsk-tsks' across my yearly review."

I tried to make light of it. "I guess I was always pretty orthodox. Some people just called me naive."

"No. You were always wiser than me. I wasn't wise. Maybe that's why my career didn't go as well. And maybe that's why I couldn't stay married. I mean, Taylor put up with Islamabad mainly because of you and Janet. When we got to Morocco a few years later, she hated the place. Pretty soon she decided she didn't much care for me either. She went back to the States and filed for divorce." He tried to make like it was no big deal, but the pain in his face didn't come entirely from the cancer. "Rabat was a bad time for me. My career was going nowhere, and after Taylor left, I went home to an empty house every night. I'm not much good at staying married, but I'm no good at living alone either.

"I met a young woman." He cast a tentative smile, looking for my reaction. "My section held a reception to thank some of the local contractors we worked with. One of the Moroccans, Miloud Benaboud, owned a transport company we used now and then. He brought his daughter with him. Chantal."

It seemed to comfort him simply to say her name.

"She was smart, charming, attractive. I fell in love." Curt made a wry smile. "I still can't imagine what she saw in me. We began to spend a lot of time together. She didn't tell her father. Our relationship became . . . intimate. I asked her to marry me. She told me no, I didn't really mean it. Maybe she was right. Or maybe I should have insisted, and I failed some test when I didn't. Our relationship cooled after that. By that time my posting to Morocco was nearly over. I was heading to Paris as the number three in the Admin section there."

He fell silent.

If this was the whole story, I didn't get it. I said, "And that was the end of it between you two?"

Curt's face twisted in annoyance. "Of course not," he snapped at me. He closed his eyes and gave a little shake of his head. "Sorry, Sam. I . . . sorry. No, that wasn't the end of it. Before I left Rabat, Chantal asked to see me one more time. A way of closing out the books, I figured. We met at a favorite café, overlooking the river. It was strange. Though she was the one who asked to get together, she seemed a long way off, had this look in her eyes like she wanted me to understand something. We had a short, awkward conversation about nothing in particular. The whole time I felt we were circling around some topic, some issue I couldn't figure out. That was the last time I saw her."

He passed a hand over his face. I could see how hard this was for him.

"A couple of years go by. Then a guy named Rick Ziglinski, who'd succeeded me in Rabat, came though Paris on his way to Washington and asked me out to lunch. A courtesy call, nothing more. He'd gotten to know my old contacts, of course, so I asked him about Miloud Benaboud, thinking he might have mentioned Chantal to him and he could tell me how she was doing. At the mention of Miloud, Rick went quiet. I asked him what was wrong. He told me Miloud was furious with me, lashing his tail around, threatening to cancel his contract with the embassy. I asked Ziglinski what it was all about. He says, 'Jesus, Curt, I thought you knew.' 'Knew what?' I asked him. He told me the whole story. Chantal had gotten pregnant. I was the father. I was floored. Her behavior at that last meeting suddenly made sense. She'd needed me to ask her what was wrong, let her know I cared. I'd have done it if I'd only known. When I didn't ask, she was through with me."

His voice had grown softer as he spoke, and his last words were almost inaudible. I felt helpless in the face of my old friend's pain, physical and spiritual.

"Of course, when Miloud found out about the baby, he was enraged, humiliated. He threatened to kill me, kill her, sue the embassy. Out of shame, he disowned her and packed her off to France to have the baby. It was a boy, Ziglinski told me. They were living in Paris with a cousin who's apparently part of a really bad crowd."

He had become increasingly wound up as he spoke. But now, as if suddenly remembering how sick he was, he closed his eyes, exhausted by the effort of telling his story. I started to say something sympathetic, but he waved me down and continued.

"At the time Ziglinski told me all this I still had a few months left in Paris. I should have spent them looking for Chantal. For the boy. My son. But I was too ashamed. Yeah, pretty cowardly. I left

Paris and took up my assignment here in Washington. I kept telling myself I needed to go back and find them. But then this hit me, hard and fast." Curt looked at his form under the thin blanket as if it belonged to someone else. "I got too sick to work and had to retire. Now I can't do any of the things I meant to do."

However much this mess was Curt's own fault, I still felt awful for him.

"What is it you want me to do, Curt?"

"I need you to find the boy."

Only sleep deprivation can explain my surprise. He hadn't called me all the way to Virginia, passport in hand, simply to tell me this tale.

"Find the boy for me, Sam. He must be about five now. You know I never had any kids with Taylor or Ann. He's the only thing I'm leaving behind in this world. And I have to take some responsibility for him. Find out where he lives. Give me an address." He lay back, looking at the ceiling.

"My exes get alimonies from me. They'll get my pension and the life insurance. That doesn't leave much. This house, some savings. I want the boy to have them. My lawyer tried to talk me out of giving it all to someone I've never seen and can't locate. But I'm insisting. Like I say, Ziglinski told me he thought this cousin of Chantal's is part of a bad crowd in Paris. I want something better for the boy."

"Curt, I'm not sure I'm the one to—"

"Go to Paris. Find the boy. My lawyer says all I need is an address. He can arrange the rest from here."

"That's it? His address?"

"My lawyer has contacts in France. He'll work with them and get it done."

"Can't I just get a phone number?"

"No. I have no idea what her number is. Anyway, if you call Chantal and she knows it's about me, she probably won't speak to you."

Curt had made a life of playing things fast and loose. It had cost him two marriages and professional success. But whatever Janet might have thought of him, I'd always felt he was at heart a decent guy. And this, about his son, was eating him worse than the cancer.

"I know it's a lot to ask," he said.

"I'd be nuts to take this on, wouldn't I?"

He gave a flash of his old charming smile. "You'd have to be."

But I'd already made up my mind. "I'll do whatever you need me to do."

The enormity of the promise hit me only after I'd made it. Once said, though, there was no taking it back.

He reached up and gripped my hand. "Thanks, Sam. I'd ask someone at the embassy to do this, but all the Americans I knew there are gone. And I don't want to tell any of the local employees about this. They looked up to me, and . . . well, I don't want them to think so poorly of me now. Bad for the raj," he said, trying to make a joke of it.

I told him not to worry.

"You don't know what this means to me." He must have seen something in my face as I tried to take all this in. "I know it's too much to ask. But I haven't got anyone else to turn to."

"I'm glad I came. But how do I do this? Where do I start?"

Gritting his teeth against a spasm of pain, Curt leaned over and drew a couple of pieces of paper from the mess on the nightstand and handed one of them to me.

"I've got two addresses here. One is a shipping company out by Charles de Gaulle Airport. When we had the occasional truck shipment from Rabat to Paris, this is where Miloud would send it. Maybe someone there will know something about Chantal. The other address is a garage near Montmartre. When Miloud's drivers needed to spend the night in Paris, he would have them leave their trucks there. There might be someone at the garage who can tell you something."

I looked blankly at the piece of paper. Two addresses, no names. No guarantee anyone will know what I'm talking about.

"I'm sorry I don't have more, Sam. Not even phone numbers for them. But I think you might have better luck just stopping by and asking."

"And if they don't know anything?"

"This might help," he said and handed me the second piece of paper. It was a photo of a young woman seated at a table in what appeared to be a crowded restaurant. She looked to be in her early twenties, round-faced, with lively, intelligent eyes full of good humor. At the edge of the photograph was Curt's hand resting on hers, wearing the sort of fancy signet ring a guy like Curt would wear.

"This is Chantal a few years ago. If those other two places can't give you anything to work on, maybe you could ask around the Montmartre area—in shops, restaurants. A lot of North Africans live around there, especially at the bottom of the hill, an area they call la Goutte d'Or."

"'A drop of gold.'"

"Yeah. Funny name for a neighborhood. Someone may recognize her, give you some idea of where she lives. But you have to be discreet. She's probably there illegally."

"I'll be careful. And what's the boy's name?"

Curt dropped his gaze. "I don't know."

His words hung in the air. To get past them, he reached toward the table again and gave me a third piece of paper. It was a check for five thousand dollars.

"What? No, Curt. I can't."

"You have to. Booking a flight this late and getting a hotel, you'll run through this pretty fast." He tried to smile. "We both know a foreign service pension doesn't go very far. I can't ask you to spend your own money. Take it."

The gesture seemed excessive. He wanted this too much. His desperation was frightening to see. But who was I to judge the yearnings of a dying man?

Reluctantly, I took the check, setting the seal on my offer to help.

A few moments later the nurse poked her head in the door and asked Curt if he needed anything. I knew she was telling me it was time to go.

Curt thanked me again, and I repeated my promise to do everything I could. Neither of us had to say I didn't have much time.

There was another thing that didn't get said. Curt's request opened up a different possibility for me, something entirely apart from finding the boy, a possibility I hadn't allowed myself to consider for many years. No, Curt couldn't have known that I had my own, very personal reasons for going to Paris.

CHAPTER THREE

CHEZ MOMO

A FTER THE LONG flight from Dulles, I staggered like one of the living dead out of the terminal at Charles de Gaulle and into the gray half-lit morning, the air a mix of cool country breezes and kerosene fumes.

I could have gone straight to the shipping office Curt mentioned, a company called Trans-Maghreb, no more than a mile away. But the toll of another all-night flight had left me in no condition to ask anyone about anything. So I took the long cab ride into the city, to the Hotel Brighton, a place Janet and I had stayed at several times while transiting Paris on the way to or from various posts.

Though it had been several years since my last visit, the staff at the Hotel Brighton greeted me like an old friend, letting me check in early and giving me a room overlooking the gardens of the Tuileries on the other side of the rue de Rivoli.

Determined to stay awake until a reasonable hour, I quickly un-packed, then lurched across the street and into the gardens, walking as clumsily as a windup toy, my head and body only loosely connected.

Carnival workers were opening the rides and game booths of the pocket-sized amusement park just inside the gates, showing their working-class disdain for the suit-and-tie crowd in the nearby offices by making as much noise as humanly possible.

Loopy with fatigue, I tottered along the dirt paths that crisscrossed the park, losing myself in the quiet, orderly grid of tightly pruned trees.

As I came out onto the park's broad central path, I noticed a young bearded fellow sitting on one of the metal chairs near the Octagonal Pond, a backpack at his feet. Few of the homeless inhabit the parks in Paris, though there's no lack of people who seem to have nowhere they need to go—few vagrants but many wanderers. His long hair needed a wash and his clothes had suffered a lot of wear. Yet he was free of that hollow, haunted look you see in so many drifters back home, and he looked at peace. To my surprise he nodded rather formally as I passed. Summoning the scraps of my most dignified manner, I nodded back.

Gradually, the cool air braced me half awake and it was pleasant walking along the earthen paths among the fallen leaves, which lay like asterisks on the ground, each one begging the question, What in the hell are you doing here?

In the morning light, my pledge to track down a five-year-old boy and his mother, last seen in a city I didn't know well, struck me as inexpressibly foolish.

For all Curt knew, Chantal Benaboud and her son had moved to some other part of France or off to Belgium or Who-Knew-Where. And if her father had relented and forgiven her, as seemed perfectly plausible, she might have long ago returned to Morocco.

Curt's charm and persuasiveness needed no better measure than the fact that only after I had arrived in Paris did these questions occur to me. And this: though everything he told me seemed to add up, something in the equation seemed wrong, although I couldn't think of what.

But I'd promised. No dodges. After a night's sleep, I would start my search.

And anyway, I had agreed to come because I had ghosts of my own to chase.

———◦◦◦◦◦◦— —◦◦◦◦◦◦—

Near the northern limits of Paris, beyond the steep hill called Montmartre, lies a thicket of apartments and local businesses. Among them was the Garage Momo that Curt had listed on the scrap of paper he'd given me.

A dingy concrete structure crouching in the shadows of taller buildings, the garage held four repair bays and a pocket-sized office with grimy windows. Behind the garage two freight trucks idled on an open expanse of pavement.

Uncertain what to do next, I stood on the opposite side of the street for some time, watching the mechanics at work. I felt a little envious of men working at a job they understood.

One of the mechanics, a short, wiry fellow with a pepper-and-salt mustache, glanced across at me a couple of times as he worked under the hood of a delivery van. Finally, he said something to the guy working opposite him, and after wiping his greasy hands on a greasier rag, he came out to the curb, his hands on his hips, and looked at me narrow-eyed from across the busy street.

Caught, I crossed the street to talk to him.

With a sharp uptick of his chin, he wordlessly asked me what I wanted. I noticed that his mustache only partly concealed a cleft palate that probably made him shy about speaking. A patch on his grimy overalls indicated his name was Eddie.

"I'm looking for someone," I shouted in French over the rumble of the traffic.

An eloquent shrug asked me what this had to do with him.

Thinking it would be easier to ask after the boy's mother than to track down a nameless five-year-old I couldn't even describe, I pulled out the photo of Chantal Benaboud. The mechanic regarded the picture for a moment, looked up at me, and raised a second shrug that lifted his shoulders to his ears. "*Bof!*" he said, an all-purpose word with a wide range of meanings, all of them dismissive. It's one of my favorite words in French, except when directed at me. As used by Eddie, it clearly meant I'd mistaken him for someone who gave a *merde*.

"Is there someone else I could speak to?" I asked.

Before I'd even finished my question, I got my answer. A short, compact man with the build of a fire hydrant, the jaw of a Neanderthal, and a nose that looked like it had broken several times lumbered out of the office heading in our direction. He was an odd-looking fellow, but the most remarkable thing about him was that his curiously unlined face was totally hairless, not only perfectly bald, but lacking eyebrows, whiskers, or even eyelashes. It gave him the look of a malignant newborn.

He too wore mechanic's overalls, though his were clean, and he carried himself in the stalking, flat-footed manner of a boxer who led with his face. The patch on his chest told me this was Momo himself.

Momo gave Eddie a look that sent him scurrying back to the van he'd been working on. "What do you want?" he asked. Without waiting for an answer, he snatched the photo from my hands and, one eye still on me, gave it a long look.

His reaction was remarkable. As if an overloaded circuit in his brain had tripped a breaker, his face went blank. Catching himself, he reassumed his tough-guy thing.

"Where'd you get this?" He had a thick, guttural accent—Eastern European?—that added to his air of menace.

I snatched the photo back. "That doesn't matter."

"Am I supposed to know who this is?"

If he'd wanted to convince me the woman in the photo meant nothing to him, that should have been his first question, not his second.

"And who are you?" he added, suspicion rolling off of him like steam.

"That doesn't matter either."

Momo didn't like my attitude. I could see he wanted to tell me to get the hell out of there. But he couldn't figure me out, and it made him uncomfortable. "You're from Garonne, yes?" The big man's voice caught on the question, as if he had invoked Beelzebub. "You tell him there's no trouble here. Everything's fine."

"I don't know anyone named Garonne. I only know I need to find this woman."

Momo gazed at me warily, trying to decide whether to believe me. When he spoke again, he'd managed to cover up his unease and had ticked back to his previous surliness. Nodding at the photo in my hand, he said, "I never saw that woman in my life."

Whatever he might say, the picture of Chantal Benaboud had set off a reaction he wanted to conceal.

"I need to find her."

"So find her. It's nothing to me." He jerked his chin toward the street behind me. "Now, get out of here."

Yet his hands undercut his tough words, nervously clenching and unclenching. Like the photo, the name Garonne seemed to carry a load of associations, none of them welcome.

I wanted to leverage his obvious discomfort to get more out of him, but I didn't know how to do it. I only understood that I'd stepped on a sore spot.

There was no point pressing him further. I put the photo back in my pocket.

"I must have been mistaken," I said, a lie for which we were both grateful.

Covering his retreat with an assertive tilt of his head, Momo lumbered back to his garage.

I recrossed the street but stopped half a block away, keeping the place in sight. Once I'd left, Momo went straight into his office and picked up the phone. As he did, he looked out the window and caught me watching him. He hung up and glared at me until I walked away.

CHAPTER FOUR

THE REDHEADED MAN

THE ABRUPT DISMISSAL I'd received from Momo still rankled the next morning. Curt hadn't prepared me for hostility, and it puzzled me. Part of my irritation came from the dashing of any hope that my task would prove easy, that someone at the garage would say, "Chantal? Sure. She lives over on the rue de Whatever. Let me give you her address. You should meet her son. Great kid."

Another part of my foul mood came from confronting my diminished status. That Gallic grease monkey wouldn't have dismissed me so easily if I'd told him I'd come from the American embassy.

But I hadn't. I was just some fiftyish American with an old photo. The upside to no longer being a diplomat? No one was insisting that I make some eight thirty meeting in a windowless embassy office.

After dawdling over breakfast, I slouched off toward the shipping office near the airport to inquire again after Chantal Benaboud.

The second address Curt had given me led to a long, low warehouse with a row of offices facing the loading docks. Over the distant roar of departing jets, I cupped my hands around my mouth and told the cabbie to wait. I went up a short flight of steps and walked along the loading docks until I came to a badly scratched metal door marked Trans-Maghreb Shipping, the name listed on Curt's piece of paper, and walked in.

Behind a plastic countertop marred by cigarette burns and coffee stains, two men sat at wooden desks, banging away at a couple of scuffed-up desktop computers. The nameplates on their desks identified them only by first names, Mohamed and Hassan. At the back of the office, a third man, with pale, freckled skin and thinning red hair, sat in a small glass-enclosed office.

All three of them looked up at me, then at each other as I entered, apparently unaccustomed to anyone coming into their office, unexpectedly or otherwise.

Thinking to ingratiate myself, I played a hunch and addressed the men behind the counter with a bit of North African Arabic. Bad idea. Their curiosity at my presence immediately veered toward suspicion. Reverting to French, I told them I was looking for someone and had been told to come to this office.

The one nearest me, Mohamed, screwed up his face in puzzlement and asked, "Here?"

Before I could reply, the redheaded man in the glass-enclosed office rose from his desk and came out to the counter. Perhaps thirty-five years old, his bulk testified to his fondness for food and drink. His still-powerful build told me he had likely spent a few years on the loading docks himself before coming to rest behind a desk.

"Can I help you?" he asked in a tone that said, *This had better be good.*

I drew the photo out of my pocket. "I'm looking for the daughter of a Moroccan named Miloud Benaboud. I understand his trucking company sometimes sends shipments from Rabat to this warehouse. I was wondering if maybe you knew her."

The previous day Momo had nearly ruptured himself trying to suppress his surprise at seeing the photo. The redheaded man's reaction was, if anything, more dramatic. His eyes widened and his mouth dropped open, though he recovered more quickly than Momo had. He glared at Mohamed and Hassan, who had been watching our little scene. They quickly turned back to their computer screens.

Nodding at the photo, the redhaired man muttered, "Put that away." With a brusque flip of his hand, he indicated I should come around the counter.

Without waiting to see if I was following, he stalked back toward his office. As I trailed him, I noticed that one of the men in this outer area, Hassan, had stopped banging at his keyboard and was looking at me closely. His eyes darted to the photo in my hand, then back to me. I had the impression he wanted to say something. Before I could ask what, his boss stopped in the doorway of his office and cocked his chin at me, telling me to get moving. The moment, and whatever it held, was lost.

The redheaded man nodded me into a scarred wooden chair and took his place behind the desk. His office smelled of cheap aftershave and old cigarettes. A small placard on the desk indicated his name was Maurice Girard.

He got to the point quickly. "Who are you? What do you want?"

The ill will he radiated surprised me less than Momo's the previous day. But I was again left with the feeling I had missed part of Curt's story. Or he had neglected to tell me something important.

Trying to ignore his aggressive tone, I told him, "My name is Sam Hough. As I told you, I'm searching for someone, the daughter of a man who runs a trucking company in Morocco." I didn't see any point in confusing things by saying it was actually her son I needed to find. "This Moroccan, her father, sends occasional shipments through here."

Girard looked at me, trying to process the question and why I was asking it. "I'm supposed to know who this man's daughter is and where she lives?" he said, the words coming out with more mockery than hostility, though they carried a strong hint of both. "What did you say his name was—the father of this woman?"

"Miloud Benaboud."

He tried to appear indifferent, but the rapid tapping of his fingers on his desktop told a different story. "And what's the name of his company?"

I was sure he knew the answers to both questions before he asked them and was just trying to figure out how much I knew.

Curt hadn't thought to give me the name of Benaboud's company, and I was forced to confess, "I don't know."

Girard's flickering smile said he'd sized me up now and knew what tack to take.

"I have no idea what you're talking about."

His evasions reminded me of something Momo had said the previous day, and I decided to play a new card. "I suppose you think this has something to do with Garonne?"

Girard covered better than Momo, but for a long, suspended moment he said nothing, only looked at me, trying to assess what I knew. In fact, I knew nothing except that this name made people swallow their chewing gum.

He cleared his throat, buying enough time to figure out which lie he wanted to give me.

He chose, "I don't know anyone named Garonne. And I don't know the woman in your photo."

I waited for more. His face made clear there would be no more.

Frustrated, thinking further conversation pointless, I got up and started to walk out.

"No." Girard waved me back into my seat. "Tell me why Gar . . . tell me why you want to find this woman. You're a detective, yes?"

I told him, "I have a friend in the United States who believes he's done a disservice to the woman and wants to make amends." Or at least that's what I meant to tell him, but after several years back home my French wasn't entirely up to speed yet, and I wasn't sure how my words came out.

Whatever I'd managed to say, and in whatever language, the name Garonne had clearly made Girard as uncomfortable as it had Momo, and he wanted to know what lay behind my mentioning it. While Momo had wondered if I worked for Garonne and fobbed me off with assurances that everything was fine, Girard seemed to think my mention of the name meant I was some sort of investigator. Working for the police? Working for this man, Garonne? I wanted to ask him which version would bother him more, but I was sure he wouldn't give me a straight answer. In any case, his guardedness gave me the feeling I was walking across ice with no idea how thin it might be.

Trying to strike a casual pose, he said, "Let me see that photo again."

Uncertain where this was going, I handed it over.

"This was taken a few years ago," I told him.

He wasn't listening any longer. He was looking at the photo of Chantal Benaboud. After several moments ticked by in silence, he tossed it back to me with a contemptuous huff meant to say that the woman meant nothing to him.

But his casual air had deserted him.

"And who are you?" he asked.

"As I said, my name is—"

"No. I mean, who are you?"

"I told you. I'm doing a favor for a friend who's unable to travel and has asked me to help."

"Who is this friend?"

"It doesn't matter."

"And he's unable to travel," Girard repeated, letting me know he didn't believe me. He waited for me to give him more, but after a moment he understood that, just as he had stonewalled me, I could do the same to him.

Abruptly, he stood up. "I can't help you."

Throughout our exchange the redheaded man had been deflecting my questions rather than answering them, telling me nothing but clearly wondering who I was and who I represented. It seemed that my willingness to pretend I was familiar with Garonne put me on her wrong side.

Maybe Girard was simply trying to protect the privacy of a client from a snoopy foreigner. Or maybe he didn't like strangers coming into his office unannounced.

Whatever the reason, I could see I wasn't going to get anything further from him. I thanked him for his time and said goodbye. This time he didn't try to stop me.

As I walked back along the loading docks toward the waiting taxi, it struck me as odd that Girard had never asked me why, if this woman's father, as well as her father's company, were Moroccan, I was looking for her in Paris. The question answered itself. He didn't ask because he already knew.

With all this playing through my mind, I almost didn't hear the sound of the metal door closing behind me. I turned around at the sound of it clicking shut.

Hassan, the man in the outer office who had looked like he wanted to say something to me, had come out onto the loading dock. He took a packet of cigarettes from his pocket and looked over his shoulder toward the office door before nodding in my direction.

"Monsieur," he said, beckoning me.

I'd taken only a couple of steps toward him when the door opened again and Maurice Girard came out. He must have seen Hassan leave the office as soon as I'd left and didn't like it.

The redhead gave me a look that didn't need any words to say, *Get out of here*, then turned toward Hassan. Hassan held up his pack of cigarettes to Girard as token of his innocent intent, shook one out and lighted it. Girard looked at me again, then at Hassan, and with a quick nod ordered him back inside. The North African dropped his cigarette, ground it under his heel, glanced once more in my direction, and went back into the office.

The favor I'd so willingly taken on for Curt had begun to look like a darker and more difficult mission than I had imagined. Whatever Maurice Girard's denials and Momo's evasions, I was thinking that if Chantal Benaboud had fallen in with a bad crowd, these guys were part of it.

CHAPTER FIVE

LA GOUTTE D'OR

WALKING ALONG THE Seine the following morning, watching the commercial barges push their way downriver, I thought of the solid wall of hostility I'd run into over the previous two days. Yet, the reactions I'd seen in the eyes of Momo and Maurice Girard told me that Chantal and Curt's son lay just on the other side of that wall.

I'd scoffed at Girard's suggestion I was a detective. But if I went around knocking on the doors of shipping offices and garages asking about a woman in a picture, what else was I?

As much as I wanted to tell myself I had nowhere else to search, I knew I'd left one stone unturned. From his sickbed ... Who was I kidding? From his deathbed, Curt had told me that if I got nowhere with the two contacts he'd given me, I should take the photo around Montmartre and see if anyone recognized Chantal.

I disliked the idea of wandering around a foreign neighborhood shoving a photo of a girl in strangers' faces, like a beggar holding out his bowl. Half the people would look at the picture and likely think I was pimping for her. The other half would assume she was a daughter who had run away from home, probably for good reason.

But I'd promised a dying friend I'd do what I could.

So far my attempts to fulfill that promise had raised a lot more questions than answers. For one, why did Curt assume that the woman and the boy lived around Montmartre? The fact that it was the part of the city nearest the airport and the offices of Trans-Maghreb offered no more than the thinnest logic, unless Curt had neglected to tell me everything he knew, an uncomfortable thought that was gaining increased traction in my mind.

Second, Curt's certainty that Chantal Benaboud had fallen in with a bad crowd gnawed at me. Momo and Maurice Girard struck me as people who lived like cockroaches, hiding under the baseboards of society, people I would normally avoid.

So, why was I aggressively seeking them out without much thought to the trouble I was courting? Agreeing to meet with the mythic delegation from Peshawar years earlier looked perfectly reasonable compared to this.

Mumbling curses to myself, I headed toward Montmartre.

The crest of Montmartre overlooks Paris from the old city's northern boundary. Its slopes rise too high to allow a Métro stop under the hill, so it's ringed with half a dozen stations from three different lines. I chose one no more unlikely than the others and, after getting off the train, trudged up the hill toward Sacre Coeur, the mosque-like church at the crown of the hill, visible from almost every point in the city.

Someone said history repeats itself, coming first as tragedy, then as farce. Maybe the same could be said of neighborhoods. Over the decades, this onetime impoverished slum, a low-rent refuge for the starving writers and artists who would revolutionize the way we looked at the world, has transformed itself into a tourist attraction.

Along its short, narrow streets modest restaurants offering over-priced lunches alternate with souvenir shops selling cheap prints of paintings by those who had lived on the hill a century earlier, the shops often charging more for these copies than the desperate artists had dared ask for the originals.

With the coming of fall, most of the tourists had gone home, leaving the quarter nearly deserted. My brief stops in a couple of shops brought me a studied welcome from the people behind the counters that quickly turned to ice when they realized I'd come to ask questions. They glanced indifferently at the photo, then suspiciously at me, before shaking their heads and pointing me toward the door.

Outside, a scattering of caricature makers and amateur painters dotted the quiet streets and small squares. The caricaturists offered to passersby the sort of clever five-minute drawings you can find at state fairs or the edges of a farmer's market. The somewhat more serious painters, many of them affecting berets and smocks like historical reenactors at a theme park, worked at small cityscapes done in a bygone style, selling them for a few euros.

I showed the photo to a few of them and got nothing but offers to make a caricature of her—or of me. But I already felt sufficiently ridiculous and had no need for a picture to prove the point.

An ill-spent hour trudging around the crest of the hill led only to a weary walk toward the nearest Métro stop back to the Brighton.

As I came down a long, steep stairway leading to a street below, I discovered a far different Paris than I'd seen before. People of every hue, age, and stature crowded the streets of this residential area—the Goutte d'Or that Curt had spoken of. Here were Blacks whose families had come from Sub-Saharan Africa and North Africans from Tunisia, Algeria, and Morocco, many of them in the brightly colored clothes of their homelands, sporting hairstyles foreign to the more conservative—and whiter—parts of the city.

The prejudice these immigrants and children of immigrants face in Paris hangs over the city like a cloak, but I knew North Africa, or at least Tunisia, better than I knew France and felt more at home in this neighborhood than I had among the shopkeepers on the hill. It was like running into old friends in a foreign city.

Buoyed by a sense that I was among people I knew, I showed Chantal Benaboud's photo in a hair salon, a pocket-sized electronics store, a newspaper kiosk. At each of them I found that my comfort with them did not translate into any comfort they might feel toward me. A couple of the shopkeepers refused at first to look at me or the photo. When I insisted, they took a cursory glance, shaking their heads even before they looked at it. They made it clear that, however I might deny it, they regarded me as a police officer, my presence unwelcome. With one more figurative door slammed in my face, I headed for the Métro, rehearsing my conversation with Curt in which I expressed regret at my failure and told him I didn't see much choice but to head home.

I knew, however, that whatever my failures, I couldn't leave yet. I had one more failure to redeem, this one more a failure of nerve than of luck or determination. Yes, I'd come to Paris for Curt, but also for my own reasons. While I could tell myself I'd done what I could for Curt, I hadn't yet found the nerve to do the one thing I'd promised to no one but myself, to make the phone call I truly needed to make, my yearning neatly balanced by my fear.

With these ideas tumbling through my head—of staying and not staying, of doing and not doing—I was angling toward a short street at the bottom of the steps below Montmartre, heading for the Boulevard Barbès and the Métro.

I'd gone no more than a couple of blocks when I came upon a tiny grocery tucked between two larger shops. Its wide metal shutter, much like a garage door back home, was rolled up, making the place open to the air. Baskets of fruits and vegetables hung near the counter. Milk, bread, and a few other staples lined the store's two aisles, both empty of customers. A young woman in a djellaba leaned on the counter, wistfully watching the passersby. After a morning of cold looks and closed mouths, something about her open, friendly face told me I should inquire one more time after Chantal Benaboud.

"Bonjour, monsieur," she said as I crossed the threshold.

"Bonjour, mademoiselle. Maybe you could help me with something," I said and produced the photo, asking if she knew the woman pictured in it.

Still of an age where her emotions declared themselves on her face, the young shopkeeper's eyes lit up.

"Yes. Or I think so. She comes to buy vegetables and fruit from us and talk to my mother."

I nearly danced a jig. "Does she come with a little boy?"

The young woman held her hand waist high. "Like this? Yes, sometimes." She cocked her head good-naturedly. "But with her husband, never."

Husband. That stopped me.

"She's married?"

"Of course," she said, a little shocked at the notion that a woman with a son might not have a husband.

This complicated things. If nothing else, Chantal's name would not likely be Benaboud any longer, making my search more difficult.

"I'm looking for her on behalf of a friend," I said. "Would you happen to know where I might find her?"

Regret written on her young face, she said, "No, monsieur, I don't know where she lives."

"But she must live somewhere nearby."

"Yes, I suppose so." Her eyes brightened with an idea. "It's possible, monsieur, that my mother could tell you. She knows our customers better than I do."

"Could I speak to her?"

"I regret she's not here right now. But she will be back tomorrow. I'm sure she will be happy to help you."

Feeling like a prospector who, just as he was about to give up, has discovered a nugget of gold, a *goutte d'or,* I bought a few apples from the young woman to show my gratitude and told her I'd be back in the morning.

I celebrated by stopping at Angelina, on the rue de Rivoli, home of the world's best cup of hot chocolate. As I took a table, I looked at my phone and saw I'd received a text from my son. I'd told Tom I'd flown to Paris for a few days to do a favor for a friend, but no more than that. Now he was checking up on his old man, making sure everything was all right.

Texting doesn't come naturally to me, but I laboriously tapped back that I was enjoying Paris and would be home soon—the first an exaggeration, the second more a wish than even a guess.

After sending the text, I sat for a long time, phone in hand, until I worked up the nerve to punch in the number I'd promised myself to call since the day I'd agreed to come to Paris.

CHAPTER SIX

A DRAWING ROOM ON THE SEINE AND A KIR ROYALE

———◆◇◆———

T HE ÎLE SAINT-LOUIS lies in the middle of Paris, a small island in the Seine a few hundred yards long and a couple hundred wide, a quiet haven for some of the city's wealthiest residents.

I'd walked the mile or so from my hotel rather than take the Métro or a taxi, as if getting there too quickly might induce a case of the psychic bends. Even so, when I arrived at 16 Quai d'Anjou, I needed to take a breath and collect myself before pushing the button marked "d'Alembert." The buzzer sounded and the door clicked open.

Though I had told myself to take things easy, stay cool, I ran up the stairs two at a time to the third floor.

She stood in the open doorway of her apartment, greeting me with a smile at once wonderfully familiar and oddly unreal, a smile I had long thought I'd never see again.

We shared a weighted pause as we each assessed the changes the years had wrought in the other. Her face was a little fuller and etched with parenthetical lines around her eyes and mouth. The honey hair showed a few strands of gray. Yet, after a moment, it all fell away, like a disguise she'd put on as a little joke, and I saw the young woman I'd known so well so long ago. Though she must have noted my graying hair and the extra pounds I carried, I felt an illusion of the decades falling away from me as well, making me, for a heady instant, once more a young man of twenty-seven, back when we had shared our first diplomatic posting in Copenhagen.

We might have stood like that all afternoon, on opposite sides of the open doorway, unable to close the last few inches—and the many years—separating us if she hadn't broken the spell.

"How are you, Sam?"

I managed to pull myself together and utter the comfortable banality. "I'm fine, Gwen."

Saying her name for the first time in years stopped me, and I barely had enough wit to add, "It's good to see you."

"Come on in. You look like you could use a drink."

The ornate, high-ceilinged apartment evoked *ancien regime* dignity and relentless good taste. Tall windows looked out on the Seine, letting in the fading afternoon light. A couple of floor lamps lent a warm chiaroscuro to the room, giving it the look of an Old Masters painting.

We exchanged chaste, bird-like pecks on the cheek, and Gwen led me into a large drawing room. At home I'd have called it a living room, but the richly appointed space would not allow such a mundane term. Between the tall bookshelves, heavy with leather-bound volumes, hung paintings of another age, their lavishly dressed subjects flirting in gilded salons or mounted on finely caparisoned steeds, looking down on us with stern but tranquil gaze. The furnishings, like the paintings, spoke of wealth generations deep.

Yes, I'd heard Gwen had married well.

"Please, Sam, have a seat. A glass of wine?"

It seemed like the kind of place where a servant would appear at the merest whisper. But when I said yes, she went to get it herself.

Her absence allowed me to take a breath and tell myself that I was simply in the home of an old friend. But of course, there was no "simply" to it.

The Department of State is a small family, and gossip its common coin. It's easy to keep track of those we no longer serve with. I had been sure since the day I met her that Gwen would advance quickly in the service. And, indeed, she had eventually risen to the jewel-in-the-crown position of deputy chief of mission in Paris, the embassy's number two. Under a political appointee ambassador, she was the person who really ran the place, CEO to his chairman of the board.

And there, two years into her tenure and at the apex of her career, she abruptly and shockingly resigned her commission and married a count or some such thing, more than a decade older than herself. She somehow got my address and sent a wedding invitation to me in Oregon. To my surprise she had written her phone number on the back and expressed the hope we might see each other again one day. I mined the message for unspoken meaning and concluded that it spoke to nothing more than friendship.

A tinkling of glasses on a silver tray brought me back to the present. She set the tray on a side table. "Kir Royale. They say it's an old lady's drink, but the cold champagne makes it refreshing."

She handed me a glass and curled up on the love seat opposite my chair, her legs tucked under her. We spoke carefully, sketching in our lives over the last couple of decades, what we'd done, where we'd been, skirting around anything too personal, not wanting to presume the other still cared to know such things.

"I was so sorry to hear about your wife," she told me, a remark both caring and safe, yet tentatively opening a more personal door I could choose to step through or not.

"It was hard," I said. "We'd been very happy. It's been almost five years, but I miss her every day."

She repeated how sorry she was. I asked about her husband.

Like a student surprised to get called on, she sat up a little straighter and said, "Ah! The Marquis Philippe Georges Henri Something-I-Can-Never-Remember d'Alembert." She recited his name and title with a roll of her eyes that didn't entirely conceal a hint of pride, before adding, "Or, if you're in a hurry, Georgie."

"A marquis?"

"Yes, or he would be but for the nuisance of the Revolution." She arched an eyebrow. "Most of my friends back home thought a marquis was something that hung over the front of a theater. They were quite distressed to hear I'd married one."

How easy it was to laugh together again.

Good sport that I am, I said, "I'd like to meet him."

She suppressed a smile. "Alas, he's with his sons down at le Brede, his place near Bordeaux. He loves it there, hunting with his boys—he'd been a widower for years when I met him—and looking after the vineyards. Frankly, it's all a bit bucolic for me. I prefer it here in Paris." She felt the need to add, "He's a very good man. Older than me," with a smile. "We've reached a great comfort with each other." A remark notable for what it said and what it didn't.

She caught it too, and before I could reflect further asked, "What brings you to Paris?"

She might have asked, *And why did you look me up?* but didn't want to force me into an answer that might have made us both uncomfortable.

"I'm doing a favor for a friend. Did you know Curt Hansen? An American. He used to work at the embassy here."

She squinted, calling on memory.

"I know the name. I think he was something over in Admin when I first came to post. Why?"

I told her how he'd summoned me to his home outside Washington and of his cancer, told her of Curt's son and of Chantal Benaboud, of the hostile reception I'd received at Momo's garage and the Trans-Maghreb offices, and my certainty that the people I'd spoken to, despite their denials, knew the woman in the picture.

I ended with a puzzled shake of my head. "Why would they say they didn't know her? What's so important that they need to lie to me?"

Gwen lay back and stretched out her legs, her drink cradled in her lap. "You say Hansen's afraid this woman has fallen in with a bad crowd?"

"That's what he said."

"I believe it." She raised her glass to her lips and hesitated. "I'd tell you to forget about it and go home, but I know you, Sam. You've made a promise, and you won't have enough sense to give up."

I wanted to object but wasn't sure to what.

"So, where does all this leave you?" she asked.

"That's the funny thing. Curt suggested that if I didn't get anywhere with the garage or the shipping company, I might show her photo to people around Montmartre, see if anyone recognizes her."

Her narrow-eyed gaze told me what she thought of this idea.

"Tell me you're not going to do that."

"Too late. I went up there this morning."

"And?"

"And I found a young woman in the area below Montmartre—the Goutte d'Or—who said she recognized her. I'm supposed to go back tomorrow. Apparently her mother knows the customers better and might be able to tell me more."

Gwen looked out the window at the fall afternoon and for some time said nothing, making me wonder if she didn't know what to say or didn't know whether she should say it.

"It doesn't strike you as odd, Sam?"

"What's that?"

"He directs you to two places where he probably already knew they would recognize her, and probably knew they would stonewall you. So he tells you to wander around Montmartre and the Goutte d'Or waving a photo at strangers. Tell me why he didn't call these two places himself?"

"He's a sick man. I'm not sure he's up to it. And I suspect he was afraid they wanted to talk to him even less than they wanted to talk to me."

"Your friend sounds like a real charmer."

I wanted to say, *he is*, but thought it best not to bring that up.

"So, when you actually found someone willing to talk to you, it was more or less by chance." Gwen chewed on her lip, thinking it through. "Something about this smells very strange." She looked at me with unsettling directness. "Drop it, Sam."

"Really?"

"Drop it."

"I can't."

Her sigh ended with a shake of her head. "I know. You're too good a man to do the smart thing. That's what I always—" She cut herself off, knowing whatever she said next would take us back to Copenhagen and a time when we were both young—something we had both so far avoided. She brushed some imaginary crumbs from her lap and, in a bright tone, asked, "How long do you think you'll be in the city?"

"If this pans out tomorrow, I suppose I'll leave in the next couple of days." I tried to judge how, or whether, to say what I'd wanted to say all along. "I was wondering if, before I go, I could ask you out to dinner."

In the long pause before she replied I nearly took it back, ready to claim I wasn't serious. But she said, "I'd like that. Very much."

"Tomorrow perhaps?"

"I can't tomorrow."

"How about the next night?" If I came across like an overanxious teenager, she didn't let on.

"All right. I'll make a reservation."

"I'll pick the place."

"I think you'd better let me do that," she said. "I'll text you."

We shared a smile that grew broader as we looked at each other, like a couple of kids planning a prank—until we caught ourselves at it and laughed out loud.

We talked for a few more minutes about things unimportant in themselves—the weather, my flight over, my home in Oregon—all of them pretexts to spend a little more time together. Eventually, I said I had to get going. In fact, I had no other plans, but I knew it was the right moment.

As I left, I couldn't help turning in the doorway, casting an appraising eye over her apartment and saying, "Nice place you've got here."

She looked around as if she had never considered the idea, then turned back to me and with a smile said, "Yes, but it's not Badger Cottage."

I wasn't ready for that. She could see it and laughed, turning her head away and making a vague wave of her hand to dismiss her remark as a joke. But she knew better. She'd known better before she said it.

CHAPTER SEVEN

BADGER COTTAGE

MY FIRST DIPLOMATIC posting had been a one-year junior officer assignment to the Public Affairs section in Copenhagen. Like most JOs, the other dips regarded me as a cross between a respected colleague and a stray adopted from the local Humane Society.

Among the first people I met was the embassy's other JO, Gwen DiCarli, who had arrived a couple of weeks ahead of me, posted to the Political section, where the Department grooms future leaders.

The two of us were lowly apprentices, and we felt it. Within the pocket-sized universe of the embassy we gravitated in the same orbit, sitting in the back row of the same meetings and, at official dinners, placed across from each other, well below the salt.

Thrown together by the benign neglect of those above us, we found that we enjoyed each other's company, could make each other laugh, and faced the same challenges of being taken seriously. I thought she was a delight. She thought I was charming.

Under the warmth of her attention, so did I.

One of the few nuggets of advice I gave my son regarding the opposite sex must have struck him as odd: "Try to fall in love with someone you actually like." So it was with Gwen and me. We advanced from lunches with colleagues to dinners alone and increasingly ardent good-night kisses, though, for the moment, no more. I knew not to push it. The regret on her face as she reluctantly backed toward her door seemed unfeigned and served, it seemed, as a promissory note written on her heart.

———◇◇◇◇◇—— ——◇◇◇◇◇———

A couple of weeks after we had started seeing each other, our work, already consuming, lit the afterburner.

A presidential visit is like an oncoming black hole, sucking everything into its gravity. Every embassy on the itinerary of the president and his traveling circus required reinforcements. Though it's one of the largest American embassies in the world, even AmEmbassy London, to use diplo-parlance, required extra staff. As the lowest creatures in the food chain, Gwen and I got tapped. I made some joke about the old movie *They Were Expendable*. Two days later we flew to Heathrow.

No other experience could have better dispelled any lingering notions about the glamor of diplomatic life. Most of the burden of a presidential visit consists of drudge work—making sure everyone's luggage gets from Air Force One to the appropriate hotel, seeing that mics and podiums are properly set up when someone needs to brief the press, and running off copies of the ever-changing schedule.

The days stretched to sixteen, eighteen, twenty hours, the work both urgent and trivial. As a political officer, Gwen fell into the gravity of the Secretary's orbit, while I assisted the embassy press office. On the few occasions we saw each other over those four hectic days, we only had time to exchange winsome looks and surreptitious waves. At night we kept to our assigned rooms, as we needed nothing so much as a few hours' sleep.

When it was over, we rode out to Heathrow with the sixty-car presidential motorcade for more luggage wrangling and last-second demands for this or that, until the whole fiasco was wheels-up, heading for Berlin or Brussels or Rome, whatever city came next. None of us really cared, so long as they were gone.

Unknown to the others, Gwen and I had our own agenda. While they were still on the tarmac, anxiously watching the president's plane fade into the distance, half afraid it might turn around and come back, the two of us had already absconded, picking up a rental car and running off like kids playing hooky.

Air Force One had hardly disappeared from sight before we were motoring across the English countryside, its bright springtime greens and burgeoning new life so closely echoing our own ardent mood that we felt we'd entered into a new kingdom.

Gwen had been the one to suggest a five-day vacation in the Cotswolds, telling me she had been driving herself, not to mention me, mad with the need to redeem the promissory note we had been making to each other over the last few weeks, and we would finally have the chance for time together. If our mutual absence allowed folks back at the embassy to put two and two together, we didn't care.

After a couple of hours driving the narrow highways and downright terrifying country roads—two lanes squeezed into a space for one, and no shoulders—we arrived at Badger Cottage, a two-story stone farmhouse near the wonderfully obscure hamlet of Temple Guiting.

Our hosts, a graying, vigorous couple named Molyneux, were as unassuming and solid as their home. They greeted us with a pot of tea and a pleasant chat that left us with the impression they had turned over one of their upstairs bedrooms for a B and B less for the extra income than for the promise of occasional company. We of course thought of them as quite elderly. Now we would regard them as contemporaries.

We soon pleaded exhaustion, though in fact we were fairly twitching with anticipation, and asked to be shown our room. Mr. Molyneux favored us with a deadpan wink when Gwen and I registered under different surnames.

Though it was still late afternoon, we went straight to bed and, after a session of first athletic, then languorous, lovemaking to christen our hideaway, slept for fourteen hours. We awoke famished for the country breakfast of eggs and sausage and bacon and beans and tomatoes and toast and tea.

Over the next few days, we hiked the ancient public pathways that cut across fields and hills, reveling in the discovery of birds and badgers and each other. We borrowed bicycles and rode past stone cottages older than almost any city in the US, the countryside silent but for birdsong and the whirring of our tires on the pavement.

On a cool, lightly raining day we made the longer pedal down to Stratford-upon-Avon, where, over a ploughman's lunch in a dark and cozy pub, we talked of Shakespeare and his sometime patron Good Queen Bess, and of books, and laughed about our time in London. We spoke of everything but the future.

———◦◦◦◦——— ———◦◦◦◦———

Perfection is not sustainable. Idylls end. Two days before we were scheduled to leave, Gwen got a call from the embassy Pol section, telling her they needed her back in Copenhagen to play sherpa for a summit of NATO political leaders.

While she talked on her phone, I lay in bed reading. When she'd hung up, I said, "I thought you told them you'd be out of cell phone range."

"We're in England, not up the Amazon. They know better. And they need me."

"No, they don't. They just want to feel important by insisting people cut their vacations short and run back to the mother ship."

Her shoulders slumped and she said, "It would look bad if I didn't go back."

Despite our sardonic jokes about the presidential visit we had just escaped, I could sense her excitement about again working with the high-ranking and powerful, and felt a sense of impending loss I couldn't have explained at that moment.

"Look bad to who? Them or me?"

"We already look bad enough to them, outing ourselves by disappearing like this."

"You think they're shocked?"

"It's different for a man. They give you a wink and a grin and a thumbs-up. For a woman, the same people decide you're not serious. If I tell them I'm not coming back, they'll write me off."

Our exchange was as close to an argument as we'd ever had. Neither of us raised our voices. We remained calm and cordial. We were, after all, perfectly reasonable people. Diplomats.

Afterward, she lay beside me, pained both to leave and to have me unhappy with her. She kissed me, her eyes seeking forgiveness. And I loved her all over again.

The following morning we said goodbye to the Molyneuxs, who refused our offer to pay for the remaining night we'd reserved, and headed back to Heathrow and a plane for Copenhagen.

We got over our disappointment, though she perhaps recovered more quickly than I did. But the incident made clear to us that we had reached that uncertain point where parallel lines meet, where we committed to each other or did not. I could see myself asking her to marry me. Gwen must have considered it too.

To take that next step, though, would require us to ignore our natures and the nature of the lives we had chosen. As intent as I was on my career, I knew that the heart of Gwen's ambition beat even more strongly than my own. Her need to leave the idyll of Badger Cottage and return to Copenhagen foretold the pattern of whatever future we might share. In a hierarchy like the foreign service, we would each feel the compulsion to follow our increasingly divergent paths to advancement. And we would inevitably part. We needed to see that clearly, needed to be sensible. And being sensible is death to love. Though we didn't speak of it, we knew our relationship would last no longer than the end of our year in Copenhagen, with me off that summer to Delhi and Gwen to a posting for rising stars in Berlin.

———◦◦◦◦◦—— ——◦◦◦◦◦———

On the day she left, I asked Admin to stand down and let me take her to the train station myself. They said that was fine. Everyone knew about us.

Unwilling to face the reality of farewell, we made love one last time in my apartment and arrived at the station late, walking down the platform hand in hand. We made no empty promises to spend our holidays with each other or to try to get posted together somewhere. The tears in her eyes gave me permission to believe she felt the loss as keenly as I did.

I almost proposed to her right there, nearly persuaded myself that the look on her face said she wanted me to. We both knew she would have to say no, but I would at least have asked.

In the end, though, I said nothing, and she boarded the train while I stood on the platform, watching as she found her compartment and waved to me through the window. I waved back and watched her train until it disappeared from sight. When it was gone, I took a taxi back to the embassy.

———◦◦×◦◦—— ——◦◦×◦◦———

That had been twenty-six years ago. I hadn't seen her since.

And now she had mentioned Badger Cottage, and I could lie awake all night trying to figure out why.

CHAPTER EIGHT

STONEWALLED BY THE VEGETABLE LADY

———◦◦◦◦———

ARLY THE NEXT morning I headed off to the Métro and the Goutte d'Or, trying to repress a great sense of anticipation.

Even more than the day before, the area near the base of Montmartre looked like a street fair, with sidewalk vendors offering sweets, cheap jewelry, and designer knockoffs. Africans in multi-colored knit hats demonstrated windup birds that flew through the air with a charming rattle of plastic wings. All of these goods were offered from cheap fold-up stands, perfect for running off should a police officer demand to see a business license.

After stumbling onto the little grocery by chance the previous day, it took me some time wandering around the oddly angled streets before I found it again. I hoped to see the same young woman and ask her to mediate my acquaintance with her mother, who might confirm that indeed it was Chantal Benaboud who frequented her shop. Instead, I found a thin, sharp-featured woman standing behind the counter, framed by hanging baskets of fruit and vegetables.

She appeared to be something like my own age, though she might have been younger. The life of an immigrant can be a hard one.

While she dealt with a customer, the two women speaking Arabic, I stood back, waiting my turn. They continued to talk even after the woman behind the counter had bagged her customer's purchases. For a while I took it as simple courtesy, but after several minutes had passed I understood that she knew who I was and hoped I would go away.

It began to rain. The customer left. I did not. Without acknowledging my presence, the woman disappeared through a door at the back of the shop. When she returned, she frowned to see me still there.

My "*keif al hal?*"—a standard Arabic greeting—broke against her scowl like a pane of glass against a rock. As at Trans-Maghreb, I found that trying to ingratiate myself by using a little Arabic only raised suspicion.

Switching to French, I said with what I hoped was a winning smile, "I'm wondering if you could help me. I'm looking for the woman in this photo. Her name is Chantal."

My smile won me nothing.

"I've never seen her," the woman said, a claim that might have been more convincing if she had actually looked at the picture.

She busied herself rearranging the modest pyramids of pears and oranges on her counter, avoiding both me and the photo.

"Your daughter thought she recognized the woman and said you might tell me where she—"

"My daughter was mistaken. I sent her home." With that, she turned on me, the set of her face sharp as a slap. "She's never seen the woman, and neither have I."

For the third or fourth time during our brief conversation she glanced at a man standing a few feet behind me, making clear she had paying customers and I should move on.

Having persuaded myself that I might be able to finish the whole business—find Chantal and book a flight home—that morning, I was unwilling to give up. "I'm not a policeman. I only want to—"

"I don't care what you call yourself. You're a *flic*. I'm not talking to you!"

I didn't believe she meant literally that I was a cop, only that I seemed like someone who held authority while she had none, and she would rather spit than help me.

For a moment longer I stood in the rain and tried to think of another tack to try. But there was none. Grinding my teeth at the futility of dealing with people who knew more than they would say—Maurice Girard, Momo, and now the Vegetable Lady—and fuming with frustration at my certainty that the boy and his mother lived within a few hundred yards of where I stood, practically in plain sight, yet invisible, I turned and walked away.

I didn't buy any apples this time.

Not ready to head back to the hotel and spend the afternoon staring at the ceiling, I wandered the streets like a drifting balloon.

Among the voices around me I heard just enough of the language and accents I'd known in Tunisia to feel I was walking through a familiar neighborhood. Could I have imagined as a kid that Arabic might sound more familiar to me than French, or that I would feel more at home in Tunis than in Paris?

Frustrated by my failure, I tried to imagine that I might run into Chantal on her way to buy groceries or returning home to make lunch for her son. Hoping for a stroke of luck, I peered at every woman I passed, until a young Arab woman's offended huff and sharply tilted chin told me that my searching gaze begged to be misunderstood.

Her rebuff, like a dash of water to the face, made me look around to see if anyone else had witnessed my comeuppance. What I saw disturbed me more than any momentary embarrassment.

On the opposite sidewalk, amid the figures scurrying for cover from the rain, stood a short, lean man of Mediterranean complexion—from North Africa? Marseille?—sheltering under an awning, staring at me.

Hadn't I seen him a few minutes earlier, watching me with the same narrow gaze as he stood behind me at the little grocery, the man the Vegetable Lady kept glancing at?

I told myself I'd grown oversensitive, if not downright paranoid, seeing things with my imagination rather than my eyes.

Certain I would make no more progress that day, I decided to head back to the hotel. Searching for someone who might not want to be found was dispiriting enough, but to do it in the rain made me feel like a damned fool besides.

As I headed toward the Métro I couldn't help looking over my shoulder. My heart fluttered as I saw the man again, hands in his pockets, hair slicked by the rain, walking half a block behind me.

I crossed the street, then crossed back. The man followed me, first one way, then the other, making no attempt to conceal himself. He wanted me to see him, his presence some kind of warning.

As I descended the steps toward the Métro, I lost him in the crowd—though I couldn't rid myself of the feeling that he hadn't lost me.

Still wondering if I was being followed—or if, in my current state of suspicion, I had ever been—I changed Métro lines and came up at the Place de la Concorde. I entered the Tuileries through its broad main gate, rather than going straight to the hotel and revealing where I was staying to anyone who might be tailing me.

The park's open spaces and the cool, rainy air slowed my heart. I strolled along the paths between the rows of trees, telling myself that my worries were baseless.

Yet, when I caught a movement out of the corner of my eye I nearly yipped.

Resting under a tree, as still as the Buddha in one of the park's metal chairs, sat the young bearded man I'd seen near the Octagonal Pool a couple of days earlier. He seemed to recognize me too. As before, we nodded in a cordial but distant way.

As I passed, he asked in English, "How ya doin'?"

He smiled at my surprise.

"I'm okay," I managed to say. "And you?"

"I'm *fine*," he replied with curious emphasis.

I supposed him to be a few years older than my son. His weathered face spoke to a great deal of time outdoors.

"How did you know I was an American?" I asked.

He smiled at the question. "Your clothes. The cut of your hair. Something about the way you carry yourself."

None of us likes to be so quickly—or so accurately—pegged. Yet his judgment shouldn't have surprised me. Being an American had for years been my métier. As diplomats, our Americanness stood out as a professional trait, something expected, even required of us, until it became as distinctive as a sailor's rolling gait or a cowboy's bowed legs.

"Your accent tells me you're from the States too."

He made a slight bow to acknowledge this truth and leaned back in his chair. "What brings you to Paris?"

The question seemed broader than its literal meaning. "I guess I'm trying to solve a mystery."

The fellow thought about this for a moment and nodded. "Me too." He cocked his head to one side. "But you're worried about yours."

"And you're not?"

He shook his head. "Nah." A faint smile. "Different kind of mystery."

"Yeah? Maybe I could use some advice. Tell me what you're doing to solve yours."

The young man regarded himself in the chair and looked up at me. "I'm sitting."

His Delphic manner irritated me even as it made me smile. Something in the kid's tone said he was making a joke that I hadn't caught onto.

I couldn't help thinking that in all the classic mysteries the detective has an acquaintance, someone who acts as a Greek chorus, warning him to be careful, reminding him there was a real life outside the world of his obsession. For Sam Spade or Philip Marlowe it would be a shoeshine boy, a news vendor, a parking-lot attendant. But this was Paris, so I got a philosopher.

We seemed on the verge of an interesting conversation I wasn't sure I wanted to get into. However our exchange might go, it would almost certainly end with this vagabond asking me for money.

I was checking my pockets when he surprised me again, this time by grabbing his knapsack and rising to his feet.

"Gotta go. Good luck on that mystery," he said before walking off toward the gate by which I'd entered.

The oddness of our exchange, and its abrupt end, made me ready to believe it had all been imaginary, a momentary product of a mind blinking red with jet lag, fatigue, and unease after my escapade near Montmartre. Yet, if nothing else, it made me wonder— thinking of Chantal Benaboud and her boy, of Curt, Gwen, Janet— exactly what kind of mystery I was pursuing.

CHAPTER NINE

FIREHOUSE DOGS CATCH THE SMELL OF SMOKE

———◦◦◦———

BY THE TIME I found the restaurant near the Place de la Bastille that evening, Gwen had already arrived.

"I thought you'd choose some tony restaurant near your apartment," I said.

She gave me a wry smile. "Too many people know me around there."

"And you don't want them to see you having dinner with a strange man while your husband's away."

"It's a tiny island. People talk." She grinned and looked away. "It's as bad as an embassy."

The waiter lit the candle on the table and took our order, returning moments later to open our bottle of wine.

We touched glasses, neither of us sure enough of where we stood to propose a toast beyond "*salut*." Our conversation hewed to safe banalities—about the wine, the day's rains, and the state of French politics—until Gwen looked at me over the rim of her wineglass and asked, "So, how's the detective business? Are you more the Sherlock Holmes type or the hard-boiled gumshoe?"

"More like the baffled rube coming into town on a load of turnips. Looking for this boy and her mother is like living in a *Where's Waldo?* book."

I described my conversation with the Vegetable Lady and how her daughter had apparently been banished for telling me too much, told her too of wandering through the Goutte d'Or in the rain, certain that Chantal Benaboud and her son lived close by. Manufacturing an offhand attitude, I mentioned the man who had followed me, trying to turn it into a humorous story.

Gwen frowned.

"You think I'm wasting my time," I said.

"I think you're going to get your head bashed in if you don't watch out. They don't like inquisitive strangers around here, especially in a neighborhood like the Goutte d'Or."

"You figure they don't like to talk to someone they don't know?"

"And a foreigner besides? No, Sam, this is trouble you don't need." The waiter came with our dinners, and she paused until he was out of earshot. "You should go home, Sam."

"You keep saying that."

"Start listening."

"I can't, not until I find the boy, or decide I never will."

"I guess we've been over that one already and decided you're too pigheaded to have any sense."

"I liked it better when you called me noble."

"I'll bet you did." She sat up straight, suddenly businesslike. "Okay, let me at least do something for you. Georges and I have a friend with the police, a sort of deputy chief. I'll tell him what you've told me and see what he thinks. Will you let me do that?"

Though reluctant to rope Gwen into my windmill-tilting, I was grateful for the offer. "If you'd like."

"I'd like." In that cool, quick tone she had begun to develop even as a junior officer, she said, "I'll call him first thing tomorrow. I've got your cell number. You can let your friend Hansen know what's going on. But don't do anything until I get back to you."

I had to smile. "You've gone into full professional mode."

Abashed, she sat back in her chair. "I'm sorry. I didn't mean to seem..."

"It's all right. Maybe we're both a couple of old firehouse dogs wagging our tails at the smell of smoke."

Gwen chuckled, but I could see her embarrassment at devolving to her former self, the one she had cultivated for years.

I didn't want to come on like I was nosing into her private life, so tried to say the next casually.

"Why did you resign, Gwen?"

At first, I thought she wanted to pretend she hadn't heard me. Eventually, though, she paused and set down her knife and fork. "A question of principle, I guess." She flashed an ironic smile, as if admitting to a fault. "Our work is—was—to defend and promote American foreign policy. I did it faithfully for years. But I got to the point that I couldn't do it anymore. The last administration..." Her voice trailed off, then came back strong. "It's one thing to disagree with the policies we promote. We all had to do that sometimes. It's another thing to abet actions you believe not only folly, but morally wrong. It had been killing my soul for nearly four years. When I got to the point where I was avoiding mirrors, I did the only thing I could do and quit."

"Why did you stay here? Why not go back home?"

"To Indianapolis?" She crossed her eyes and made a strangling sound. "Indian-No-Place? Tell me you're kidding."

"'*How ya gonna keep 'em down on the farm / after they've seen Paree?*'" My singing voice is regrettable, but I got a smile out of her before she turned serious again.

"I guess I was like most of us. I'd lived overseas so long I didn't really have a home to go back to. Not like you did. I envied your sense of belonging somewhere. I'm not sure that, in your heart, you ever left Oregon." She cocked her head to one side in an ambiguous way. "And I met Georges. This was the year before I resigned. We met at a reception and he invited me to a party at his place. We began to see a lot of each other. He was widowed and lonely. I was single and the same. We enjoyed each other's company. After two months he proposed and I said yes. We married and came to love each other." A little too quickly, she added, "I don't mean to say it was in that order."

"Any regrets?" I asked.

"About what?"

"Resigning."

"No." She shook her head and repeated, "No," giving the impression she needed to deny it to herself as much as to me. "I suppose if I'd stayed I'd have made ambassador, been sent off to some West African country where you never stop sweating. The capstone of my brilliant career." She flicked me a look under her brow. "Or were you asking about Georges? No regrets there either." After a moment she asked, "And you?"

Buying time to pull my thoughts together, I ran my finger through the candle flame a couple of times. Trying to purify myself, burn away the past? "After Janet died the light went out in my life. I stayed in Tunis another year, but I wasn't worth a damn anymore. I suppose I could have stayed, played out the string a few more years to get a bigger pension. But, maybe like you, I couldn't have looked at myself in the mirror. Besides, I didn't want to be ten thousand miles away when Tom went off to college. As you say, I had a home. When Tom graduated from high school in Tunis, it was time to go back to it."

"You live in Portland?"

"I guess someone else must have addressed your wedding invitations," I said with a laugh, unable to avoid the little dig. "No, I live in a little town called Walterville."

"Walterville?" Gwen leaned back in her chair and laughed. "Oh, that's too precious."

"I wouldn't use that term around there if I were you. They think of themselves as hardworking and decent, not precious."

"I'll be careful if I ever come to see you." She caught herself. "I mean, Georges and I . . . if we come see you."

"Sure. He spends a lot of time at your place near Bordeaux?"

She caught my drift too easily.

"Georges says the problem with American marriages is that the husband and wife see too much of each other." When I didn't laugh, she said, "It's a good marriage. Very comfortable for us both." She caught the ambiguity in her words and added, "You must have someone back there in Waldoville, someone you see."

"No. Friends, yes, but no one I . . ."

Exhausted by the possibilities and impossibilities of what we'd said and what we hadn't, we turned the conversation back to other topics. For the first time we spoke of Copenhagen, of mutual friends, what had happened to them, rehashed a few funny stories. We said nothing about ourselves back then.

"I heard you almost got killed in Pakistan," she said.

"I can make that sound pretty funny too. But it wasn't. Like I said, Curt was there with me. We nearly got killed together. Makes for a different kind of friendship."

"One where you'll come to Paris and go up against a bunch of bad customers to find his son."

"I guess so."

The waiter placed a little dish with the check at my elbow. Gwen set a finger on one end of it and drew it toward her. I put my finger on the other end to stop her.

"I invited you," I said.

"My city, my tab. Besides, I chose the restaurant."

"And I ordered the most expensive item on the menu."

"Yeah, I saw that. But when I spilled the sauce on my skirt, you were gallant enough to act like you didn't notice."

"I *didn't* notice. In fact, I think you're making it up."

We started laughing, and for a wonderful and terrifying moment we were young and in love again. The weight of it silenced us both and we looked at each other over the light of the candle, a little shaken. We both reapplied to the other's face the crow's-feet, the receding lips, the graying hair, doing it as hurriedly as we used to scramble back into our clothes and return to work after a lunchtime tryst.

We retook our roles as simply onetime friends at the perilous twilight of middle age.

In the end, I allowed her to pay for dinner, telling myself it was the best neo-macho thing to do. And her eyes warmed when I made the paleo-chivalrous gesture of helping her into her coat.

We stepped out of the restaurant into the autumn night, the cool air still damp after the day's rain. Both of us understood I would walk her home. We walked slowly, saying little, crossing over the ancient Pont Marie onto her island and along the Quai d'Anjou until, too soon, we stood outside her door. Gwen looked up toward the window of her apartment. I watched her consider whether to invite me up and saw her decide no. I felt oddly relieved. We had split the emotional tab of the evening down the middle and we'd each paid with the last of our reserves.

But when I put out my hands to take hers and say good night, she put her arms around me and placed a lingering kiss on my cheek. She whispered in my ear. "It's been a good evening, Sam. A little too good." I could hear her smile.

We said good night, not goodbye.

CHAPTER TEN

THE RUINS OF NOTRE DAME

---◇◇◇---

THE NUMBER WAS easy to find, and someone answered on the first ring, "Trans-Maghreb."

"I'd like to speak to Hassan." I'd remembered his name, the guy who had followed me out onto the landing, wanting to talk to me.

"This is Hassan."

"This is Sam Hough."

A pause.

"I'm the American who came by your office a few days ago and spoke to Maurice Girard."

A longer pause. "Yes?"

"You seemed to want to talk to me."

The silence lasted so long I thought he'd hung up.

"Yes," he said, his voice muffled, and I knew he'd cupped his hand around his mouth so as not to be heard by the man who worked next to him. "I can't speak now."

"Tell me where and when to meet you."

A Promise to Die For

He gave me the address of a café in Clichy, a suburb on the north side of the city. I was to meet him there the following afternoon, a Saturday. He hung up without another word.

Gwen called later that morning, saying she needed to talk to me, but not over the phone.

"Seriously? Is this secret shit?" I asked, the vulgarity denatured by common use as a foreign service term for anything classified.

"Sorry," she said. "Old reflex."

I knew what she meant. Ingrained habits meant to keep us safe overseas don't go quickly away. When I'd first returned to Oregon, I came back to the house one afternoon after a walk to find a small pickup parked in front of my place.

Without thinking, I got down on my hands and knees to inspect its underside. After a moment, as if waking from a dream, I asked myself what in the world I was doing.

Yes, of course, just as I would have done for years overseas on finding an empty truck in front of my residence, I was checking for a bomb.

Gwen brought me back to the present. "I spoke to my friend with the police. The one I mentioned."

A private telephone line in Paris poses no security risk, but if she wanted us to get together I wasn't going to tell her no. She said to meet her at three o'clock at a bar-café on the Left Bank.

"If I get there first, I'll order Kir Royales," I told her.

"Better not. It's a working-class bar. They'll string you up by your balls if you ask for something like that."

"Two beers and a hard-boiled egg?"

"That's more like it."

"I'll see you at three."

We took a sidewalk table across the river from the wounded monument of Notre Dame, both of us quiet in the shadow of its ruin.

"The cathedral's a monument to an old way of thinking, an old way of living," Gwen said. "As long as it stood as it was, the French found it easier to kid themselves that they were still the same people who had put it up. It's been a huge blow. So much has already changed here. Now this. Like a portent. People are on edge, wondering who they are." She sipped at her beer. "It's almost as if the fire had to happen—the question had to be raised. What will it mean if we can't rebuild it? What will it mean if we can? Will it just be a replica of something that used to be important?"

I noticed her use of "we" in speaking of the French.

"It's not so different back home," I told her. "We have that same sense that we used to be something, but we've lost the what and the why. Is this why you couldn't come home? You didn't want to see what had happened to us?"

"Home?" She shrugged in a way that said she had once known what the word meant, but no longer. "I spoke to Marc."

"Your friend with the police? What did he say?"

"You may be stepping into trouble. Drugs are coming in from the Stans, North Africa, other places. Marc says they've been keeping an eye on this Trans-Maghreb place."

After the suspicion I'd raised by simply walking into the office, after Hassan's guardedness over the phone, Curt's warning that Chantal may have fallen in with a rough bunch, Gwen's news shouldn't have surprised me.

"They're running drugs out of the place?"

"He only said that they've been watching it, and I knew not to ask anything more."

"How about the other place I went to?"

"The garage? I didn't think to ask. Sorry."

"So, for now it all may boil down to nothing."

"Sure. And it all may boil down to real trouble. I mean, here you are, some official-looking guy . . . Don't give me that look. I hate to tell you, but you could put on clown makeup and a pair of size fifty shoes and people would still catch a whiff of the upright bureaucrat."

"Okay, I'll have to be a little careful around these people until I can find Chantal and the boy. But what Curt asked me to do has nothing to do with their business."

"You may have a hard time convincing them of that." Gwen pushed aside her half-finished beer. "Marc knows an inspector who's following this stuff. He asked if you might want to talk to him."

"No. I don't want to start talking to the police about any of this."

"Maybe if you help them, they could help you."

"I don't want to get mixed up in any of that. I just want to find the boy, tell Curt where he is, and get back home." I considered telling her of my hunch that Curt's truest desire was a reconciliation with Chantal before he died, even if only by proxy. But I decided I wasn't sure and, anyway, it had nothing to do with what we were talking about.

Gwen waited, giving me a chance to change my mind about getting help from the police. When I didn't, she said, "Okay. I'll let him know to leave you alone."

We talked for a few minutes longer about nothing in particular, and she started to reach for the bill.

I whisked it away. "Nothing doing. You paid for dinner the other night. I intend to pay for your beer and call it even." I nodded toward the Île Saint-Louis and her apartment a few hundred yards away. "Can I walk you home?"

"In broad daylight? No way in the world, pal."

"Ah, yes, what would the neighbors think?"

"I know damn well what they'd think. And I'm not going to give them a chance to think it."

She gave me a flirtatious smile as a consolation prize and we got up from the table.

"Be careful, Sam," she whispered in my ear as I kissed her on the cheek. "Not everyone is honest and forthright. I think you forget that."

CHAPTER ELEVEN

QUIET DAYS IN CLICHY

CLICHY ON A Saturday morning is a quiet place, and it only took a few minutes and an online map to find the dimly lighted café. I could feel Hassan's eyes on me the moment I stepped in. Nervous as hell, his gaze darted around the room as I took the seat opposite him in the booth. I ordered a café crème. Hassan was working on a double espresso, though he seemed plenty wound up already.

"Thanks for meeting me," I said. "I had a feeling you wanted to talk to me the other day when I came by Trans-Maghreb."

He waggled his head equivocally.

"Have you worked there long?"

"Three years," he said, closing his mouth so quickly he appeared to grudge even these two syllables.

"You're from Morocco."

"Yes."

"Rabat?"

"Meknes."

Whatever it was he wished to say, he wanted me to drag it out of him.

"What do you do for Trans-Maghreb?"

"I do the accounts. I'm an accountant." His French carried the accent of North Africa.

"You like working there?"

"No."

"Your boss, Monsieur Girard, seemed—"

"I hate Maurice Girard!"

His vehemence startled me. "But you've been working there for three years."

"He's only been there a year."

"So he's fairly new."

"Girard is a terrible man. I hate my job. I hate France. I hate my life."

His outburst had compromised his dignity and he looked away, angry with himself.

I let the words settle for a moment. "Why don't you go home?" I asked, skipping past the irony that I was suggesting something I refused to do myself.

"There's no work there. Not for a man like me." He said everything between clenched teeth, the words coming out like the hiss from a pressure cooker. "You have to have connections." He spoke with a poor man's disdain for those better positioned in life. "I have a wife and son in Casablanca. I had to leave my family and come here to make enough to feed them. I send them most of my money every month. I live in a place not fit for dogs." He huffed with the pain of his humiliation. "I can either care for my family or live with them. Not both."

"Couldn't you find another place in Paris to work?"

"I'm here illegally. You know that."

"How would I—"

He spoke over me. "If I try to quit, if I tell anyone what they're doing at Trans-Maghreb, they'll turn me over to the police."

Thinking of what Gwen's friend had said, I asked, "Are you telling me they're doing things they shouldn't be doing?"

He aimed his laugh at me like a dart. "Don't pretend you're ignorant. I'm a good Muslim. They've forced me to do what I'm doing. I hate it. I hate them all. But I can't do anything about it."

"So why are you talking to me?"

"I don't know," he answered with a twist of sarcasm that said I was only pretending not to understand.

Unable to fathom what he was thinking or why, I bulled ahead. "Hassan, I'm looking for someone. A Moroccan woman and her son." I pulled the picture from my pocket. "You saw this when I showed it to Girard. He said he didn't know her, but I don't believe him. Maybe you've seen her."

His eyes shifted around the room before taking the photo from my hand and looking at it closely. After a moment he frowned and shook his head. "No, I've never seen her."

I believed him.

"Do you know a man named Benaboud? A Moroccan."

His answer needed no words. At the mention of Benaboud's name his head snapped up and he leaned back from the table, wariness sharpening his every move.

"This is his daughter, Chantal," I said, indicating the photo.

"I told you, I've never seen her. I don't know her." He licked his lips as he spoke. While I still believed what he chose to tell me, I tried to guess what he was holding back.

Avoiding my eyes, he asked, "If I talk to you, can you help me stay in France?"

"Sorry?"

"If I cooperate, can you make sure they don't deport me?"

Now it was my turn to lean away, confused. "I think you misunderstand who I am."

"I can tell you a lot—about that pig Girard and the things Trans-Maghreb is doing. And how Girard and his friends are doing things their bosses don't know. I'm caught between them and can't say anything. He doesn't care what happens to people like me." His terror showed in his eyes. "I can tell you what Garonne—" He looked around, as if he had invoked the name of the devil. His voice dropped to a whisper. "I can tell you that they think someone's working for Garonne, someone in their own group."

"What? Everyone talks about Garonne. Who is he? I don't understand what you're trying to say."

Hassan's eyes narrowed with suspicion. "You think I'm a fool? You know what I mean." Shifting uneasily in his seat, Hassan whispered. "A bald-headed man—completely bald—came in and talked to Girard. At first they whispered, but they got more and more excited and we could hear what they were saying. Something about Garonne. Something about someone working for him and they didn't know who. And it scares them."

The bald man he described could only be Momo.

"Tell me who Garonne is."

Hassan searched my face. Whatever he found made him turn away, and he gave no reply.

"Okay," I said. "So, tell me about Girard. What do you know about him?"

Hassan appeared confused at my changing questions, and it made him all the more suspicious. "I think he lives up near Montmartre somewhere," he said grudgingly.

Thinking of Chantal and her son, of the Vegetable Lady and her daughter, of the man who followed me to the Métro, I asked half-jokingly, "Does everyone live up near Montmartre somewhere?"

His brow furrowed. I was losing him, and I didn't know why.

"What are you getting at?" he asked.

"Nothing. Never mind."

"You haven't answered me," he said. "Will you help me?"

"Help you how? Who do you think I am?"

Hassan looked offended, as if I were mocking him. "You're the police. That's all right. I don't care. I'll help you. I can tell you how they bring things in, how they sell them all over Europe. They talk about selling them even in America, but I'm not sure they're serious."

"Sell what? Drugs?"

Too taken up with what he needed to say to hear my question, he shook his head in annoyance and continued. "I can tell you about Trans-Maghreb, about Garonne." Desperation darkened his voice.

"Hassan, I'm not the police."

"All right. The CIA. The FBI. Whatever you call it."

"I'm none of those things. You heard me tell Girard, I'm looking for Chantal Benaboud on behalf of an old friend. That's all there is to it."

He simply looked at me.

"I don't believe you."

"Start believing. I don't care about Trans-Maghreb or what they're doing. Truly, I don't. You can tell them that if you like."

I watched his face fall with the collapse of his hopes of currying favor with the police. He'd made a fool of himself and it made him angry.

"You should go back to America and forget about this," he said.

I wanted to ask him if he'd been talking to Gwen.

"Look, Hassan, I just want to find the girl and her son. That's it. That's all I'm here to do."

"So do it," he snapped.

"Will you help me?"

"Why should I help you if you can't help me?"

I had no answer to that, but pulled out a pen and tore a page from a pocket notebook. "Here's my name and cell number. If you think of anything that might help, call me."

I pushed the piece of paper across the table. He acted as if I had shoved a tarantula at him. With a furious glance at me for my lack of discretion, he snatched up the note and stuffed it in his pocket and looked around the room to see if anyone had noticed. In fact, no one in the little café had been paying the least attention to us. But as he looked past me and toward the door, he froze.

I looked over my shoulder in time to see a man standing in the doorway, glaring at Hassan. When he saw I'd noticed him, he quickly walked away.

"*Kuns maei ya allah,*" Hassan whispered, his voice hollow with fear.

I recognized the Arabic for "God be with me."

"What's wrong?"

He looked at me, eyes filled with fear. "Damn you!" he said. "Damn you!"

He jumped up and ran out the back door of the café.

———ooo○o——— ———ooo○o———

Curt's call that evening took me by surprise.

"How ya doin', Sam?"

Though he wanted to come off as jovial, the same old Curt, the weakness in his voice carried a note of pathos, and he paused between words to catch his breath.

I gave him a rundown of my visits to Trans-Maghreb and the garage.

"And they didn't know her?"

"That's the funny thing. I think they did." I told him about meeting the Vegetable Lady and how, when I asked about Chantal, she had given me a look to turn me into a pillar of salt.

"Maybe she didn't like the idea of a fifty-something American talking to her daughter," Curt said, but I could hear an edge of excitement in his voice, a startling rush of energy. "If this younger one says she's seen Chantal, that tells us we've got the right neighborhood. We're close."

"Maybe. If the daughter was right about recognizing her, that means the mother is trying to hide something and I'm at another dead end."

"You're beginning to doubt everyone, Sam, becoming too suspicious."

"I don't think so. Tell me why some guy would be following me."

The line went quiet. When Curt found his voice he tried to make a joke of it. "I don't know. Maybe you should ask him." But I could tell he was worried.

"And get my chops busted for an answer. I'm running into a lot of interference, maybe not because of the girl, but something to do with the people she hangs out with."

"Sam, I'm beginning to think I've put you in the middle of something I shouldn't have."

"I've met an old friend here, told her what I was doing. She knows someone with the police and she asked him if he knew anything about Trans-Maghreb. Turns out their narcotics squad, or whatever they call it here, is keeping an eye on them."

"What? Jesus."

"I wonder if Chantal's father is somehow caught up in this."

"No way. Forget about that."

I didn't find it half so unbelievable as Curt seemed to.

"So, who is this friend that knows a cop?" Curt asked.

"Just an old friend who used to work in the embassy here."

"Anyone I'd know? American? French?"

"An American. No, no one you'd know." I waited for a response, got none. "How you feeling, Curt?"

It took him a long time to answer. "I've stopped taking treatments. Just palliative care now. Trying to keep the pain down." He paused. "Sam, I should never have sent you out there."

"This needed doing, Curt, and you can't do it yourself. What's more important than helping a friend?"

"That's exactly why I shouldn't have asked you. I should have asked someone with enough sense to say no. I didn't expect this to get risky."

"It's not half so dangerous as having a building burning down around our ears. You understood better than I did the risk we were taking that day, and you came anyway. I can take a few risks for you. Anyway, it beats sitting around at home watching the History Channel. This is the most excitement I've had in years."

"You're out of your mind, Sam. But thanks." Curt's long sigh hissed over the line. "I'm pretty tired now."

The rush of energy I'd heard a few moments earlier had run its course, leaving him exhausted.

"Okay. Rest easy, old friend."

"So long, Sam."

CHAPTER TWELVE

AN ENCOUNTER WITH ULYSSES, AND A SPEEDING FIAT

A FTER A TROUBLED night's sleep, I woke in the morning to the sound of car tires on wet pavement. It had rained during the night, stripping the leaves from the trees in the Tuileries, warning that winter wasn't far off.

After breakfast, I headed in the direction of the Octagonal Pond, vaguely wondering if—hoping that?—I might run into the American I'd met earlier, spend a few minutes talking to someone who had nothing to do with my troubles.

But the metal chairs were empty and there was no one around except a young mother walking her son down the broad central path.

Disappointed, I made for the main gate.

"Ah, you're back!"

The voice came from above me, on the earthen rampart that slopes up on either side of the wide gate and overlooks the Place de la Concorde.

In a city of strangers, several of them harboring ill will toward me, I was unreasonably happy to see the young wanderer. More curious, he seemed happy to see me.

"Yes, and you're back too," I called up to him.

He was sitting on a bench, looking around him as if overseeing his estate. "How you coming with that mystery?"

"I'm more baffled every minute."

"Sounds like you're making real progress."

"I wish I was as sure as you are."

He squinted at me. "Maybe you're not asking the right questions."

"What do you mean?"

"If you're not looking at things from the right angle, you can't ask the right questions and you'll never see them clearly."

"Yeah?"

"Yeah. Sometimes you need to shift your perspective, and everything will come clear."

A cog in my mind slipped and I had a momentary vision of myself thrashing around Paris, asking all the wrong questions, seeing everything the wrong way. I felt again that the young man was playing Greek chorus—or at least shoeshine boy—to my baffled detective.

"I thought it was the old sage who dispensed wisdom to the young man. Not the other way around."

"The truth is always the same age," he said.

Maybe everyone becomes a philosopher if they stay in Paris long enough.

"How you coming with your own mystery?" I asked.

"It gets deeper all the time." The idea appeared to give him satisfaction. "I'm almost ready to ask the right questions."

"You live here in Paris?"

He thought about it. "I live wherever I am."

I wanted to kick him in the pants for his smugness, but couldn't help chuckling at his oracular ambiguity. Wanting to bring things down to a less esoteric level, I called up, "What's your name?"

He tilted his head back as if trying to recall—or uncertain I was ready for the answer.

"Ulysses."

"Like General Grant."

He shook his head. "No, the other one."

"Ah! The great voyager in search of his home."

He raised his chin in acknowledgment.

I doubted this was the name given to him by his parents, but all the better for it. Maybe we should all give ourselves truer names as we come to understand ourselves better, changing them as we ourselves change. Not a bad idea, though it would be hell on the DMV.

"And what's yours?" he asked.

"Sam."

"Like Uncle Sam?"

"No, just Sam."

He seemed disappointed at my lack of imagination.

"You're heading somewhere," he said.

"Chasing down a part of my mystery."

"Then you'd better get going. Take care, Sam."

"You too, Ulysses."

"Doin' my best," he said. "I'll see you again."

"You sound pretty sure."

He smiled, though more to himself than to me. "I'll be around if you need me."

It sounded like a promise.

I left the park, walked around the Place de la Concorde, and found I was drifting once more toward Montmartre. Maybe I'd leave tomorrow, but today I'd give Chantal and the boy—give Curt—one last chance.

It's not a long walk from the Tuileries to the streets below Montmartre. But it's one thing to walk a couple of miles on the planned grid of an American town, and something else to find your way through a city that has grown up organically over the centuries. Its streets, once cow paths and pilgrims' trails, meet at odd and deceptive angles, constantly beckoning you in the wrong direction, and I ended up bouncing around from one corner to another with all the blind relentlessness of a Roomba.

It started to rain again, a soaking shower that made the already slick streets even more treacherous. As it soaked my pant cuffs and cold drops went down my neck like an electric shock, I thought of the guy who had followed me down to the Métro. If I saw him again, I might ask him why I seemed so interesting, and to whom.

I walked past the Place Pigalle and the Moulin Rouge and around the slope of Montmartre, edging away from the tourist haunts toward the color and bustle of the Goutte d'Or.

I found the hole-in-the-wall grocery without much trouble this time. As before, the woman who ran the place had a customer at the counter. In the shadows of the narrow shop the daughter, her back to me, was taking a broom to the tile floor. As she turned to sweep down the other side of the aisle, she saw me and froze. I opened my mouth to say hello, but she scurried through a back door like a mouse down a hole.

The older woman finished with her customer, then took out her phone, turned her back on me and pretended to make a phone call. At least I assumed she was pretending, though I would soon have to rethink that.

While she made a study of ignoring me, I asked myself what I'd expected—that she'd laugh and tell me she'd only been pulling my leg about not knowing Chantal Benaboud, then give me her address and wish me good luck? Maybe give me an apple? A handful of magic beans?

I waited a few minutes but understood that she could pretend to talk on the phone as long as I could stand there. Knowing I would get nowhere with her, I walked away.

Shoppers, mostly women and, by their dress, mostly Muslim, jostled me as if I were invisible while they went from one market to another, buying what they needed for lunch. I towered over most of them, walking among their open umbrellas like an airplane skimming over a sea of nylon. I still nursed a hope of running into Chantal, though it occurred to me that, even if I should walk right by her, I probably wouldn't see her below the cover of her umbrella.

The rain began to fall harder. The few remaining shoppers made their last purchases and ran back to their apartments. Shopkeepers started to lock up for the afternoon.

As I breathed the once-familiar lunchtime aromas of roasting lamb and cumin drifting from the nearby apartments, I wondered if I might, even at that moment, be walking under Chantal's window, she and the boy sitting down to lunch, unaware that a passing stranger wanted to offer them the means to change their lives.

And, with that thought, I decided to give up. The day had been a bust and I had no reason to think tomorrow would be any better. Hassan and Gwen and even Curt had all told me to go home. Maybe it was time I listened. I'd done what I could and gotten nowhere. Or, more accurately, I'd come tantalizingly close but no closer. I'd spent a good hunk of Curt's money with nothing to show for it but dead ends, hotel bills, and the unkindness of strangers.

And I'd seen Gwen, which had proved sweeter than I'd allowed myself to hope. But she was a married woman with stepsons, a place in the country, and a marquis for a husband. For all the people I'd been pursuing in Paris, her younger self and mine were the ones most beyond reach. And, if trying to break through all the stonewalling I'd gotten from Momo and Girard and the Vegetable Lady was pointless, chasing down the ghosts of the past might yet prove sheer folly. And regarding my fruitless search for Curt's son, Gwen was right. Honesty and nobility are fine, but there's no point making a damn fool of yourself.

With the rain coming down hard, my hopes of finding the woman and the boy were replaced by a longing for a pair of dry socks. I turned down a narrow lane heading toward the Métro and found, as in residential areas all over Paris, that the locals had parked on the sidewalk, leaving pedestrians like me to walk in the street.

The car might have been following me for a couple of blocks, waiting for this chance. I'll never know. But as I stepped into the middle of the narrow street, the whine of an accelerating engine made me look over my shoulder just in time to see a small Fiat bearing down on me. I dodged to the edge of the street and hugged a parked Renault. The speeding car dodged too, coming straight at me. Moving more quickly than I thought I could, I scrambled into the tiny space between the Renault and the car parked in front of it. The Fiat passed so close its mirror clipped my sleeve.

Having missed me by inches, the car quickly veered back toward the middle of the narrow street, but the abrupt maneuver caused the tires to lose their grip on the wet pavement. With a loud slur of rubber, the car fishtailed. The driver nearly righted it, but before he could straighten the car out he ran into a delivery van.

With the Fiat's transmission howling in protest, the driver tried to jam the car into reverse, but it only shuddered and died, steam rising from the radiator in the pouring rain, one tire flattened by the impact with the van.

For several seconds both the driver and I were too stunned to move. Then the door of the Fiat popped open and a short, wiry guy staggered out. Steadying himself against the side of the van he'd hit, he gaped dumbly at the ruin of his car. With a woozy shake of his head, he looked up the street and appeared startled to find me standing only a few feet away.

It wasn't the fact that he had nearly run me down that made me angry, but something about the slack-jawed stupidity in his face. As I tried to shrug the whole thing off as an accident, the sort of motorized savagery you see all over Paris, I got a good look at him, saw the pepper-and-salt mustache only partly obscuring the cleft palate. A shock of recognition sent me reeling back. This was the mechanic who had first confronted me at the Garage Momo. And I abruptly saw things for what they were, a deliberate attempt to run me down.

"Eddie, you hare-lipped sonofabitch!"

With a growl of rage I hardly recognized as my own, I ran at him and took a looping swing at his jaw. Addled by shock and anger, I missed by about two feet and nearly spun myself into the ground. My errant blow caused Eddie to jump backward into the side of the van. I swung wildly again and struck a glancing blow off the top of his head.

Knowing I had recognized him probably staggered him more than the blow I'd landed. Panicked, he reached into his pocket and fumbled for a small revolver, which he waved at me as if it were a magic wand that would make me disappear.

Though I should have been frightened, the sight of the gun in the hand of this inept little weasel only made me angrier. I made an off-balance backhanded swipe that, by rights, should have made the gun go off in my face. Luck was with me, though, and I knocked it out of his hand. The gun hit the pavement and slid under a parked car, the impact causing it to go off, the bullet whining off after hitting the underside of the car. Eddie threw a punch at me, but he proved himself no steadier than me, and missed.

We were in no position to appreciate the absurdity of our clownish fight in the rain, but a small crowd had formed and seemed to be enjoying it. Neither of us wanted the attention, and we were both looking for a way out. The driver of the van, a young woman in a brown uniform, ran out of a nearby shop. Shouting and waving her arms, she whacked Eddie across the head with her clipboard.

Above us, another car turned onto the narrow street. Finding his way blocked by our street fight, the driver leaned on the horn, tipping our little scene further into chaos.

Thoroughly undone, Eddie pulled his arm back to throw a punch at the van driver, but even in his addled state he apparently had scruples about hitting a woman. She had none about hitting Eddie, and gave him another whack to the head. He responded with a feeble push, then scampered around in the rain trying to find his pistol.

The car horn continued to blare, and the van driver, shouting that she was going to kill him, scampered around behind him and continued to bash him around the head and shoulders. With the rain coming down like a waterfall, he gave up on the gun, turned and ran. I was in no emotional or physical state to chase him.

With a final bleat the honking car skittered past the dying Fiat and moved on. The van driver got on her cell phone to report on the damage to her van.

I was left standing in the middle of the street, soaking wet, puffing from exertion and shock. Every eye had turned in my direction. I might have sensibly told someone to call the police and made a report. But at that moment I wanted no more to do with the police than Eddie did and, like that crapulous little bastard, I took off running, not stopping until I had jumped onto a Métro heading downtown.

Back in my room, I tried to steady my trembling legs, still vibrating from an overload of shock, fear, and anger.

Though Eddie's car might have missed me, it had thoroughly overturned my decision to go home without finding the boy. Damned if I would give up now, I told myself, trying not to consider at what point commitment and determination become stupidity.

When my heart rate returned to something like normal and I had regained control of my hands I called Gwen to tell her about my afternoon. Her long, hopeless sigh knocked the props out from under me more than any lecture on my lack of judgment and general foolhardiness could have.

"I'm getting close now," I insisted against objections she hadn't uttered.

"Yeah, to getting yourself killed."

"That's not what I want to hear right now."

"I'll bet it's not. Look, Sam, if Trans-Maghreb is really dealing in drugs, they have to think you're after them."

"No. They've got to know I'm just trying to find the girl."

"Explain to me how they know that. Even this Hassan fellow didn't believe you."

"That's not the half of it. Hassan said there was someone working for this Garonne guy, someone Girard didn't know about. Like a mole in their organization."

"Mole. Gopher. Sewer rat. Whatever he is, don't get caught up in this. You say you want to keep your distance from the bad guys, so do that." She said it sharply, before letting her tone soften. "Ah, Sam, half of me wants you to stay, but the other half knows you need to go back home."

I allowed myself a glimmer of speculation that her insistence that I go home had more than a hint of self-protection to it.

"I can't," I said. "I promised Curt I'd find his son. It's become a point of honor."

I hadn't seen Gwen angry more than once or twice, but I knew it when I heard it. "Honor? More like idiocy and arrogance. I hope you're starting to understand why it couldn't have worked out between us. I couldn't have stayed with a self-righteous prig who hasn't got the sense to stay out of trouble—or come in out of the rain. I can't imagine how Janet put up with you!"

Her agitated breathing spoke to all the additional words she managed not to utter.

"Say something, Sam!"

"Are we still on for dinner?"

"Sure. See you this evening."

CHAPTER THIRTEEN

A CRYPTIC NOTE AND A PUNCH
IN THE GUT

W ITH DUSK FALLING, I got dressed for dinner and stepped out onto the rue de Rivoli an hour early, planning to buy a paper, then stroll leisurely toward the Marais and the restaurant on the Place de Vosges where the hotel had made reservations for us.

Given their difference in age, and the apparently considerable time they spent apart, I sensed—no doubt because I wanted to—that Gwen and the Marquis Georgie shared one of those world-weary upper-class French marriages based less on love than on affection and a concern for appearances. Which French nobleman was it who walked into a drawing room to find his wife in *flagrante delicto* and told her, "Please, dear, use some discretion. I could have been anyone"?

Whistling to myself, I paused halfway down the block to look into the display window of a men's clothing store, thinking what a fine—or perfectly ridiculous—figure I would cut in Walterville with a couple of French shirts. As I leaned closer to the window, I was startled to see in its reflection a man standing a few feet away, looking at me. More by reflex than real alarm, I turned to face him.

The thin, sallow-faced man didn't run but kept his eyes fixed on me. I recognized him as the one from the Goutte d'Or who had followed me toward the Métro a few days earlier. Despite my efforts to elude him that day, I realized he must have followed me back to the Brighton and had returned this evening, waiting for me to come out.

It had been a trying day and I'd had enough. The adrenaline rush from nearly getting run over in the rain came back on me like a locomotive, and I teetered between opposing urges to give him a piece of my mind or punch him out.

The man must have sensed my mood and gave me a warning look that made me hesitate long enough for him to cross the sidewalk, stuff a piece of paper in my hand, and walk away.

When he'd gone, I looked dumbly at the crumpled paper in my hand, then unfolded it. What I read so surprised me that I forgot about any leisurely stroll toward the Marais. Clutching the paper, I hurried toward the restaurant.

By the time Gwen arrived, I'd had a couple of drinks on an empty stomach and needed to grab the edge of the table as I rose to greet her.

"Hi, Sammy." An old greeting, one she used occasionally back in Copenhagen when she wanted to be endearing.

She ordered a Dubonnet. I asked for another glass of red and put on an act of conversing normally. But I couldn't fool her.

"What's up, Sam?"

"I'm a little drunk."

"Besides that."

I pushed the piece of paper across the table to her. She shot me a quizzical look, then picked it up and read it. Still puzzled, she asked, "That's it?"

I nodded.

"Two o'clock tomorrow afternoon at a café in Montmartre." She frowned. "Nothing more?"

"Some guy shoved it into my hand outside the hotel on my way here."

"Tell me you're not going to go."

"I have to."

"No, you don't. What did we talk about just this afternoon?"

"You sound like my mother."

"I wish she were here to take you by the ear and lead you to the airport."

"No you don't."

That hit too close to the truth.

"What a damned fool you are, Sam."

"Gee, dear, you're homely when you're angry."

Her mouth dropped open and she had to look away to keep from laughing.

When the moment had passed, I said, "You know I have to do this."

"I don't understand why."

"Yes, you do."

"The note doesn't even say who you'll meet there."

"I think I know."

"But you're not going to tell me."

"I don't want to jinx it."

"You'll feel plenty jinxed if there's someone waiting for you in a dark corner with a knife."

"If they kill me, you can tell me you told me so." This time my attempt to make her laugh didn't work.

Her elbows on the table, she looked at me over the rim of her raised glass for what seemed like a very long time. "I won't change your mind, will I?"

"No, I don't reckon you will."

"You won't take advice. And yet here I am giving it to you anyway." The shake of her head pronounced us both fools.

The drinks had made me reckless. "Advice? You should have advised me to get on the train with you that day in Copenhagen. I would have done it. I would have left everything behind and gone with you."

Until that moment we had danced around any impulse to speak about what we had once meant to each other. Now I had violated that vow of silence.

For a moment Gwen looked shocked, then simply shrugged and turned away, suddenly unable to look at me. "That's the romantic in you speaking, Sir Galahad."

To my surprise she pulled out a pack of cigarettes. She hadn't smoked when we were younger, and the commonplace gesture of lighting one up brought home to me as nothing else could the passage of time and the different people we had become.

She looked at the cigarette in her hand, blew a single long stream of smoke, and stubbed it out. "I forget. I'm not supposed to smoke in here." She tilted her head back and watched the slowly swirling wisp of smoke dissolve. "The truth is I wanted you to get on the train with me that day. We were in love. Nothing else mattered. But I didn't ask. And it's a good thing I didn't. You and I never had to make the adjustments it takes to live together, the disagreements about money, housecleaning, cooking, our careers. Children. Migod, children. You never had to see how different we were. You served for love of country, duty, honor. I never told you how much I admired you for that, maybe because your idealism made me uneasy. I like to think I had some of those qualities too. But I was also ambitious as hell. I'd have been hard to live with."

With every word she spoke she sounded more distant, as if she had held this conversation with herself many times and no longer allowed it to touch her. After a moment, she flipped her hand to wave away the smoke that had already dissipated and resumed her humorous, ironic manner.

"Believe me, you were better off with Janet. I wish I'd had the chance to meet her."

"You'd have liked her. Everyone liked her." I let it rest a moment. "You never married? I mean before . . ."

"Before Georges?" She took a long time answering. "Once. For a year. We didn't make any announcement. That should have told us that we knew it was a bad idea." She cocked her head to one side as if looking around a corner to catch a glimpse of herself. "I had other . . . relationships. They would last for a few months, a year, then one day the man would go off to another post, another country, or I would. And that would be the end of it. The foreign service is great that way. Lots of tearful goodbyes, few regrets." Before I could decide if she was talking about us, if she was trying to tell me that our love was no different from these other brief encounters, she sighed and said, "Well, as my military buddies at post used to say, you never talk about casualties."

Her gaze drifted off, but she placed her hand over mine and held it there. We ordered dinner and moved on to lighter topics, saying nothing more about Copenhagen or Janet or Georges or anything else too real. When the waiter brought the check I made a show of sweeping it up and holding it to my chest.

Gwen's crooked smile glowed with the candlelight. "Aren't you a dear?"

"I really am."

It's a short walk from the Marais to the Île Saint-Louis, through one of the most ancient parts of this ancient city. We didn't say much, the echo of our footsteps a sufficient exchange. I took her hand as we walked. I think we were both content. Still, I couldn't help but look over my shoulder as we crossed the bridge onto the island. At that hour there were few people out, but after the events of the day every one of them appeared animated by evil intent.

I didn't want anyone following us, didn't want them knowing where Gwen lived. Even more, though, I didn't want to miss the chance to hold her hand and walk with her in the cool night air.

We arrived at her place more quickly than I wished and stopped in front of her building. A gust of wind stirred the tops of the trees along the street. A new front coming in. We looked up and watched the last leaves stripped from the branches by the cold wind, the leaves swirling around us like windblown birds.

We said good night, but neither of us moved, our eyes asking something of each other and of ourselves. Like a flower blooming, Gwen's expression slowly transformed into a look I hadn't seen from a woman in such a long time—the Look—and I took her in my arms and kissed her, a lingering, serious kiss that she returned with inter-est. After a wonderfully long time, she stepped back, still holding my hand as well as my eyes, and started to draw me up the steps toward her door. My old heart beat so hard I was sure she could hear it.

Perhaps she did, and it woke her to what we were doing. With an embarrassed laugh, she broke away, dashed up the steps, and buzzed the door open. For a moment she stood in the open doorway and looked down at me with a wicked grin.

"Be careful, Sam. This could get dangerous."

"You mean all those bad guys I keep running into?"

Her smile lit the whole street. "Ah, yes. Them too."

She let the door shut behind her, and I watched her walk up the steps until I'd lost her from sight.

Who needs to be young when you can feel immortal?

Ready, from sheer exuberance, to run all the way back to the ho-tel, I forced myself to walk in a dignified manner toward the bridge.

As I passed a darkened doorway, I saw a short, thin man stand-ing in the shadows, looking at me as I walked by. Feeling like every man's friend, I called to him, "Don't you have better things to do with your evenings than follow me around? Tell your bosses to send me whatever they're paying you. I'll tell them where I am."

The man—I saw now that he had a buzz cut, lending him a sinister air—came out from the doorway into the light of the streetlamp, and I knew I had spoken to the wrong guy. Nevertheless, he smiled as he approached.

I think he was still smiling when he hit me in the gut and walked off.

The force of the blow knocked me over, but it was more of a push than a real punch and, through my overcoat and sport coat, it didn't hurt much. I got up chuckling. Like I say, on this beautiful evening I was everyone's friend.

CHANTAL

———◦◦◦◦◦———

THE PREVIOUS NIGHT'S winds brought cold, clear morning skies. Out my window, a lingering ground fog hung over the Tuileries, making the gardens look like one of the moodier Impressionist paintings.

It would have made sense to take the Métro toward Montmartre, but I would have arrived too early for my rendezvous. Besides, given recent experience, I didn't like the thought of being hemmed in underground, unable to get away if someone approached me with dark motives. So I decided to walk the couple miles toward the café mentioned in the note shoved in my hand the previous day.

Until Gwen had said something the previous evening, it hadn't occurred to me that my meeting might turn into an appointment with trouble. So I made a point of arriving a few minutes late and walked up to the place cautiously. Nothing about the modest café raised alarms, though that only made me wonder how I'd know what to look for.

I took a deep breath and went in.

———∞∞∞∞— —∞∞∞∞—

It seems we always recognize someone who is looking for us, even if we've never met. The woman at the back table knew immediately who I was and raised her chin in mute greeting, though she didn't smile.

Her hair was shorter, her face thinner, but Chantal Benaboud looked much as she had in the picture.

She brushed her hair back nervously and sat up straight as I walked past the scattering of other customers toward her table. Though not beautiful, her face spoke of intelligence and strength and a good heart battered by experience. Yes, she was the sort of woman a man might easily love.

I took the seat opposite her and introduced myself. Knowing there was no need, she did not.

Any sense of accomplishment I might have entertained in finally meeting her faded at the realization that, though I'd been searching for her since the day I'd arrived in Paris, it only now occurred to me that I hadn't given much thought to what I would say when I found her. A dozen lame phrases came to mind. In the end, I uttered the lamest.

"I've been looking for you."

"I know. What do you want?"

"Curt Hansen asked me to find you."

I'd wondered how she would react to hearing the name of her former lover. I quickly found out.

She twisted her mouth in distaste. "Why?"

"He wants to do right by his—your—son. He's asked me to contact you and get your address so he can arrange to send money for the boy's care."

She dug her fingernails into her palm. "Why now?" she asked. "And why didn't he come himself? Are you helping someone else?"

"What? Who else?" I asked even as I guessed what she meant.

"I don't know. The police. Someone else."

The "someone else" came out too casually to be casual. The specter of the mysterious Garonne loomed behind the thoughts of almost everyone I talked to. But if she could avoid saying his name, so could I. "I don't have anything to do with anyone else. And Curt can't do this himself because he's dying."

She looked at me hard and decided I was telling her the truth. "I'm sorry," she said. I thought I heard sincerity in her voice.

When she didn't say more, I added, "He didn't know about the boy for a very long time. And I think, at first, he was too embarrassed to reach out."

The hardness in her manner returned. "*He* was embarrassed."

"He knows now what he's put you through, about your father banishing you here. All of it. He regrets it very much and wants to make it right before he's gone." I was pleading for him more forcefully than I had imagined I would, perhaps less defending Curt than trying to justify my decision to come to Paris.

"Now he regrets it," she said with a snort.

"Chantal," I said, wanting to use her name, put our talk on a more personal level. "I may be making people at Trans-Maghreb suspicious."

She suppressed a smile, the first crack in her guardedness. "At least you know that much, Monsieur Hough."

"Call me Sam. Look, I'm not interested in Trans-Maghreb or Momo or anyone else. This has nothing to do with them or whatever they're doing. Can you tell them that?"

My words implied knowledge of the business they wished to hide, and carried an assumption that she knew of it too.

She ducked her head and murmured, "They want to know what you're after."

"It's about Curt and you and your boy. Nothing more."

She took a long time to process this, my words like a suspicious package that needed close inspection.

"You say Curt wants to help us." She shook her head. "No. Curt always wants something for himself. There's always an angle."

"He wants to die with a clear conscience, to know he's taken care of his responsibilities. That's his angle." When she said nothing, I added, "He still loves you, Chantal."

She opened her mouth to speak, but some things are too complex for words, and after a few moments she muttered only, "It's a little late for that."

She sipped at her coffee to give herself time to think. I couldn't help putting in a plea for myself. "Anyway, for now, can you get these people to back off? They tried to kill me yesterday."

Her surprise seemed genuine, but she shook her head. "If they'd wanted to kill you, you'd be dead now."

"The man—a guy called Eddie—pulled a gun on me."

"Eddie's an idiot."

"Whether I get shot by an idiot or a genius, it's pretty much the same to me."

That finally got a real smile out of her, one that she immediately erased, as if it were a sign of weakness.

"Just before that, he tried to run me down."

"He was trying to scare you."

"He did a damn good job of it."

"They wanted to make you go away. When they saw you wouldn't, they told me to talk to you."

It was a peculiar conversation. Her moods swung like a wind-blown leaf, wavering between hostility and something more sympathetic. Several times she looked away while she collected her thoughts or repressed her emotions. Eventually, I saw that her gaze always ended on a tall young man sitting at a table a few feet away—a man who, as I looked in his direction, quickly put his nose in his newspaper. When Chantal saw that I'd noticed him, she gave me a look that said, yes, he's been listening to us. I understood. She was here on their insistence, to sound me out, and they wanted to make sure she stuck to her script.

I needed a way to elude her gatekeeper. Though it had brought me nothing but distrust at Trans-Maghreb and with the Vegetable Lady, I took a chance and switched our conversation from French to Arabic.

"What's your boy's name?"

She blinked in surprise at my use of her native language.

"Nassim," she replied, with the first true warmth I'd seen from her.

"How old is he?"

Talking about her son seemed to relax her. "He's five now."

"Let Curt help him."

She shifted her eyes toward the guy sitting at the other table. He continued to stare at his paper, his brow furrowed in consternation now that he could no longer understand us.

Chantal smiled at his confusion, though, if she was supposed to let him listen to our conversation, she had to know she might pay a price later for this evasion.

"You're aware of what they do at Trans-Maghreb?" I asked.

"I'm not stupid," she said. "But they think I am because I'm a woman. And an Arab. They try to keep secrets from me. But then they forget and they talk about what they're doing, the drugs, right in front of me. I know more than they think." She turned away and murmured, "More than I want to."

"Have they mixed you up in what they do?"

"No," she said hurriedly, but ducked her head while she said it, and I knew she was lying.

"Tell me something," I said. "Who is Garonne?"

Chantal's eyes locked on mine and widened, but she said nothing.

I insisted. "Momo brought up his name while I was at his garage. For some reason, he seemed to think Garonne had sent me. The next day, just to see if I'd get a reaction, I mentioned the name to the manager at Trans-Maghreb, a guy named Maurice Girard. You know him?"

She looked at me, startled, then gave a barely perceptible nod.

I should have pursued whatever lay behind her surprise, but instead said, "When I mentioned Garonne to Girard the day after I'd seen Momo he couldn't speak for a moment. Then he denied knowing him. Just like he denied knowing you. I didn't believe him on either count. Later, I brought up the name with another guy who works at Trans-Maghreb. He acted like I'd tried to whistle up the devil."

"You had." Chantal glanced at the man at the other table to see if he had caught any of this. Her voice fell to a whisper. "Be careful. It can be dangerous to speak that name."

I tried to keep a calm demeanor, but her words left me shaken.

"Dangerous to me? To you? Who is he?"

It took her a long time to decide if she wanted to say anything more. "He's the head of the largest trafficking organization in Paris. Maurice Girard, some others, are trying to break away from him, start their own organization. They can't let Garonne know. If he knew . . ." She became more agitated as she spoke, and finally left her thought unfinished.

Pressing the issue, I said, "This other man I spoke to, the one from Girard's office. He seemed to think someone in Girard's group was actually working secretly for Garonne. Like a spy. He says they're scared to death about it."

Chantal took a breath and held it for a long time before saying, "If Girard and Momo really thought you were working for Garonne and might catch on to what they were doing . . . Well, maybe you're right. They would have to be thinking of killing you."

A hot flush went through me, followed by a second wave, cold as the grave.

Chantal stirred her coffee far longer than necessary. Then she said quietly, still in Arabic, "This is the only reason they're letting me talk to you. As I say, they want to know who you are and what you want."

"Tell them I'm exactly who I say I am, that I'm acting on behalf of Nassim's father. Nothing more."

"I'll tell them. It may not help. They deal in lies. They lie to everyone, and they assume that everyone is lying to them."

I tried to take it all in, figure out where it left me.

"And what about your cousin? Is he part of all this?"

She frowned. "My cousin?"

"I was told your father sent you here to live with your cousin."

She shook her head. "No. No cousin."

"Then . . ."

"When my father found out I was pregnant he sent me up here to marry a man who worked for him. For appearances' sake. He didn't want to marry me any more than I wanted to marry him, but between my father and this man's own people here in Paris, they could force both of us into it." She saw the expression on my face and gave me a look warped by bitterness. "There's no love between us. He wishes I wasn't around. He's got a girlfriend. He stays with her a lot. When he's home he acts like a tough guy, putting on this act to convince himself."

"He beats you?"

She shook her head. "No, nothing like that. We've become used to each other. And he's good to Nassim. Nassim thinks he's his father. He adores him," she said, her mouth warped with the irony.

The man near us snorted in frustration as we continued to speak in Arabic. Under different circumstances it might have been funny.

"Chantal, give me your address. That's all Curt wants."

With the mention of Curt, her wariness returned. Her eyes darted to the man at the other table and back again.

"Not here."

I reached into my pocket for a pen and a bit of paper. "Can you call me?"

"Please don't do that. He'll see it," she said, shifting her eyes toward the unhappy man with the newspaper in his face.

"Can we meet again, somewhere else?"

"Maybe." She licked her lips nervously. "Maybe in a couple of days."

"And if you do, you'll make sure no one follows you?"

"I'll try," she repeated. "They control me by controlling Nassim."

"And they keep a close eye on you too."

"They didn't until you came around asking after me."

"I'm sorry if I've made your life more difficult. That's not what I want. If you can't call me, leave a message at my hotel. I'm at the—"

"I know where you are."

Our conversation had grown easier as we spoke in her language, forming a bond of trust between us, however tenuous. She actually winked at me as she switched back to French and brusquely told me she had nothing more to say to me.

Assuming my role in the charade, I protested, "But you don't understand!"

"I don't want you doing anything for me. Ever! Do you hear me?" She pushed her chair back and walked quickly out the door.

The man at the other table left a few moments later, probably thinking how discreet he'd been.

———◦○◦○○○◦—— ——◦○◦○○○◦———

I spent the rest of the day not calling Curt. When I had a little extra time, I used it to not call Gwen too.

What was the point in phoning Curt simply to tell him I'd found Chantal but failed to get her address? Her agreement to see me again offered the possibility I'd get another chance. I'd call him after that, not before.

As for Gwen, I didn't want to play the lovesick schoolboy looking for excuses to call a girl. We were adults treading on morally unfirm ground. I guarded a guilty hope she was struggling not to call me too.

In the end, I couldn't entirely hold out. Taking out my phone, I laboriously tapped out a text, telling her I'd gone to the meeting with Chantal and that no one to speak of had tried to kill me. She didn't reply.

CHAPTER FIFTEEN

PEOPLE WHO GO MISSING

———∞∞∞———

THROUGH ALL THE run-ins, runarounds, and roadblocks I'd faced, I had assumed that, once I met Chantal, everything would fall into place. I'd call Curt with her address, book my flight out, and free myself of this whole mess.

Instead, my quest had become a chain around my neck, and unsavory characters could yank on it to pull me ever more deeply down their rabbit hole. Chantal had said she would call "in a couple of days," the vaguest of promises. Already, two days had gone by without any contact from her. If this had been the fallout from a first date, I'd have recognized it as a brush-off. Yet, I'd felt an urgency on her part that made me hope her offer was serious.

Speaking in Arabic may have been a mistake. The eavesdropper at the other table might have reported that we'd hidden our conversation from him. It might go hard on her if he did. On the other hand, maybe our bit of theatrics at the end, when she claimed she had nothing more to say to me, had worked.

"Maybe! May have! Perhaps!" I shouted to the walls the words that haunted every moment of my time in Paris. Nothing was certain. No one knew anything. I was strangling from an ever tighter string of unanswered questions. I grabbed my hat and coat and, wearing my frustrations like a hair shirt, blew through the Brighton's lobby. Only as I reached the door did I realize the desk clerk had been calling my name.

"Monsieur Hough. Monsieur Hough, you have a message."

I tried to appear calm as the clerk handed me a slip of paper telling me to go the following afternoon to a café at the Gare de l'Est, a train station about a mile from the Goutte d'Or.

"Did the caller leave a number?"

"No, monsieur."

"Was it a man or a woman?"

The clerk spread his hands in a gesture of helplessness. "I don't know, monsieur. I wasn't the one who took the message."

I persuaded myself the message must have come from Chantal. Yeah, just like I persuaded myself the rioters from Islamabad were a bunch of wonderful guys from Peshawar. I thanked him and went out onto the street, heading for the Tuileries.

"Ulysses! I was afraid I wouldn't find you."

The bearded young man sitting on the bench in the sunshine looked up from his book. "Didn't I tell you I'd be here if you needed me?"

I couldn't decide if he was the most irritating character I'd ever met or one of the most ingratiating. He had a wizard's gift for ambiguity.

"I'm hoping you can help me out with something tomorrow."

"This has to do with your mystery?"

"Yes."

"You're coming close to clearing it up?"

"No. It gets darker all the time, edging toward danger."

"Existential danger?"

"No, the real thing."

He let out a low whistle. "Are you sure you're doing the right thing?"

"The morally right thing or the smart thing?"

"Either one."

"Probably neither."

He smiled to himself. "The City of Light, they call it. But light makes shadows. It takes a lot of guts to rush into those shadows open-eyed."

"Don't give me too much credit. My eyes didn't open until I'd already rushed in."

He put a marker in his book and closed it. "Either way, I'm your man."

"I received a message to meet someone tomorrow, but I'm not sure the person who'll show up is the one I want to see."

"You're afraid you're being set up."

"It's possible."

"And you want someone with you, just in case."

Though I spoke of danger, my request for company sounded increasingly like a case of bad nerves. Still, I said, "I'd be grateful."

Ulysses rose from his bench. "Tell me where you need me and when."

———◦∞◦—— ——◦∞◦———

Half a dozen railway stations ring the periphery of Paris, each one dedicated to a different arc of the compass. As its name implies, the Gare de l'Est was built to serve the great capitals of now-fallen empires—Vienna, Athens, Istanbul—their names still resonant with

Old World intrigue and romance. The Orient Express had once departed from these platforms.

This might have filled me with a sense of excitement, the thrill of adventure. Instead, I felt a deep sense of dread. The cryptic message I'd received at the Brighton contained nothing to indicate it actually came from Chantal or anyone else I knew. And I hadn't forgotten that there were people in Paris who wished to harm me.

Flocks of travelers and well-wishers swarmed the station's platforms and grand halls, their cries of greeting and farewell echoing from the soaring ceilings of the nineteenth-century secular cathedral, its great spaces now modernized to the sterile anonymity of a shopping mall.

Ulysses waited for me under the station's great clock. With no more greeting than raised eyebrows, he fell in beside me as we walked toward the café specified in the message.

We must have made an odd sight, me in slacks and sport coat and dress shoes, Ulysses in shapeless dungarees, stained raincoat, and a pair of down-at-the-heel Nikes, but I was glad to have him with me. The harshly lighted café offered a display case of plastic-wrapped sandwiches and the aroma of wretched coffee—but no sign of Chantal Benaboud.

After a moment of indecision, we sat at one of the plastic-topped tables. I asked the bored waiter for tea. Ulysses ordered a latte. Five empty minutes passed, then five more.

Ulysses asked, "So, where is this woman you were hoping to meet?"

I flexed my hands, trying to release the tension building in me. "We're still a little early."

"You said you weren't sure the message really came from her?"

"No, I'm not."

"And you're afraid whoever sent it might be trouble." He adopted a relaxed slouch and threw his arm over the chair next to him.

His insouciance bothered me, speaking to a skepticism about my concerns.

"It's possible. Maybe." I blew out a breath. "Probably not."

Ulysses stretched as languidly as a house cat and looked around the nearly empty café. "I've read that if you want to kill someone and get away with it, a public space is a great place. The killer fires a couple of quick shots, then melts into the crowd, and the witnesses are all too shocked to give the police any kind of description."

"That's supposed to make me feel better?"

"Nah. Just sayin'."

Gradually, the other customers looked at their watches, paid their bills, and departed. Soon we were the only ones left, sitting alone in the middle of the empty room.

Embarrassed, I told Ulysses, "Okay, maybe no one's going to show. Sorry, I've dragged you out on a fool's mission."

The young man shrugged equably. "It's not like I canceled a bunch of appointments to get here."

"And it turns out I didn't need you."

"Yes, you did." He had again slipped into his guru persona, and I had to smile.

He actually offered to pay for his coffee, but I insisted.

We had started to leave when a tall, heavyset man in an ill-fitting jacket came through the door as if running late, nearly knocking me over in his rush. Startled, he squinted at me for a moment. Then his eyes widened and he fumbled for something in his jacket pocket. When he noticed Ulysses he hesitated an instant before starting to draw his hand out.

Ulysses didn't hesitate. He shoved the man in the chest, knocking him out of the doorway. With a volatile mix of surprise, confusion, and anger, the guy looked for a moment as if he were thinking of running, then took a swing at Ulysses, delivering a glancing blow in the side of the head.

Occupied with Ulysses, he didn't see my punch coming. The blow to his chest sent him stumbling farther backward.

For the second time since I'd arrived in Paris, a small crowd gathered to watch me get in a fight. As I began to think that I should start charging admission, a little guy with gray, curly hair, apparently the café's manager, came out from behind his counter, shouting something I couldn't catch and trying to shoo us away from his door.

Our attacker looked from one of us to the other. Apparently not liking the odds, or maybe the fact that we'd attracted a crowd, he turned and ran, shoving aside a couple of bystanders as he fled.

With the resilience, and the testosterone, of a young man, Ulysses quickly shifted from the attacked to the attacker and took off after him. I ran after Ulysses, hoping to stop him before he got himself hurt.

Weaving through the throngs in the main concourse, I lost sight of both of them and was about to give up when I came upon Ulysses standing near the ticket windows.

"I lost him," he said.

"Just as well. The way he went for his pocket, I think he was armed."

Breathing hard from the stimulus of the last couple of minutes, Ulysses grinned. "That was fun."

He had left behind him any hint of the self-contained Tuileries guru, and was just a young guy enjoying an adrenaline rush. "Who was he?" he asked.

"No idea."

"But you were right. Someone was setting you up."

"Looks like it." With the excitement over, I began to wonder what we had actually seen and done. "We don't really know. He might have been some friendly Parisian reaching into his pocket to hand us a couple of tickets to the ice follies."

Ulysses snorted. "I don't believe it."

"Neither do I," I admitted. "Thanks for being here, Ulysses. You might have saved me from some serious harm."

"Glad to do it, Sam."

I offered to head back to the Tuileries with him, but he said he'd promised to meet a young woman at the Trocadero. As he walked away, he stopped and turned back to me. "Like I say, I'll be there when you need me." With that, he waved and disappeared into the crowd.

———⊶⊶⊶—— ——⊶⊶⊶——

Trying to get back on track after Chantal's no-show, I pulled my phone out and called Trans-Maghreb as I walked back to the hotel. "Could I speak to Hassan?" I asked the voice that answered the phone.

After a long silence, the voice said, "Hassan no longer works here."

I recalled the fear in Hassan's face as he fled the café in Clichy and wondered how dearly he had paid for speaking to me.

"Do you know how I can reach him?"

Another long pause.

"No."

"Where has he gone?"

The man at the other end of the line—it had to be Mohamed, the one who sat next to Hassan when I visited Trans-Maghreb—breathed unsteadily into the receiver. "Maybe he's gone back to Morocco."

Wasn't anyone in this town sure about anything?

"Why did he go back to Morocco? Did Girard fire him? Did the police pick him up?" A far worse possibility entered my head, one that said he hadn't gone back to Morocco at all but, thanks to me, might be at the bottom of the Seine.

Before Mohamed could answer or, more likely, refuse to answer, I heard a voice in the background asking, "Who are you talking to?"

The line went dead.

———◦◦◦◦◦◦— —◦◦◦◦◦◦———

That night I phoned Curt. During our previous conversation I had all but promised to call him with good news, but I had none. I filled him in on my contact with Chantal at the café and her failure to show up at the Gare de l'Est. I told him, too, of Hassan, his nervousness at our meeting and his subsequent disappearance.

"You've developed a real knack for getting in touch with people who go missing right afterward," Curt said.

Before I could stammer a defense, he cut in. "But you finally found Chantal. Did you get her address?"

"No. Someone was watching us."

"Watching you?"

"Like I said, the crowd she fell in with is rougher than either of us thought. They're mixed up in drug trafficking."

"You didn't sound half so sure about that the last time we spoke."

"Chantal more or less acknowledged it. I think they've forced her to get involved too. Curt, this is getting dangerous. Someone tried to run me down the other day, then pulled a gun on me before he ran off. What the hell's going on?"

"Jesus! Sam, I had no idea things would get like this. I figured Chantal would be happy to tell you where she lived, she'd give you her address, and you'd be on your way."

He sounded shaken, and I didn't want to add to his distress. "It's okay. This is still a lot more interesting than raking leaves back in Walterville."

"I want you to stay safe."

"You and me both. By the way, one thing I found out from Chantal is that her father didn't send her off to live with a cousin. There was never a cousin."

"Really?"

"Her father needed to save face by finding her a husband. He set up a forced marriage for her here in Paris. That's bad enough, but it seems her husband's caught up in this drug racket too. I know you don't want to think so, but it looks like there's a connection between Benaboud and these guys."

"You're sure? I didn't think he would . . ." Curt sounded querulous, starting to express thoughts he couldn't finish, showing no sign of the quick-witted rogue I'd known so well.

Between the search for his boy and the progression of his illness, it was clear he was trying to tap psychic and physical reserves he no longer possessed.

His voice abruptly came back strong and insistent. "I've got to get that address."

"I'm working as hard as I can," I told him, knowing I sounded not only inept but defensive. "You haven't got any ideas about some other person, some other approach to this thing?"

Curt's tense, shallow breathing came over the line as a prolonged hiss. "Okay. There's one more person you could talk to. But I don't know if he . . ." His voice faded to silence.

"Who is he, Curt?"

"A French employee in the embassy's Admin section. Used to work for me. Name of Paul Forestier. But . . ." Again, he left his thought unfinished.

"But?"

"I don't know if he's going to want to talk to anyone who knows me."

"Why is that?"

"Wait a minute. I think I still have his phone number here."

He hadn't answered my question, but I let it go. "No. I don't want the number. If what you say is true, he might hang up on me. Do you have an address? I'd rather just show up at his door."

I heard him put the phone down and rustle through some papers. "Here it is," he said, "Ten rue Daguerre, an apartment in the Fourteenth Arrondissement. Thanks, Sam, for not giving up on this. Not giving up on me."

"I'm glad to do it." An exaggeration, but not entirely untrue.

"Keep your head down," Curt said, the standard foreign service sign-off to someone in a hazardous post.

"But you have to tell me how talking to Forestier has anything to do with finding your boy." When he didn't reply, I told him something that had increasingly come into focus over the previous couple of days, an idea that should have struck me from the beginning. "There's something more to this, isn't there? Something you didn't tell me."

"What do you mean?"

"You told me about the boy, but I know it's at least partially about Chantal. You still love her. That's why you want me to talk to her. So you can reconcile with her before . . ." I didn't want to finish the sentence any more than I wanted to talk about the hazards of trying to regain lost love. "But there's something more to this, and I can't see it."

For a long time he said nothing. Then he took a deep breath and said, "Hurry, Sam."

"Curt—"

But he had already hung up.

CHAPTER SIXTEEN

THE MAN WITH A SIGNET RING

LOCALS MAKE UP the great majority of employees in any American embassy. Many of them work with us for decades, developing long-term relationships with our most important contacts, relationships they maintain for us while we Americans come and go. Working in cultures we'll never fully understand, we rely on their judgment and experience to keep us out of trouble. Forestier would be someone Curt trusted, someone with deep contacts, developed over years, someone who knew things we Americans, in our three-year assignments, would never have time to learn.

Curt's insistence that I should talk to a former embassy employee gave me a good pretext to call Gwen. She had said Curt's name sounded familiar. Maybe she knew things about him I didn't. And there seemed an even better chance she would know Forestier.

We hadn't spoken since the evening she had started to lead me up to her apartment and then run away, leaving me wondering where that left us.

I punched in her number and braced myself for a myriad of possibilities—flirtatiousness, contrition, stony distance—but after six rings I got nothing but a recording asking me to leave a message. Hoping all the while that she would pick up, I described my conversation with Curt and gave her Forestier's name. While I tried to think of more to say, the beep at the other end of the line told me I'd run out of time.

If this was the detectives' life they could have it. A few phone calls, some scattered conversations, a lot of walking around and tedious hours of nothing—unless I counted the occasional attempt to run me down. I smiled at the skill of mystery writers to make it all sound exciting. The lying bastards.

The ringing of my phone startled me from a deep doze. For a few bleary moments I had no idea where I was or whether it was day or night. Eventually, I located myself at the Brighton Hotel on an autumn afternoon in Paris, lying fully clothed on the bed.

I picked up my phone and muttered, "Yeah?"

"It's Gwen."

"Gwen." My head still cloudy, I asked, "Why are you calling?"

"You called me, remember? You wanted to know about Paul Forestier."

"Oh, yeah."

"This somehow relates to finding your friend's son?"

"I hope so. Curt gave me Forestier's address but didn't tell me why I needed to talk to him. Any chance you know him?"

"I know who he is, anyway. The famous Paul Forestier."

"Famous?"

"Or notorious. He had a genius for getting himself into trouble, then popping out of it again. The Houdini of bureaucrats."

"That would make him Curt's kind of guy. I can see them working in the bowels of the embassy like the witches in *Macbeth*, cauldron bubbling, scheming up ways to get around the Foreign Affairs Manual. They must have made a real pair."

"Too great a pair. Forestier nearly got fired about the time I arrived."

"What about?"

"Something to do with establishing an improper shipping contract for friends of his."

"This was when Curt was still there?"

"Must have been. As I say, Hansen left the same summer I arrived. But before leaving post he went to the mat to save Forestier's unworthy behind."

"Why?"

"You're asking why Forestier did what he did, or why your friend protected him?"

"Either one. Both."

"Everyone assumed Forestier was getting some kind of kickback for writing up this shipping contract outside the regs, but they could never prove anything. Your friend Hansen vouched for his employee's unwavering honesty, if not his methods. From Hansen's point of view the whole ruckus was probably about turf protection. You know, 'No one fires my people but me.' He was able to show that Forestier's friends actually charged less than others did, and said he deserved an award for saving taxpayer money."

"So Forestier kept his job."

"Temporarily. Once Hansen left, they showed him the door." While I thought this over, she added, "Look, Sam, I'm sorry, but I'm almost out the door. I'm taking the train to our place near Bordeaux for a few days."

"You have to go right now?"

"I need to remind my husband he's a married man."

"And to remind yourself you're a married woman?"

She took a long time before saying, "Sam, promise not to leave until I get back, okay?"

"I promise."

———∞∞∞—— ——∞∞∞———

The rue Daguerre is a pedestrian street, blocked off during the day to form an open-air market for vegetable, fruit, and seafood mongers and busking musicians.

With darkness coming on, the owners of the food stands were taking down their awnings and throwing canvas covers over their refrigeration cases. A few dawdling shoppers wandered around, trying the patience of sellers anxious to go home for dinner.

The door to number ten, a solid middle-class apartment building from the 1920s, stood between an upscale wine shop and a bakery. I pressed the buzzer next to the name Forestier.

"*Oui*?" asked a voice over the speaker.

"Monsieur Forestier?"

"Yes."

"My name is Sam Hough. I'd like to talk to you."

I felt his wariness through the silence.

"Why?"

"I'm a friend of Curt Hansen's."

The pause lasted long enough that I thought he'd hung up. "What does that have to do with me?"

"He told me I should talk to you."

Another pause. "What about?"

"I'd rather discuss it with you face-to-face." This sounded better than admitting I wasn't sure myself.

The buzzer sounded and the door clicked open.

"Fifth floor," he said.

I took the birdcage elevator up to the small landing in front of his apartment.

He answered the door at my first knock. Tall for a Frenchman, he was older than I had imagined, perhaps sixty-five. Thin, with an erect posture, he compensated for his receding hairline with a Vandyke beard.

"Monsieur Forestier?"

"What do you want?" he said in English, wanting to make clear that after years in the embassy his English was better than my French.

"I'm trying to help Curt Hansen on a private matter. He suggested you might be able to help me. May I come in?"

After twisting his mouth with finely demonstrated reluctance, he stepped aside and allowed me to enter.

It was a small corner apartment, a comfortable place with heavy furniture of another era and tall windows on two sides. The aromas of dinner cooking hung in the air.

Frowning at the necessity of being polite, Forestier nodded me toward the sofa. A graying woman in an apron peeked out from the kitchen. With an arched eyebrow and a click of his tongue, Forestier sent her back.

He remained standing. "What is this about?"

Ignoring his brusque manner, I briefly described how Curt had asked me to find his son, born of a woman he had known in Morocco but who now lived in Paris.

"Why isn't Mr. Hansen here himself asking me about this?"

"He's dying."

I watched the shock register on his face. "I had no idea."

"Neither did I until recently. I promised I would do what I could to find his boy."

Forestier took a seat in an armchair opposite me and sat silently for some time, his head bowed, his look turned inward. When he raised his eyes to me, he said, "I'm sorry about Mr. Hansen."

"I understand he helped you keep your job at one point."

I immediately regretted my words. Forestier bridled at my allusion to his professional difficulties. Caught between apologizing and pressing on, I pressed on.

"You got into trouble for steering things toward a company called Trans-Maghreb. Yes?"

My shot in the dark hit home, catching him off guard.

Before he could recover, I said, "They were friends of yours?"

He sat stiffly, like a hostile witness on the stand. "They were friends of Mr. Hansen's from his time in Morocco. I'd never heard of the company until he told me to contact them." Forestier's resentful expression made clear these were not happy memories. "What has this to do with finding Mr. Hansen's son?" he asked.

A good question. I wished I knew the answer. Curt wouldn't have told me to talk to Forestier without a reason. The Frenchman knew something or could do something of value for me, but I wasn't sure what it was.

"Tell me how this started with Trans-Maghreb," I said.

His lips compressed to a pair of white lines. For several seconds he said nothing, then explained, "When he first came to Paris, Mr. Hansen told me to make up a contract with Trans-Maghreb without going through proper procedures. Eventually, a Department inspector found out and blamed it on me." His mouth set grimly, he tilted his chin sharply. "Mr. Hansen saved my job, yes. But he's also the one who put me in a position where it had to be saved."

"And after he left, you were let go and—"

Forestier broke in sharply: "After he left, I retired." We both knew that allowing him to retire instead of forcing his dismissal was a convenient dodge for all concerned, avoiding the messiness of documenting cause.

"Mr. Hansen's son is by the daughter of a man named Miloud Benaboud. The name is familiar to you?"

Starting to feel the edges of the corner he was backing into, Forestier hesitated before answering. "Of course."

"The daughter's name is Chantal. That name is familiar too?"

"No."

I believed him.

"Curt didn't know anything about the boy until shortly before he left Paris and he didn't know what to do. Now he does. He wants to help the boy by leaving him a considerable sum of money."

"As I asked earlier, what has this to do with me?"

"I don't believe he wants you to do anything. But you might be able to help me." I pulled the photo from my pocket. "Have you ever seen this woman?"

He regarded the picture, then waved it away. "I don't believe so."

"You're not sure?"

"I've met a lot of people. I can't remember them all. This is Benaboud's daughter?"

"Yes. As I say, she lives here in Paris."

"And . . . ?"

"I don't suppose you would have any idea where."

"How would I know the whereabouts of a woman I've never met?" The tension in his posture, which had been building throughout our conversation, visibly eased. "So this has nothing to do with the troubles with Trans-Maghreb after all?"

"Not directly, no. Curt told me to stop by their office out by Charles de Gaulle. But they weren't of any help."

Forestier raised his eyebrows in surprise. "Mr. Hansen told you to go there?"

"Yes."

He had been leaning forward in his chair, but now sat back. "I'm puzzled they would know nothing about Benaboud's daughter if she were living in Paris."

"I think they know more than they want to admit." I didn't see any point in telling him that I wasn't being candid either, that I'd met Chantal and she'd refused to tell me where she lived. "There's some sort of guilty knowledge they wish to hide. I believe that's why Curt wanted me to talk to you, in hopes you might know something that could lead me to her."

A frown twitched across his face. "Because I know people at Trans-Maghreb."

"Something like that. You used to go out there?"

"Yes, Mr. Hansen always left it to me to contact them," he said, his voice colored with resentment. "But I don't know why he thinks I could be of any help finding her."

"As someone they know, it's possible they might tell you something they wouldn't tell me. Would you be willing to call them for me and ask where she lives?"

"No."

"Even if—"

"No."

I waited for him to relent, but he clearly felt no need to fill the silence that built up between us.

I'd come to yet another dead end. I thanked him for his time and rose to go.

Forestier's relief that I was leaving without roping him into another of Curt's schemes was palpable. He even smiled as he led me to the door.

"Please give my regards to Curt," he said as I called for the elevator. "I'm sorry for his illness. I always liked him. In spite of everything."

Like a game-show host saying goodbye to a failed contestant, Forestier apparently didn't wish to see me go away empty-handed. "By the way, as I say, I've never seen the woman in the photo, but I can tell you who the man is."

Puzzled, I pulled out the photo again and looked at it.

"It's Curt, isn't it?"

"No."

The elevator arrived with a jolt, like an exclamation mark to our exchange.

"You can't see anything but the man's hand," I said. "How can you be so sure?"

Pleased to have surprised me, he said, "The ring. It's very distinctive."

Feeling a kind of vertigo as I once more wandered out of my depth, I asked, "Who is it?"

"His name is Girard. I believe he's working for Trans-Maghreb now."

"Maurice Girard?"

As startled as I felt, he appeared even more so. "You know him?"

"We've met."

The fog I'd been wandering through began to lift and a thought came to me with sudden clarity. "Chantal Benaboud's father arranged for her to marry a man here in Paris. Someone to pose as the boy's father. Could that man be Maurice Girard?"

"Now you're asking me questions beyond my pay grade," he said, leaning on an old bureaucratic wisecrack. "But I'm sure it is he in the photo. I recognize the ring."

I thought of how much easier things might have been if I had noticed Girard's ring the day we met and guessed at his relationship with Chantal early on.

A new question occurred to me. "Did you ever hear that Trans-Maghreb might have been transporting goods they shouldn't have?"

Like a light going out, Forestier's face went blank and his wariness came back. "I wouldn't know anything about that," he said and shut the door in my face.

Feeling like a pilgrim seeking the Oracle, I searched the Tuileries the next morning, looking for Ulysses. It seemed absurd to think he could shed light on my labors. Yet, his ability to see beyond what I saw made me want to give it a try.

After half an hour of wandering around the fountains and the shuttered carnival, I found no trace of him. Left to myself, I struggled to assess my progress and realized it could be measured almost entirely in negatives.

From my stops at Trans-Maghreb and chez Momo I had learned little, except that people there were inclined toward violence when strangers sniffed around asking after Chantal Benaboud. Later, after allowing Chantal to slip away, I had burned through a series of possibilities that all led nowhere. My connection with Hassan had resulted in nothing for me and, for him, a one-way ticket back to Morocco—at best. The man sent to confront me at the Gare de l'Est remained a mystery, making me doubly regretful that he managed to slip away. I had gained little from my talk with Forestier, except the intriguing revelation that Chantal might be married to Maurice Girard.

All my efforts had led nowhere—except to Gwen. The persistence of the embers still glowing in our banked fires had startled us both, needing the merest breath to ignite them into a still-small flame. I saw it in her as clearly as I felt it in me. Despite all the imperatives of decency and good sense, neither of us did anything to put the flame out.

The thought sparked a peculiar guilt, though—to my discredit—not about the Marquis Georgie. I had loved Janet without limit or shadow. But sometimes, lying in bed on one of those nights when sleep defied me, I had thought what a shame it was that we got only one life and I could not spend this one with Janet and another with Gwen.

No matter what might pass between Gwen and me, I still felt married to Janet. However I might fight against its illogic, my longing for Gwen felt like a betrayal, one for which I could not ask Janet's forgiveness because she was gone.

The years since Janet's death had taught me a great deal about loneliness. I had even found a thin comfort in its simplicity. But I'd had enough of a bad thing, and seeing Gwen again made me feel alive for the first time in years, made me want to say, for once in my life, to hell with being a straight arrow and take another chance on life. If our arrangement might be squalid, maybe I should allow a little squalor in my life.

By her husband's absence and my own reluctance to mention or even think about him, I had nearly persuaded myself that her husband wasn't real, only an illusion that Gwen and I toyed with. I knew it wasn't true.

The desk clerk's face lit up as I crossed the lobby of the Brighton.

"Ah, Monsieur Hough, I have a message for you."

Knowing how pleased I'd been to receive my previous message, he must have been disappointed at my puzzlement. But Curt wouldn't call at this hour, and I doubted that Gwen had returned yet from Bordeaux.

Wavering between professional distance and personal familiarity, the clerk said, "The woman called not more than an hour ago. She told me to make sure I gave you her message as soon as possible."

"What woman?"

But of course I knew.

He dared a sly smile at the young woman's urgent wish to see me and handed me the piece of paper. At least Chantal had left her name this time. I was to meet her at the Place St. Pierre at the foot of Montmartre at two o'clock.

I looked at the clock behind the front desk. I had twenty minutes.

I dashed out to the street and flagged down a taxi.

CHAPTER SEVENTEEN

A CAROUSEL ON
THE PLACE ST. PIERRE

G LOWING LIKE AN oversized Christmas ornament, the carousel in the Place St. Pierre lay nestled in the curving arms of the twin staircase at the base of Montmartre.

Even on a chilly fall day the painted ponies carried a score of riders on their slow revolutions, the hobbyhorses bobbing with grave dignity. On the carousel's platform, a few parents and au pairs stood alongside the smallest children, keeping them steady in their saddles. A young couple held hands across the space between their horses.

After paying off the taxi, I searched the faces on the carousel and those of the adults standing nearby and couldn't find Chantal among them.

Thinking she had again set a rendezvous and failed to show, I started to tell the cabbie not to leave when I spotted her on one of the benches between the two staircases. She'd chosen the farthest bench, nearly hidden within the spider-work shadows of a leafless tree. She must have seen me arrive but made no sign of recognition other than to watch me closely as I approached.

Still nervous about what had happened at the train station two days earlier, and remembering our meeting at the café, I glanced around the tiny square for an eavesdropper or even a possible assailant. I couldn't help worrying that she might have been set out like the proverbial goat tied to a stake, bait for an ambush. But she sat alone, no one near her.

Still uncertain, I sat a little distance away, taking the bench next to hers, watched the carousel go around and said nothing. Though she knew I was there, she paid me no attention. At every revolution she smiled and waved to a skinny little boy on one of the painted horses.

When I'd begun to wonder if she had invited me simply to watch the carousel go around, she said, without looking at me, "I'm glad you could come."

"I'm sorry I missed you at the Gare de l'Est. But someone else came instead."

I said it to get a reaction, and I got one. The puzzlement on Chantal's face looked genuine.

"What are you talking about?"

"I got a message at the hotel the other day to be at a café at the train station. You're saying you didn't send it?"

"No, I didn't." She shook her head, confused. "But you say someone met you there?"

"Yes. I think he meant to do me harm."

"Who was it?"

"I don't know. I'd never seen him before."

"And what did he do?"

"He was looking for me. When he found me he reached into his pocket."

"And?"

I wasn't ready for so simple a question. "Well . . . I hit him." I had no wish to bring Ulysses into it.

Chantal cocked her head to one side and squinted at me. "A man came up to you and put his hand in his pocket, so you punched him?"

"I was afraid I had been set up." I could hear the defensiveness in my voice. "After nearly getting run over, and having a gun waved in my face, and getting punched, I've become a little sensitive. Besides, in spite of the note to meet there, no one else approached me."

"Maybe you were right—that he'd been sent," she said.

"By Maurice Girard's bunch? Or this man Garonne?"

"I don't know."

We fell into a long silence. She waved again at the boy on the carousel. "That is Nassim," she said.

So this was him. The goal of my search, the son Curt wanted to help to a better life. The elusive little fellow who had led me into six kinds of trouble was suddenly just a little boy on a merry-go-round. A surge of both affection and pity ran through me.

The boy smiled and waved to his mother, turning on his pony to keep her in sight as the carousel revolved.

"He's a handsome little fellow," I said. In fact, he bore a striking resemblance to Curt, but I thought it best to say nothing about it.

The wind blew a twig from the tree onto the bench. Chantal picked it up and worked it nervously in her hands.

"I'm happy you were able to get a message to me today," I told her.

"Usually, one of Maurice's friends picks Nassim up from school." She gave the word "friends" a full measure of irony. "The children have a short day on Wednesdays. Bernard—that's who picks him up—usually forgets that Nassim leaves early that day. Bernard probably dropped out of school in third grade and would have no memory of such things. So I took the chance to pick up Nassim from school myself and bring him somewhere I could meet you. That's why I called you on such short notice."

"We're not being watched?"

"With Bernard gone, there's no one left to keep an eye on me."

"This Bernard, he comes all the way from where he lives just to pick up Nassim?"

"No. Almost everyone in that bunch lives in the same building with us. Like college boys." She tossed her head unhappily. "For all the effort they put into it, they're as broke as college boys."

"I'd always thought people involved in the drug trade made lots of money."

"Only in the movies. No one's getting rich. It's a small group, just a handful. They're still part of a larger organization, but they're trying to break off and go on their own. For months they've been diluting some of the drugs they're supposed to deliver for the organization and selling the extra on their own."

"That sounds dangerous."

"It is. They spend half their time making small deals and the other half shitting their pants, terrified that the Big Man will find out. And he will." She muttered this last under her breath.

"The Big Man. That's Garonne?"

"How did you find out about him?"

"Momo mentioned him. He seemed to think I was working for him. I threw the name at Maurice Girard to see if it meant anything to him. He nearly had a stroke pretending he didn't know who I was talking about."

"You mentioned Garonne to Maurice? That was very dangerous."

"Tell me more about Garonne."

"He's the head of the organization Maurice and his friends are trying to break away from."

"What would happen if he found out about them?"

"He'd kill them. Eventually. First, though, he needs to know who's involved and exactly what they're doing." She shrugged as if it were of little concern to her, then turned and held my gaze. "If they ever decide you're working for Garonne . . ." She didn't need to say the rest. "The idiots Maurice has thrown in with, they're all young and stupid. Except for Maurice. He's older and stupid."

"Maurice Girard is your husband, yes, the man your father forced you to marry?"

Throughout our conversation her body language had revealed as much as her words, and now she looked into the sky and sighed. "My husband? According to the laws of the French Republic, yes." With a bitter smile she said, "At least he wasn't a stranger. He'd come to Morocco once or twice. I knew him slightly."

"He liked you?"

"He likes women." She worked at the twig in her hands. "Sometimes he's good to me."

The bleakness of her words chilled me.

"And, as I told you the other day at the cafe, Nassim likes him. He thinks Maurice is his father."

"How did Maurice get mixed up in all this?"

"You have to understand Maurice. His family were *pieds-noirs*."

I knew the term. Black Feet. It was what the French called the French families who had lived in Algeria, often for generations. Despised by the Algerians as colonialists and disdained in their homeland for not being sufficiently French, they were people without a country.

Chantal dug her hands deeper into her pockets. "Maurice saw how his family was treated for having lived in Algeria. The kids bullied him in school, called him an Arab, a rag head. It made him an angry child, and then an angry man, always an outsider, belonging nowhere, to no one. So he likes the idea of rebelling against his bosses, rebelling against anyone. I've pleaded with him to quit this group, not to go against Garonne. For Nassim's sake." She shrugged at her helplessness.

"You mentioned Bernard. He was the tall man sitting near us at the café?"

She nodded. "They're all like little boys, playing a game they saw on TV. They like to pull out their guns and show them off, even in front of Nassim. They have no sense at all. That's why they're dangerous, even if it's mainly to themselves."

"The man from Trans-Maghreb I spoke to about all this, he hinted that Garonne has a mole in your husband's group."

I thought the news might have shocked her, but she only asked, "Who told you this?"

"A man named Hassan."

She didn't say anything for a while, then asked, "Does he actually know? Or is he making this up?"

"He seemed to think it was true."

Chantal twisted uncomfortably on the bench. "Maybe he meant he himself was the mole. Someone working for Trans-Maghreb might know a lot without actually being part of this gang of idiots."

"He seemed to think I was working for the police, that if he gave me information I could keep him from being deported when we arrested everyone. If he believes that, he's probably too stupid to be a very good mole."

"No. He might be exactly stupid enough to do something that dangerous." Chantal blew out a bitter laugh. "Anyway, forget about this supposed mole."

"But it seems that if I—"

"Stop! If it's true, it's too dangerous for you to know anything about. Drop it."

I tried to laugh. "It's like I'm putting together a puzzle, but every time I think I'm nearly finished I find another piece and I have no idea where it goes."

"I don't know why Garonne worries about this bunch. They'll tear themselves apart soon enough without any help from him." She didn't say anything for a while, finally asking, "Can I see the photo?"

I pulled it out and handed it to her. She gazed at it so long I thought she'd forgotten about me.

I coughed into my hand to bring her back to the present. She actually jumped. Embarrassed, she returned the photo to me.

"Me and Maurice," she said with the kind of sad shrug given to things that can't be undone.

She watched the carousel slow to a stop and the riders dismount. Nassim came running to his mother, laughing and rattling away in his little boy Arabic, the words too rushed for me to understand. Though I sat only a few feet from Chantal, the boy took no notice of me.

She put her arms around him and in a conspiratorial voice said, "I'll bet you'd like to ride it again."

He nodded excitely. She put a coin in his hand. "Hurry. People are already getting on."

Nassim started off toward the carousel at a run, then skidded to a stop, ran back to Chantal, and gave her a hurried kiss on the cheek before dashing away again.

"A sweet boy," I said.

"Yes," she said, a faint smile on her face as she watched him hand the coin to the woman in the ticket booth and run onto the carousel.

"But you didn't tell Curt about him."

Still watching her son, her smile faded. "I was young and frightened." Her shoulders slumped. Unable to afford the indulgence of regret, she recovered herself quickly. "I arranged to see Curt one last time. But I didn't tell him why. I wanted him to figure it out. I wanted him to ask me what was wrong. When he didn't, I gave up on him." She broke the twig she'd been working in her hands and threw the pieces to the ground. "I can never decide if that was foolish or wise."

"When your father found out you were . . ."

"Pregnant? I thought he might kill me. That's not a joke. When other people found out about my . . . condition, my father would look like an old fool who couldn't control his daughter. In the end I was lucky. He only disowned me, sent me away, and forced me to marry a gangster." I'd never heard a more mirthless laugh. "He told everyone I'd gone back to France to continue my education and had married a fine gentleman."

"And Girard agreed to marry you."

"He was under orders as much as I was."

"So he's not the head of this breakaway group?"

"God, no. He'd like to be. It's run by a man—a boy, really—named Raoul. He's vicious and smart, except when he's on drugs himself, which is too much of the time. He's like a baker who eats his own pastries." Her smile held a bitterness hard to watch. "I hate this life."

"Chantal, if you'll give me your address, I can help you and Nassim get away from it."

"No." She shook her head. "They wouldn't stand for us getting money they didn't control."

"Could I send it to your bank account?"

"I'm not allowed to have one. Maurice insists he control all our money. He'd find out and there would be trouble."

"You couldn't explain to them where it came from?"

"I'm not sure it would make any difference to them. Or it might even make things worse." She returned to watching Nassim on the carousel and said nothing. When I wondered if our conversation was over and I should leave, she said without looking at me, "If you want to help us, there's one thing you can do."

"What's that?"

"You can get us out of here. You can get us to America."

Her words took me so unexpectedly that for a moment I couldn't reply. "I . . . I don't know that I can do that. I'm retired. I'm just a private citizen now. And, even if I weren't . . . Look, Curt tells me you're here illegally."

As if insulted, Chantal raised her chin. "No. I have a passport. Nassim too."

"Curt thought—"

"Curtis is wrong."

Curtis, she said. It struck me as speaking to their intimacy that she called him by a name that no one else did.

"You'd still need visas," I said. "Nassim would need his father's permission to go to the States."

"Curtis is his father."

"We'd have to prove that. It would take time."

"Then we have to hurry." The somewhat diffident young woman of a few minutes earlier had become animated as she plotted a way out of the life she'd been forced to lead. It struck me that if there were any brains in her marriage, they didn't come from Maurice Girard. "If Curtis has money for Nassim, tell him to send it right away, at least enough to buy plane tickets. He can send the money directly to you, then you can give it to me in cash."

She spoke with the sublime confidence of people who have no idea what they're talking about. The embassy would never give her a tourist visa when she clearly had no intention of returning to France. And getting an immigrant visa could take months. But if I told her it wouldn't work, I was sure this meeting would be our last.

"Can you do this?" she asked.

"I don't know. Maybe. I have a friend here who might still have some pull." The speck of reality in this was microscopic, but I could at least tell myself I wasn't lying to her. "I'll do what I can."

How much trouble had I gotten myself into recently with those words?

Buoyed by hope, however illusory, she said, "I'll send a message saying when we can meet again."

She rose as the carousel came to a stop. Nassim jumped off the platform and marched toward his mother, swinging his arms, transfigured with the glory of having ridden the carousel twice in one day.

Chantal held him close and nodded toward me. "Mommy met an old friend. This is Monsieur Hough."

I smiled. "It's nice to meet you, Nassim."

The boy bowed and said with grave formality, "I am pleased to meet you, Monsieur Hough."

I smiled with enjoyment at his good manners. The boy laughed and held out his hand. I offered him mine and he gave it a precociously adult shake.

These were good people and deserved better than they'd gotten. Maybe, like people say, I think I'm one of the Knights of the Round Table, but in that moment I promised myself I would do whatever I could to help them.

Chantal rose from the bench and took Nassim's hand. "Time to go home." With a distracted smile, she said to me, "Thank you. For whatever you can do," she said and headed toward the boulevard.

As I watched her walk away with the boy, the impossibility of what she was asking of me hit me hard, my promise to help them entirely disingenuous. It would never work. But there was still a way I might get her address while I hoped she was mistaken about thinking Curt's money would get her in trouble.

I let Chantal and the boy get nearly out of sight, then fell in behind them. Though the sidewalk wasn't crowded, I managed to keep several people between us, contenting myself with occasional glimpses of them as they walked along the street. After a few minutes

I began to relax, congratulating myself on my previously untapped skill at tailing someone. Maybe I'd make a good detective yet.

At a busy intersection Chantal and Nassim stopped for the light. Afraid they might turn and see me, I ducked behind a lamppost, my back to them. Yes, I was good at this.

After a few moments, I judged they'd had time to cross. I came out from behind the lamppost—and ran straight into Chantal, her hands on her hips.

"Don't do this," she said.

Embarrassed, I could only blurt, "How did you realize I was following you?"

"Because I knew you would." She glanced over her shoulder at Nassim standing in front of a store window. "I keep trying to tell you, you're putting Nassim and me in danger—as well as yourself." From the beginning of our conversation that day, I'd had the impression she was holding something back. Now it burst through. "You want to know the truth? All right. I lied to you when I said I wasn't involved with what they do. I am. I've done things I didn't want to do. They forced me, and I did them. If the gang goes down, if Girard is arrested, I'm going down with them. I'm terrified of going to jail. I lie awake at night, thinking about prison. Maybe I have it coming, but I worry about Nassim. If Maurice and I both go to prison, what happens to him? No." She shook her head fiercely. "That's what I'm afraid of, getting thrown in prison—or getting killed—and leaving Nassim with no one. That's why I want out. That's why I want to go to America. You have to help us."

I felt my face redden in embarrassment at my clumsiness in following them, and from shame at my empty promises and the danger I might yet put them in.

"I'll do what I can," I told her again. "But I'm afraid of losing touch with you. How can I help you if I can't reach you? At least give me your cell number."

She shook her head. "You can't call me. It's even dangerous for me to call you. If I get caught . . ."

"Then how . . .?"

"Through Khadija." She saw my blank look. "The woman at the grocery store in the Goutte d'Or. If either of us needs to contact the other, we can leave a message with her."

"She's not exactly my friend."

"She's mine. We're both from Rabat. She's the one who first let me know you were looking for me."

"And you told Maurice."

"I had to. I didn't know who you were or what you wanted."

"So Maurice had said nothing to you about my stopping by his office."

"No. Nothing."

"Can I at least give you my number? I know it's risky, but if something comes up I may not have time to reach Khadija. And I'm not always at the hotel. I could miss a message. I nearly did today."

Chantal worked her mouth unhappily. "All right."

I pulled out a pen and a piece of paper and wrote down my number. She looked at it, repeated the number to herself, and handed it back to me.

"I will remember. Now, please, go away."

CHAPTER EIGHTEEN

A LONG-DISTANCE CALL, AND A SHORT BATH OF SELF-PITY

C URT'S NUMBER RANG until I thought I'd end up having to leave a message. But he eventually picked up, his voice hoarse and weak.

"Hey, Sam, whaddya know? Have you had any more contact with Chantal?"

"That's why I called. I saw her again this afternoon. And I met your boy."

Curt's shallow breathing measured out the seconds. Finally, he whispered, "What's he like?"

"He looks a lot like his father."

Curt chuckled. "Poor little guy."

"He's a handsome fellow. Very sweet. Smart."

"What's his name?"

"Nassim."

"Nassim," Curt said, tasting the word in his mouth.

"Chantal is raising him well."

"Did she give you her address?"

"No. She won't do it. Says her husband and the rest of that bunch probably won't allow her to get anything they don't control, that it would be dangerous to even try."

"Damn it! Why can't she just give us her address?"

His anger toward her shocked me. "What the hell, Curt? Go a little easier on her. She's doing what she figures is best for her and the boy. She would be grateful for a little money right now. She wants you to send it through me, not directly to her. I'm sure she figures that if I get her address you'll send her the money, like it or not. And that would put her in hot water."

"That's not how this is supposed to work, Sam. I told you, my lawyer says if we can just get her address that's all he'll need to make this happen."

"Look. Curt, ease up. You need to know what's going on. She wants the money so she and your boy can go to the States. Permanently. And she wants me to give it to her directly so that the others won't know."

"That's ... No. Why does she think she can come to the States?"

"Since Nassim is your son and we're both former diplomats, she thinks we can somehow make it happen."

"You told her no, didn't you?"

"I only told her it would be difficult. She'd have to prove you were Nassim's father. And I tried to make clear ..."

I didn't know how to say the rest, so Curt did it for me.

"That there isn't enough time."

"Yeah."

He veered back to his obsession. "But she still won't give you her address."

"She says it's too risky. One, she isn't allowed to have her own bank account. Two, if you send money for Nassim to her husband's account he'd find out, and that would raise all sorts of trouble. Send me whatever you can right now and I can slip it to her quietly. I'll tell her to hold on to it until she can get a visa, but at least she'll have some money right now."

"No!"

I didn't understand why he couldn't grasp what I was trying to tell him about the dangers Chantal was facing. Or maybe he was just a dying man trying to take care of the biggest problem left to him on this earth.

As if reading my thoughts, Curt seemed embarrassed by his outburst and said the rest more quietly. "My lawyer says we need the address. Besides, if I send money to Chantal she can't just hide it under her mattress."

"She says they don't allow her an account of her own. This bunch is paranoid as hell. If her husband, or anyone in that gang, found out she'd opened one and had a lot of money it could be very dangerous for her. But, speaking of her husband, that's one thing I can help you with. I found out who he is. The odd thing is I'd already met him but didn't realize the connection. He's some sort of manager at Trans-Maghreb. Name of Maurice Girard."

I'm not sure what sort of reaction I expected from Curt, but it wasn't total silence.

"Curt? You're still there?"

"You met Maurice Girard?"

"Yeah, you know him?"

"I . . . How did you find out Chantal's married to him?"

"That was the one nugget I got out of Forestier. When I saw Chantal today, she confirmed it. Is this important?"

"And Girard works at T-M?"

"Yeah. Forestier said he started working there not long after you left Paris. You know him?" I asked again.

"I . . . I've heard of him. He was working for Benaboud back then."

"Maybe that tells you all you need to know about the connection between them. Forestier says it's Girard's hand in that photo you gave me. He recognized the ring."

"Really? I hadn't thought of . . ." Despite his momentary surge of energy, his voice sounded vague, his mind elsewhere. "Thanks, Sam. You're doing great. I'm going to have to think things through, figure out what to do. But right now, I'm really tired. I need to sleep. We'll talk again soon."

"Take it easy, old friend."

After we'd ended the call, I stood at the window and looked out over the Tuileries and the wings of the Louvre, just visible to my left, the Musée d'Orsay rising on the other side of the river, to my right the Eiffel Tower, the whole city bright with the fading patina of past glories.

Who was it who said that Europe had become the world's largest open-air museum? That made it a particularly fitting, and treacherous, place for former lovers to chase down lost opportunities—Curt's long-ago affair, my love for Gwen. Only Chantal, the youngest of us, lived in the present and knew what she wanted from the future—to leave Maurice Girard and make a new life for herself and her son in the United States. And she was the one most likely to be disappointed.

The obvious hit me like a slap to the head. I didn't need to follow Chantal. Girard's address would be the same as hers.

For a misguided instant, I thought of simply calling him at Trans-Maghreb and asking him where he lived, but I was sure he'd refuse to tell me. And my question would likely tip him off that I had figured out he was married to Chantal, which could lead to further trouble.

So I got on my phone and searched for the address of a Maurice Girard in Paris. I quickly found one. And another. And another. And another. I tried M. Girard. There were dozens of them. I checked addresses against an online map, a tedious process that produced half a dozen results in the general area of the Goutte d'Or.

After a brief but refreshing bath of self-pity, another approach occurred to me. If I couldn't find the address of Girard's place, I might get him to lead me to it.

CHAPTER NINETEEN

A STAKEOUT, AND THE AGGRAVATION
OF OFF-KEY WHISTLING

———⦿———

A LIGHT-RAIL SYSTEM leads from the airport into the city. As it was cheaper than a car or taxi, Girard would almost certainly use it to get to and from work. Coming home in the evening, he would likely switch from the light-rail to one of the Métro lines that ringed Montmartre and walk home from there. If I waited outside a different stop each night, I was bound to find him and could follow him home. Sure I could. The idea that I would spot him among dozens of other people pouring out of the Métro station seemed like wishful thinking, even to me. But it was the only plan I could think of.

My first choice for a stakeout couldn't have been worse. Two lines cross at the Barbès-Rochechouart station: one running above ground, the other below. And rather than having only one exit, it has four, which pop up hundreds of feet from each other.

Even arriving early, before the evening rush had reached its peak, I found scores of commuters emerging from each of its exits, fanning out in all directions. I retreated north, up the Boulevard Barbès, figuring it for Girard's most likely route home, and took a seat at a bar-café that faced the street. There I waited, and waited, getting thoroughly wound up on cup after cup of coffee. Several times I stood up, my eye caught by a glimpse of red hair, only to find each time that it belonged to someone else. Who would have thought there were so many redheads in Paris?

After an hour and a half I gave up.

—◦◦◦◦◦◦— —◦◦◦◦◦◦—

Bored and restless, I felt I needed to call Curt and give him an update on my lack of progress. For the first time since I'd come to Paris, he didn't answer. I wondered if, while I was trying to make sure Girard didn't give me the slip, Curt himself might have gone to the hospital—or had slipped away, and for good.

It didn't make sense to continue this increasingly hazardous quest if he was gone. Yet I refused to accept the possibility that he had died. The job had become something more than an improvement on raking leaves in Walterville. I had made a promise, and lacking any evidence to the contrary, I would assume the person I'd made that promise to was still alive. And the two people I'd come to find—Chantal and Nassim—were no longer just abstractions. They were real now, and I liked them. I wanted this to come out well for them.

Lying on my bed, staring at the ceiling, I felt the curious urge to call Gwen—the only number I had was her landline—even though I knew she wasn't home. The idea of reaching out to an empty room had a peculiar appeal directly proportional to its lack of risk.

As I started to punch in the number, an image came to me of Gwen in front of a great fireplace at her husband's chateau in the countryside, a warm brandy in hand, curled up at the feet of a man

I had no right to be jealous of. It hit me again that Curt and I were both grappling with the reverberations of lost love. He had sent me to Paris because of his, and I had come because of mine. I had a sudden intimation that none of it could end well.

I put my phone down.

There's the old joke about the guy who loses his wallet on a particular street but searches for it on another street because the light is better. Following the same logic, I decided the following evening to give up on the Barbès-Rochechouart Métro stop, with its masses of humanity, and wait instead a little farther north, near Chateau Rouge and its single exit.

I found a quiet bar with a view of the entrance, ordered a glass of wine and a sandwich and, as on the previous night, sat down to wait.

Even at the quieter stop scores of people emerged from the station at this hour, making it difficult to catch a clear glimpse of each one. I must have made an odd sight to the others in the bar as I leaned and twitched and craned my neck as the commuters emerged from below.

After an hour, Girard hadn't shown up, and the early autumn darkness had fallen, making it even more difficult to see faces. I was wavering between finding a closer vantage point and heading back to the hotel when I saw a tuft of red hair bobbing up the steps across the street. Having been disappointed so many times, I fought to keep from getting too excited. But as the head of red hair rose above street level, I could see clearly that it was Maurice Girard trudging up the steps.

Like a deep-sea fisherman who, after hours of tedium, is yanked out of his seat by a big strike, I felt a surge of energy running through me. I left money on the table to cover my check and rose to leave.

Girard had reached the top of the steps and turned up the boulevard. As he did, I saw a second man walking with him, silhouetted against the shop lights behind them, the two in deep conversation. As I wondered how this complicated matters, the two men walked under a streetlight. My legs went out from under me and I collapsed back into my chair.

For a man dying of cancer, Curt Hansen appeared extraordinarily robust. As they walked side by side, he gripped Girard's arm in one hand while gesturing extravagantly with the other. I'd seen this act before, Curt cajoling a reluctant companion into granting him a favor the companion shouldn't even consider. And I knew he would likely succeed. Did I mention he's a charming man?

Now I understood why he hadn't answered his phone the last time I'd called. He'd already left home and the ambient sounds would have made clear he was no longer on his deathbed. Something else, though, remained obscure to me. What in the hell was this all about?

They had nearly disappeared by the time I recovered from my astonishment, dashed across the boulevard, and fell in behind them. Fortunately, Curt and Girard were too absorbed in their conversation to notice me.

Whatever his talents of persuasion, Curt appeared to have his work cut out for him. While he dialed up his most beguiling manner, Girard appeared unpersuaded, frowning and shaking his head.

Staggering in disbelief, I tailed the two of them along the busy avenue until they turned up a narrow residential street, nearly deserted at this hour. My initial shock gave way first to confusion, then to an anger that grew with every step I took. Seized by a perverse impulse, I pulled out my cell phone and called Curt's.

Even at twenty yards, I could hear it ringing on the quiet street. Curt pulled it out, looked at the screen, saw it was me, and put it back in his pocket.

As my fury built, another part of me thought coolly of what to do next. Given my present mood, if I braced Curt in the street it could turn into a fight. Whatever Girard's problems with Curt, he would probably take his side, especially if he recognized me as the guy who had come nosing around his office. And if I squared off with them now, I would likely never discover Girard's—and Chantal's—address.

Then it hit me. After seeking for that particular holy grail since arriving in Paris, the address no longer mattered. Curt had found the person he had wanted to speak to all along. Not Chantal, not his boy, but Maurice Girard.

The thought left me baffled. What possible sense did this make? None to me, but evidently a lot to Curt. His story of sending me to Paris so that he could get money to his son and use my offices to reconcile with Chantal only made sense if he were dying. And clearly, he wasn't. For reasons I couldn't fathom, he had faked a mortal illness, phoned me in Oregon, and called on our bond of friendship to persuade me to take up what he had framed as a dying favor. But if he was healthy all along, why hadn't he come to Paris himself? And why, after sending me, was he here now?

After walking several blocks, still in animated conversation, Girard and Curt stopped in front of a dingy apartment building, many of its windows covered by sheets rather than curtains, bare lightbulbs shining through the windows of others. I ducked into a doorway on the opposite side of the street, where I could keep them in sight.

The two of them continued to talk. His gestures short and stiff, Girard appeared increasingly unhappy. When Curt again took him by the arm and started to walk into the building with him, Girard yanked himself free and held up a warning hand.

Curt raised his hands in an appeasing gesture, then offered to shake. With obvious reluctance, Girard took his hand and gave it a quick, single pump. Curt smiled, said something I couldn't catch, and, with a friendly wave, turned back down the street. Girard stood in front of the apartment building for some time, watching to make sure Curt kept walking, and then went inside.

His characteristic jaunty walk undiminished by Girard's resistance to whatever scheme he'd been suggesting, Curt passed by me on the opposite sidewalk.

For a moment I thought of walking into the middle of the street and calling him out, like one Western gunslinger to another, but my native caution overrode my anger. Instead, I stayed put until he was halfway down the block, then came out from the shadows and followed, hoping he might do something, go somewhere, meet someone that would make clear what he wanted, why he'd come to Paris and, most of all, why he'd lied to me. When the moment was ripe, I would walk up to him and demand that he tell me what in the hell was going on.

When he arrived at the Chateau Rouge stop I followed him down the steps.

A train arrived as Curt reached the platform. Its doors opened and he entered through the front end of the last car. I boarded at its rear. I feared he'd see me, but he didn't show the slightest concern that anyone might be following him. He stood in the middle of the aisle with a slight smile on his face, gripping a stanchion, apparently lost in pleasant thought.

He rode only one stop and got off at Barbès-Rochechouart. I let him get well ahead of me before falling in behind.

I'd supposed he had taken a hotel room close to Montmartre, but once he got off the train at the underground stop, he continued up the steps toward the line that ran above the street, one that could take him far from Montmartre and the Goutte d'Or.

Keeping well back, I followed him up to the platform, thinking I'd blend in with the crowd of commuters. But a train must have just left and the platform was nearly deserted. I ducked into the shadow of a small billboard and held my breath.

A long couple of minutes passed before a train came. He boarded at the front. I jumped on at the back of the nearly empty car and took a seat behind the largest man I could find.

We dove back underground and rode through several stops. Somehow, Curt's obliviousness to anything around him, his complete lack of concern, the absence of any indication of a guilty conscience, fed my growing anger.

Obvious questions chased obscure meanings. How much had Curt hidden from me, and why? The question that had nagged me since my arrival came back more strongly than ever: what was I doing here? Like a dark figure emerging from a darker background, a sinister pattern began to emerge in my mind, though I could not yet see it clearly.

Absorbed by my struggle to make sense of Curt's behavior, only the ringing tone warning that the doors were about to close brought me out of my funk. My head snapped up just in time to see that Curt was no longer in the car. Panicked, I looked around and found him standing on the platform, looking at a map of the station and its exits.

I jumped up and leaped toward the closing doors. Too late. They closed on me, trapping me until, with a rattle of protest, they popped open again and I stumbled out. By then Curt was nowhere in sight.

The station had two exits, one behind the train, one in front. The rear exit was closest and I ran for it. When I got to the bottom of its long flight of steps I saw no sign of him.

I turned around and shoved my way through the mob of commuters heading toward the stairs, raced toward the other end of the platform, and ran up the steps, coming out onto a long tunnel-like pedestrian passageway that led, like the platform below, in two directions.

Panting, I looked down one end and then the other of the passageway without seeing Curt's bouncing walk. The fear crept into me that he might have, after all, been wise to my presence and duped me by stepping out onto the platform then, when I took the bait and dashed out, getting back onto the train and riding away. My hopes fading toward despair, I was about to simply choose a direction and rush off when something I'd seen in my first glance down the passageway fully registered.

Paris Métro stations serve as rent-free concert halls for busking musicians, many of them surprisingly talented. A few yards down the tunnel, a young woman with long, straight hair and a fetching beret was doing a wonderful job on the solo to Dvorak's violin concerto.

In front of her stood Curt, smiling and saying something to the violinist that caused her to frown and turn away. With a laugh, he dropped a few coins into her open violin case and went on his way.

Weak with relief, I took a deep breath and hung back for a moment, then resumed shadowing him as he walked to the end of the passageway and up the stairs.

Like a recurring nightmare, I found that, when I came up onto the dimly lighted street, he had again disappeared. I looked up and down the long block and saw no one. Certain I had finally lost him, I kicked at the pavement, half expecting to break my foot as penance for my incompetence. I would have welcomed it. Furious with myself, with Curt, with Girard, with Paris, I decided I had no choice but to slink back to the Brighton.

I had turned around to head back toward the Métro when a faint sound stopped me.

Across the quiet evening air someone was whistling, badly, the melody the young woman had been playing in the Métro.

On the opposite side of the street, Curt emerged from behind the dark form of a delivery truck, walking with the same carefree stride he'd shown since saying goodbye to Girard.

Fearing he might hear my footsteps on the quiet street, I stayed back, but I needn't have worried. He continued blithely whistling off-key into the night as I stalked him from the opposite side of the street.

We'd come a couple miles since first getting on the train and were walking now in the direction of the Gare St. Lazaire. Something about Curt's heedlessness—and his awful whistling—further stoked the anger I'd been nursing since I'd seen him with Girard. I struggled to keep myself from running across the street and throttling him until his tongue turned black.

A passing train drowned out his warbling and gave me a chance to close up a little without being heard.

A moment later he turned toward the entrance of one of the inexpensive hotels that dot the streets around Paris train stations.

I had vowed earlier not to approach him until the moment was ripe. When he reached the steps of the hotel, I decided it was plenty ripe.

"Curt Hansen!"

He stopped and squinted up the street in my direction.

"Migosh!" He seemed genuinely pleased to see me. "Sam!"

When I got within arm's length, I threw the most righteous punch of my life and decked him.

He was lucky. If he'd started whistling again, I'd have killed him.

CHAPTER TWENTY

CURT HANSEN TELLS ALL

THE KNOT OF people standing in front of the hotel froze in shock. Someone muttered, "*Oh la la*," like in a movie. Another of the onlookers said something about calling the police and started toward the door.

Testing his jaw with one hand, Curt staggered to his feet and called after the man, "No!" Then, more quietly, in French, "It's all right." He glanced at me and added in English, "I had it coming."

He slumped over, hands on his knees, trying to clear his head. After a few moments he extended an arm toward me. "Come up to my room with me." I didn't budge. "C'mon, Sam. We need to talk." When I still didn't move, he smiled through his pain and said, "I never imagined you packed such a punch." He slowly stood up straight and blew out a breath. "C'mon, Sam. I'll pour us both a drink and you can give me a chance to explain."

I warned myself not to let him start his charm act on me. But I couldn't walk away without understanding what he was doing in

Paris and why he had sent me on this errand. And I needed to know why so many people were so bent on doing me harm. Curt was the one person who had the answers. I nodded toward the door, letting him know I'd follow.

He retrieved his key from the desk clerk, and we took the elevator up to the top floor, silent as a pair of strangers. Curt had taken a small rundown suite with dingy floor lamps, a couple of comfortable armchairs and, through a door, a narrow bedroom.

Telling me to take a seat, he crossed to the minibar.

"Red or white?" he asked.

"I'm not here for a drink."

He smiled indulgently. "A drink would be good for both of us. Would help us talk."

"You're the one who needs to talk."

"Okay, I'll take the red," he said with a laugh and poured himself a glass. "Yeah, I guess I need to explain myself, tell you why I needed a favor from you."

"You told me you were dying."

"Hey, aren't we all?" he asked with that charming smile, as if this were all a little joke we were playing on someone else.

"You know what I mean. You were playacting. Making me feel sorry for you. My old friend."

"I'm sorry, Sam. I really am." He said this lightly, betraying no actual regret, and settled into the chair opposite me. "You've probably guessed by now, I hired someone to play my nurse, made sure the room was dim so you couldn't see me well. The rest, like you say, was playacting. I needed a little sympathy from someone with a heart. And you have the biggest heart of anyone I know."

I wished I had taken him up on the drink so I could throw it in his face. "You mean you needed someone you could play for a sucker. If you think I have such a big heart, why didn't you level with me? I might have done it anyway."

He pulled his head back in surprise at the idea. "No." He thought it over a moment and repeated, "No. If you'd known the truth you wouldn't have agreed to come here. Honestly, Sam, I'm sorry that—"

"Enough about how sorry you are. What the hell is this about?"

With a grunt of irritation at my refusal to let him beguile me, Curt settled deeper into his chair. "Where do I start?" he asked. But he knew. "Like I told you back home, I got screwed by the foreign service. The ambassadors loved the way I brought home all sorts of goodies for them. Never took a penny for myself. Ever. Then they'd knife me in the back on my annual reviews. I never got the promotions I deserved."

He spoke with the same bitterness I'd seen in him back in Virginia. At least that much had been real.

"In the end, my exes got their alimonies, health insurance, and most of my pension." A half smile twitched across his face. "I know I wasn't a very good husband, but I never imagined I'd married a pair of bloodsuckers."

"What has this got to do with me? Or Nassim and Chantal?"

Curt cradled his glass against his chest and gazed in front of him. "I loved Chantal. I really did. I still do. But . . ." He flicked a hand to dismiss what might have been. "Like I told you, I'd gotten to know her father, Miloud. Ran a transport business. Over time we got to be friends. We'd have tea together at an open air café in the old medina, and we'd swap stories." Curt smiled. "My tale about nearly getting killed with you in Islamabad was a favorite. He had me tell it a half a dozen times. I made clear to him you were a great guy and how stalwart you were—if a little dim." Curt lifted his glass, toasting me. "In return, he'd tell me about some of his shadier adventures. Dubious shipments to unsavory people. Guns to rebels in Algeria. Then one day he dropped his voice and whispered, 'Even drugs.'"

Curt lifted his eyebrows significantly and my stomach dropped with apprehension, though I couldn't see things clearly yet.

"He'd truck them up to Europe and pray he didn't get caught. I made a joke one day about how, if it went as a diplomatic shipment, customs authorities couldn't make a search. Maybe he didn't realize I was joking. Maybe I didn't realize I wasn't. Over the span of a couple of weeks we danced around the subject. Before I knew it, I'd agreed to help him out."

He smiled sheepishly, as if confessing to smoking in the boys' room.

"Taylor had divorced me. I was paying two alimonies. My career had stalled. I needed money."

"Sure."

He caught my tone. "Don't get sanctimonious with me. In the same situation, you would have done it too."

"No, Curt, I wouldn't have."

For a moment I hoped he'd get sore enough to come for me, and I could deck him again. Instead, he gazed into the half-empty wineglass in his hand and continued. "So, okay, I let him start adding his stuff to shipments we were sending to Paris. Didn't cost the taxpayer a cent."

"Didn't cost the taxpayer a cent. That's really noble. So, when your tour ended you managed to get sent to Paris, where you could continue to run Benaboud's shipments."

Curt tried to laugh. "You make it sound like I'm some sort of criminal."

"You are."

His face reddened with anger. "Don't start coming on like all you other guys were spotless. Don't go sounding holy just because for once I broke the rules to get a little something for myself. Nobody was getting hurt. Victimless crime."

I let that slide. "And once you got your posting to Paris, Forestier found out what you were doing?"

Curt shrugged, uncomfortable with the question.

"He might have guessed something was up, but he didn't want to know exactly what, so I didn't tell him. I had him arrange a contract with Benaboud from here in addition to the one he had in Rabat. Made things easier."

"And you could send Forestier out to Trans-Maghreb to arrange the shipments."

"It's not like I could afford to be seen there. Besides, most of it was done over the phone." Something in my face made him say, "Hey, it's not like we were doing this every week. A few times a year, that's all. Minimal risk for Paul."

"He got fired for it," I told him.

"No, I managed to save his job for him."

"As soon as you were gone, they pushed him out the door."

That took Curt by surprise. "I'm sorry. I didn't know."

"And I'll bet you got paid plenty."

He slammed his hand down on the arm of the chair, sloshing some of his wine onto the floor. "What are you, the Grand Inquisitor? Okay, I shouldn't have done it. But, like I say, we weren't harming anyone. And Miloud was grateful."

"Funny, in Virginia you talked a lot about love, for Chantal, for your son. But all the time it was really just about money."

"Enough already!" He struggled to recover his temper, trying to keep me on his side. "The love was real, Sam. Give me credit for that much. And for the first couple of years I didn't know about the boy."

"But Benaboud did. Why did he continue to work with you?"

He squinted in disbelief at my denseness. "Because I made good money for him. He may have wanted to kill me, but where else could he get a deal to ship his stuff under diplomatic protection? Anyway, he and I weren't in direct contact. We did everything through Trans-Maghreb—T-M. I guess that made it easier for him to put aside the thing with me and Chantal."

A wave of disgust passed through me as he dismissed his son as "the thing with me and Chantal."

He must have seen it in my face. "Remember, I only found out about the boy when Ziglinski came up from Rabat and told me."

I was getting tired of his self-justifications, tired of his whole story. "So what does any of this have to do with needing me to come to Paris instead of doing it yourself? You didn't really want to send money to your son at all."

Curt hunched his shoulders and looked away. "Sure I did."

"You're saying that sending me here was just an exercise of your kind heart? Bullshit. Start telling me the truth."

"Don't make me out to be a villain!" he shouted, then slumped in his chair and didn't say anything for a long time. "I was short of money, okay?"

"You said that already."

He ignored me. "My posting in Paris was coming to an end in a couple of months. I'd be going back to the States, and that would be the end of my arrangement with Benaboud. But I saw an opportunity. When I left, the Department would be shipping all of my effects back home."

"My God, Curt, you're telling me you took a bunch of drugs back to Washington in your household effects?"

His shamefaced smile was designed to cajole me into seeing what he did as a minor infraction, like jaywalking or spitting on the sidewalk.

"That was the plan, anyway," he said. "We don't have diplomatic immunity at home, but you know how it is, they never inspect our stuff. I figured it would be safe."

"Tell me you didn't ask Forestier to take care of this for you."

"Of course not." Curt sounded offended. "I was afraid he'd talk. He suspected something about the shipments from Benaboud, but he wasn't sure what it was about, and he didn't want to be. Telling him to take care of this for me would have been too much. So I sent out a feeler to Miloud, figuring years had passed since he'd banished Chantal, and he'd already been dealing with me for quite a while, at least indirectly. I figured maybe he'd gotten over things and would get back to me himself." Curt gave me a wry smile. "I was wrong. He had his number two, a guy named Marrakchi, call me, ask me what I wanted. He and I arranged the deal over the phone. Benaboud wouldn't be directly involved. He'd use someone he knew in Paris as the cut-out. I'd pay for the stuff through this local guy, and he'd arrange with T-M to hide it in my household effects shipment." He wagged his head. "But Marrakchi also let me know that Miloud had mellowed over the years. Not toward me, but toward Chantal. He wanted to see his grandson. Wanted to see them both."

"But he was too proud to say this to Chantal."

"Maybe he thought I'd find her for him and tell her."

"This 'stuff' you talk about, that you were shipping with your effects—what was it?"

"At first, I just wanted some hash oil. But, hell, with marijuana legal in half the US there's no market for it anymore."

"What did you agree on?"

He waved his hands, unwilling to speak.

"What was it, Curt?"

"Heroin."

How could I have been shocked?

He saw the look on my face. "I didn't like it either."

"But business is business, right? And—don't tell me—the man he sent to arrange it with you was Maurice Girard."

"Small world, isn't it?" he said with a laugh. He blew out an impatient breath when I didn't laugh with him. "Surprised me too. But maybe it shouldn't have. I'd met him once or twice in Morocco, knew he lived in Paris and that he worked in some capacity for Miloud. Maybe it would have been more surprising if he'd sent anyone else."

"You knew he was married to Chantal?"

"No, I didn't." He saw the anger building in me and might have thought I was going to get up and pop him one if he lied to me. "Okay, maybe I knew."

"And all this time, while I've been wandering around Paris getting into deeper and deeper trouble, it was really Girard you wanted to find. Not Chantal. Not Nassim. Why?"

"Look, I couldn't send you off searching for Maurice Girard. You'd have smelled a rat. But I figured if you could find Chantal's address I'd know where to find him."

"And once I told you he worked for Trans-Maghreb, you knew where to find him, and you didn't need Chantal's address any longer."

He spread his hands to acknowledge the obvious.

Though I was seething, I resisted the urge to get up and break his jaw. "But you're not telling me why you were so desperate to find him. Let's see if I can figure it out. When Girard talked to you here in Paris about the drug shipment, he told you they wanted their money up front, right?"

"That's how it works. A hundred and fifty thousand bucks. I had to take out a second mortgage to raise the cash. But I figured it was a safe bet. Girard promised me that once I got my shipment they'd even tell me who to sell it to in the US One call and it would be off my hands. Guaranteed. I'd make five, six times what I'd paid for it. And my exes couldn't touch the money because they wouldn't know about it."

"But when the shipment arrived, the drugs weren't there."

"You could see it coming?" He cocked his head to one side. "I didn't. Funny thing, as many times as I'd broken the rules, I don't know why it didn't occur to me that someone else might break them too."

The tumblers began to click into place. Containing my growing anger, I said, "Okay, so you sent me here to get Chantal's address by giving me a cock-and-bull story about how you wanted to help her and the boy, when all along what you really wanted was to find where Girard lived so you could get in touch with him and get your money back. Why didn't you just come here and take care of all this yourself? Why did you need me?"

"You don't understand. I was afraid that if I came here myself, snooping around, trying to find him ... well, they'd know what I was up to, and they might, I dunno, kill me or something. I figured if I could talk to Girard, someone I knew, without attracting any notice, he'd help me work things out with the people who had my money. But I didn't know how to find him. I didn't know he'd started working for T-M. If I had, that would have made it easy."

"So you sent me, and they nearly killed me instead."

"Sam, I never meant to put you in danger. I'm sorry."

I believed him. And I didn't care.

"But not so sorry that you would actually tell me the truth."

He chuckled, apparently thinking I was being humorous. "No, I guess not."

"So, what makes you think Girard's going to help you?"

Curt twitched his shoulders and raised his glass to his lips, found he'd already emptied it, and set it down. "We'd gotten along well when we met in Morocco. We had, you know, a connection. I figured he'd be willing to help me out a little."

"Does Girard know you're Nassim's father?"

"I don't know. Probably. Why?"

"Just curious. Just wondering how squalid this story can get. So, now what are you going to do about helping Nassim?"

The question seemed to take him by surprise, which only confirmed my notion that, once I'd found Girard for him, he'd forgotten all about his son.

"I don't know," he said. "There's no way to bring him and Chantal to the States, if that's what you're thinking." When I didn't reply, he shrugged. "Anyway, she's married. I figure they're pretty well taken care of."

"They're not. They live hand to mouth with a bunch of criminals."

Curt looked away. "I didn't know. I thought they were fine." When he turned back to me I was struck by the pleading in his eyes. "I loved Chantal. I want to see her, try to make everything up to her. Maybe I still can."

Every nerve in my body was telling me how much I wanted to slug him. "Maybe you think this whole thing is pretty well wrapped up now. You've found Girard and now you figure you'll use him to get your money back. And you'll go home thinking you've done all right for yourself and to hell with everyone else."

"What are you, my conscience?"

"It's another little service I offer to people who haven't got one of their own."

"You self-righteous bastard! I stood by you in Islamabad when you screwed up. And now you want to leave me hanging when I'm in trouble."

"I've never forgotten that, Curt, believe me. But that was in the line of duty."

"No, not that. I'm talking about later. Did you know Diplomatic Security came to me after the library burned down? No? They wanted to nail your hide to the wall. They figured you'd been incredibly naïve. Downright stupid. The way they saw it, everything—the burning of the library, the two of us nearly getting killed, all of it— was your fault. And they'd have crucified you. But instead of doing the smart thing and agreeing with them, I defended you. I told them you knew the risks, but the meeting was one you had to take, just in case they were who they said they were. And I said I was happy to go with you, willing to put myself in danger to back up a colleague." He waved his hand to brush away the past. "So, Security backed off and the ambassador put us both up for awards. You were golden after that. Me, not so much." The bitterness in his voice nearly choked him.

The night had been a series of shocks, but this one left me struggling to find something to say. It's bad enough when you find out that things aren't what they seem. But when you find out that even the past had changed on you . . .

"I . . . I didn't know. About Security, I mean."

"Damn right you didn't know. I made sure you didn't. You were my friend."

It took me a while to sort through the confusion, the shock, the anger and think clearly.

"That doesn't excuse what you're doing now."

"In other words, what have I done for you lately?" He leaned forward in his chair, ready to make his pitch. "Look, I can cut you in on this. I've already given you five thousand. How about I give you five more?"

In fact he was doing me a favor, but not the one he thought. His cravenness freed me from any last tatters of our friendship.

"Go to hell, Curt. I'll repay your goddamn five thousand as soon as I get home. I don't want your money. Any of it."

His face turned red and he opened his mouth, no doubt to tell me again about my smugness. I didn't give him the chance.

"You sent me out here to see that Nassim and Chantal were taken care of. And that's what I'm going to do. Maybe you don't give a damn about them. But I do. Whatever deal you make with the people who screwed you over, I mean to see you do right by the woman and the boy. Now, tell me what you and Girard agreed to tonight."

His eyes popped in surprise. "You saw us?"

"I've been following you since you came up from the Métro at Chateau Rouge. I was trying to find Girard by keeping an eye on the Métro stops around Montmartre. Follow him home, get his address. I didn't imagine he'd have company."

A slow smile spread across Curt's face. "You sneaky bastard."

I ignored his attempt to beguile me. "Tell me about your talk with Girard. What's supposed to happen now?"

Curt's manner eased, ready to talk business. "He said he'd set up a meeting with his boss in the next day or two. He'll let me know where and when."

"I want to be there."

Curt actually laughed. "You're out of your mind. These guys aren't a bunch of yahoos claiming they're from Peshawar. They're professional criminals."

"And what are you, some sort of tough guy? Never mind, don't answer. Whatever it is you think you are, I want to be there when you meet them."

"Why?"

"To see that Nassim and Chantal get what they have coming to them. They deserve part of this."

"How dumb are you, Sam? These guys'll say, 'Sure, we'll give them twenty thousand,' or whatever, and it'll just be money I won't get back. Chantal and the boy won't get it either. These guys will promise me anything, then keep it for themselves. Why shouldn't they?"

"Because you say Girard will be in the meeting, and when we insist that his wife and Nassim get some money, he'll be all for it because he'll have access to the money too."

It sounded weak even to me, but it was the best I could come up with.

"Meaning you trust these gangsters more than you trust me. You think you have to be there to hold my feet to the fire."

"Let's say I think you might forget. And this way we don't have to find a way to sneak the money to Chantal. It'll all be in the open."

With an unhappy grunt Curt got up and poured himself another glass of wine. "Okay. I'll let you know about the meeting as soon as I find out."

With our deal sealed, the doubts crept in. "Why in the world do you think they'll say yes?" I asked. "What leverage do you really have?"

"I'll tell them I'm still connected to the embassy, that we have DEA there, and I can make things uncomfortable for them if they try to screw me." He downed the wine in a long gulp.

"Yeah, that'll really put them on the spot, won't it? They may decide the easiest thing to do is kill us both, right there. You're not going to get far trying to claim diplomatic immunity with this bunch."

"They're businessmen, Sam. It's a business deal. They respect us more if I stand up for myself."

"Look, I've got a friend here. No one they'd know. Once they tell you the time and place of this meeting, I'll tell her where we'll be and why. Then we can tell Girard and his friends that if anything happens, if we don't get in touch with her after a certain hour, she'll call the police and they'll know exactly where to come."

Curt thought it over. "I like it. Should help keep things business-like."

As I put on my coat, he told me again he'd let me know about the meeting. He didn't offer to shake on it. He knew I was in no mood to shake his hand.

CHAPTER TWENTY-ONE

NOSTALGIA AND ITS PLEASURES

A GRIM LID of gray had replaced the cold, clear weather of the previous few days, making me feel like someone living inside a drawer that no one cared to open. Even the Tuileries felt oppressive as I roamed up and down the allées between the rows of trees and circled the Octagonal Pond. Only when I'd given up did I see Ulysses sitting on a bench along the broad central path, watching me. I fought the eerie notion that my wish to find him had made him materialize in front of me.

When he'd originally told me he'd be there if I needed him, I'd brushed it off as another of his mystic pronouncements. Now I'd begun to believe.

I crossed the path and sat down beside him on the bench.

"How are you, Ulysses?"

"I am fine," he said in that assertive way of his.

"I wanted to thank you again for being with me at the train station the other day."

"Glad I could be there." He cast a sidelong glance at me. "But you don't look so good."

I wanted to steer the conversation away from my own miseries. "Are you always here in the park?"

"Only when I need to be."

I had to chuckle. "And when you're not?"

"One place or another. Parc Monceau. Champs de Mars. The museums. But I like it best here." He leaned back on his bench and let his gaze wander around the park. "Sometimes, if I have a little extra money and need a shower, I'll spend a night at a youth hostel. Most nights I spend here. The carny workers let me keep my stuff under one of their booths. If it's raining, I can sleep under a counter after they've closed. That way I can keep an eye on things at night for them. They appreciate it, give me a few euros."

While we talked, we seemed to trade roles, with me asking questions and Ulysses telling me about himself. I sensed he, too, wanted to talk to a fellow countryman, someone not quite a stranger, someone he could speak to without fear of consequence. He talked about the books he read, what he had learned during his travels, the places he'd seen—Spain, Corfu, Sicily. He said he'd been kicking around Europe for two years but would likely only manage a couple more months before his money ran out.

"And where will you go then?"

"Home." Ulysses picked up a handful of gravel and tossed the pebbles one by one back onto the path. "Traveling is like gathering treasure. You have to take it home and look it over before you really understand what you've found."

As to where he came from in the US and what he would do when he got back, he said nothing. I smiled, understanding that he wished to remain mysterious a little longer, at least until winter came and he would have to head home, filled with tales of adventure and acquired wisdom.

Something both alien and familiar emanated from the young man, though at first I couldn't define it. Eventually, as we spoke, the notion came over me that I was talking to a kind of alter ego, someone whose wanderings echoed my own.

Yet, like the relation between a photo negative and its original, he had done it in a way entirely contrary to my own. He had avoided the bonds of an entangling bureaucracy, of assignments that froze him in place for years at a time, leaving him free to go where and when he wanted, able to speak his mind rather than trim his public words to fit policies made thousands of miles away by people he would never know. I was glad for him, enough so that I questioned the validity of my own life.

For all my travels and the elevated status laid on me as a diplomat, I had taken the safer route. Should I, too, have traveled alone, without a job, open to whatever experience came my way? Too late to worry about that now.

"I hope I'll see you again before I go home too," I told him.

"Careful what you wish for. If you see me, it'll probably be because you need me again."

"I'll take my chances."

Ulysses smiled and returned to throwing bits of gravel onto the path. Was he thinking something over? Or was he able to simply empty his mind whenever he wished? In any case, for the moment, my Greek chorus had gone quiet.

I reached into my pocket and asked if he could use a few euros. "Maybe I can help you extend your stay in Paris a day or two."

He stiffened and gave a little shake of his head. "I never take money from friends."

I felt both embarrassed and flattered. Like I said, he had a real gift that way.

As before, we nodded rather solemnly—each of us recognizing a bit of ourselves in the other?—and parted.

Wondering if I was being followed, I crossed over the river, thinking I would notice someone tailing me on the bridge.

From the opposite side of the Seine the Tuileries looked more formal, something from an earlier time, making it easier to imagine its history as a trysting place for nobles and their lovers—easier, that is, if you could ignore the Ferris wheel rising above the trees.

The Left Bank was a favorite part of the city from past visits, but one I'd hardly set foot in this time. After grabbing a bite to eat at a bistro, I continued along the river, pausing at the Pont des Arts to watch the old men fishing off the end of the Île de la Cité under the watchful gaze of the equestrian statue of Henri IV.

It was only as I crossed the Boulevard Saint-Michel that I realized where I'd been heading all along.

The quiet streets of the Île Saint-Louis calmed my mind and made me forget the weariness in my legs after the previous night's long walks and short runs. Still, my foreignness made me feel uncomfortably conspicuous walking across the narrow waist of the island toward the Quai d'Anjou. It seemed ridiculous to think that one of Gwen's neighbors might see me and, in a flash of prurient insight, guess where I was headed and why, but still I pulled my hat low over my eyes.

As I got closer, I mulled the paradox that while I had resisted calling her since she had left for Bordeaux, I would readily walk up to her door. No doubt, as with the phone call I'd nearly made, the appeal of reaching out without any risk of actually making contact made it all easier. Could my behavior have been any more adolescent? Was I getting perilously younger every day? Around Gwen I had felt like a young man again, edging toward acting like a teenager in love. And now I was making like a twelve-year-old with his first crush. Soon I'd be going around in short pants and carrying stuffed animals.

Whatever the embarrassment of my devolution, only the certainty that Gwen was hundreds of miles away gave me the nerve to push the buzzer to her apartment so that I could walk away, kidding myself I had tried.

I waited a moment, imagining its ring echoing through the empty rooms, leaving me free from any fear of either rejection or acceptance. I wasn't sure which prospect frightened me more.

Curiously satisfied, I started back down the steps.

"Yes?"

The voice from the speaker stopped me.

For a moment too shocked to speak, I turned back and managed to whisper, "It's me."

A pause even longer than mine followed. Then the door clicked open, and I took the stairs to the third floor.

Gwen stood half hidden behind her partially open door. The light from the landing illuminated only one side of her face, leaving the other in shadow, the perfect image of our longings and hesitations. As we had on that first day I'd come to visit, we stood silently, taking each other in, our thoughts more complex now, our emotions both more powerful and more uncertain than a week earlier.

"Well, hello," she drawled.

From where I stood, I could see only half a smile.

"I hadn't expected you," she said.

"Any more than I expected you."

"Yet you pushed the buzzer." Her gaze fixed on my eyes for the span of a deep breath. "I guess you'd better come in." She stepped back and opened the door just enough to let me enter.

However much I'd told myself she wouldn't be home, I had of course nursed a dream that she would. But I hadn't known, or at least not realized, what I would do in that moment until the moment came. I pushed the door closed behind me, took her in my arms and kissed her.

Our kiss knew no age, but was fresh, new, ardent, erasing all the years between our first kiss and this one. She squeezed me as if to force out the last trace of every breath I had taken between then and now.

We finally broke, both of us gasping with a heady mix of delight and confusion.

Holding my hands, Gwen took half a step back and looked at me in something like wonder.

"Hello indeed," she murmured, her smile wavering between pleasure and something else I didn't want to ask about. "I was going to offer you a drink, but now I think I'd better not."

"When did you come back?"

She looked at me for a long time before saying, "I never left, Sam."

I was startled by how little it surprised me. "And this whole time..."

"I've been here."

"You didn't want to see me."

"I wanted to see you very much—too much."

I looked into her eyes. She didn't look away. I asked, "Like the old song says, 'Should I stay or should I go'?"

She pulled me close and whispered, "I think you'd better stay."

There are many motivations and manners for making love. Nostalgia can prove one of the sweetest, reawakening dormant senses and remembered pleasures. Did Gwen share my sense of delicious dislocation, as if I were making love to two people at once—the Gwen I'd cherished many years ago and the one I held in my arms now—in love with them both?

Afterward, I pulled the rumpled bedspread over us. At our age it was perhaps best not to see each other in too much light. Gwen rested her head on my chest and I put my arms around her. We lay like that for a long time, neither of us ready to restore time or thought. But however much we might tell ourselves we wished to stay like this all afternoon, the unwelcome present slowly reasserted itself.

"Maybe it's time for that drink," she said. She kissed me on the cheek and rose from the bed. With beguiling deftness she whisked the bedspread off me, wrapped it around herself, and headed for the liquor cabinet, the end of the bedspread trailing behind her like a queen's train.

I was left to decide whether to crawl further under the covers or get up and put my clothes on. An easy decision. I crawled under the covers.

Though luxuriously appointed, the room to which she'd taken me held few personal touches, no photos, no books on the bed-stand—clearly a guest room, not her matrimonial bed, freeing us from conjuring with truths we didn't wish to face.

And in that moment I felt a terrible longing for Janet. I wished her here with both of us. I don't mean to say in the bed with us. She'd have cracked me over the head for any suggestion like that, though she might have laughed while she did it.

I simply felt the need for her presence, the restoration of that part of me that resided in her, so that I could better negotiate the excitement and disorientation and, yes, the guilt of this too-heady moment.

Before I could follow these thoughts further, Gwen returned with a large snifter of warm brandy and, letting her bedspread-gown slip to the floor, got under the covers with me. We took turns sipping from the single cup in contented silence until she gave me a smile whose warmth was matched only by its wavering complexity, like the patterns in a wheat field tossed by opposing winds. "And I always took you for the eternal Boy Scout."

"I'm working on a special merit badge."

Her laugh was like rain on the parched earth of my heart.

It was not the moment to ask where we went from here. For now, the world came down to this moment, this room and the two of us. Reality could cool its heels.

Or so I thought. Gwen knew better. "How's the detective business coming?" she asked.

Yanked unwillingly into the world outside, I told her everything—about Curt's betrayal of both me and Nassim and the foreign service, me knocking him down and our long talk in his room. I described his deal with drug dealers, his desire to make contact not with his son but with Maurice Girard, ending with my insistence on attending his meeting so I could see that Chantal and Nassim were treated right.

At the end of my confession, Gwen looked at me with an expression so forlorn that I turned away. "Sammy, my Sammy, you don't jump into trouble halfway, do you?" She took my hand and held it to her breast. "There's nothing I can say to talk you out of this?"

"No, but go ahead and try. I love the sound of your voice."

"This isn't funny."

"No. It's not."

"You used to have such good judgment," Gwen said.

"Sure I did. We both had great judgment. That's how we ended up waving goodbye on a railway platform."

She tried to frame a sensible reply but ended up lying back against the pillows and looking at the ceiling. "Yeah."

"You tell me I was better off for it."

"I'd have broken your heart, Sam. Mine too." It took her a moment to add, "And you wouldn't have met Janet."

It was an iceberg of a conversation, with the words we spoke barely rising above the thoughts we didn't express.

"Where does that leave us?" I asked.

"Us? I don't know. Me? I'm even less sure. And you? You have to go ahead with what you're doing, ill-judged or not."

She said all this hardly above a whisper, her quiet voice weighted with apprehension. For the first time I felt the full weight of the danger I insisted on facing.

"How are you supposed to find out about this meeting?" she asked.

"Curt has my number. He'll call or text."

"So, you don't have to go back to your hotel tonight."

I looked at her to be sure I understood. She didn't look away.

"No, I guess I don't."

"Don't worry, I'll find you a toothbrush."

Gwen made a wonderful dinner, which we ate at the kitchen table. We laughed a lot, talked of people we'd known, things we'd done, of Badger Cottage and more. She spoke of the history of the Île Saint-Louis and I of my place in Walterville, both of us happily avoiding anything of consequence.

Yet, every reference to our past pushed it farther over the horizon, leaving us, at the end, talked out and washed up on the perilous shore of the present.

Gwen asked again about the meeting with Curt. She reminded me she had friends with the police. I wanted to tell her, yes, I could use their help, but felt strongly that they posed a danger to Chantal and the boy. So I said no.

Exasperated, Gwen said, "Sam, there's no merit badge for being a damned fool."

"The police will be the police. When they show up they'll arrest everyone. Chantal too, if she's anywhere in sight. With her and Girard both in prison, the boy will be worse off than if I'd never come. Anyway, Curt says these guys are businessmen. They don't want trouble from an unhappy client. They'll cut a deal and close the books on this thing."

"And you believe this."

Before I was forced to admit to being either naïve or less than honest, the phone on the kitchen wall rang.

Gwen stiffened but made no move to answer. The phone rang again. We both sensed who was calling.

It would be up to me.

"You'd better get that."

It was the landline, with an extension in the kitchen, but she went out to the drawing room to answer.

"Oh, hello, darling." The muffled sound of her voice told me she had her hand curled around the mouthpiece as, her voice fading, she walked farther away, her words swallowed by distance and discretion.

When she had hung up and returned to the kitchen, neither of us spoke of the call or, for a moment, of anything else. Such a deep and sudden silence is said by the superstitious to be the sign of someone walking over your grave.

We tried to regain the carefree tone of minutes earlier, but, aware now of what we were doing, betraying one love for the memory of another, it was hard work, and our laughter rang false, our voices pitched artificially high, straining to sound natural.

I looked at the kitchen clock. "Maybe I'd better . . ."

She put her hand on mine. "No, Sam. I want you to stay."

We talked a little more—perfunctory, listless talk, mentioning everything but Janet and Gwen's husband.

When we went to bed we made love again, and it was wonderful and we loved each other and we both knew it was no good.

We slept well and woke late. Gwen took me up on my offer to make breakfast.

While I fumbled around the unfamiliar kitchen, she made a couple of phone calls, looking in on me once, rolling her eyes at the mess I was making.

After breakfast—coffee and toast and scrambled eggs that were supposed to be an omelet—I wanted so much to stay that I knew I needed to go.

I put on my coat and Gwen followed me to the door and put her arms around me.

"I love you, Sam. Not just from years ago, but I love you now. I know I shouldn't say it, and I don't want to think of where it can't lead, but there it is."

I kissed her gently. "Then you and I are in one hell of a fix, because I love you too."

Reluctantly, we broke our embrace. As I opened the door to leave, my phone beeped, telling me a text had arrived. Gwen and I looked at each other as if we'd heard the peal of doom.

I pulled the phone from my pocket and read the message, aware of Gwen's eyes on me.

"It's this evening," I told her. "I'll find Curt at a bar near Chateau Rouge at seven. We'll go to the meeting from there."

"And you're going to do this?" When I didn't answer, she added, "You can still say no."

"No, I can't. Not now." I remembered my last conversation with Curt. "I have an idea that might make you feel better, something I mentioned to Curt. We can tell the people we're meeting that you'll know where we are and that if you don't hear from us by nine o'clock, you'll call the police."

"They'll believe that? I mean, you won't know where you're meeting until you get together with Curt."

"As soon as he tells me, I'll call you."

"All right," she said, though I could see in her face what she truly thought of this half-baked plan. "Are you going straight back to your hotel?"

"No. I need to walk for a while. I'll probably get back to the Brighton after lunch. Why?"

"No reason," she said, her brow furrowed with worry. "I just . . ."

"I'll call you as soon as I know where the meeting is. And I'll call you afterward to tell you everything went fine."

"I won't be able to sleep until you do." After a moment, she added, "And don't be mad at me."

"Why in the world would I be mad at you?"

She replied with a kiss and shut the door behind me as I left.

Once outside I wandered aimlessly, caught between fierce but inchoate emotions about Gwen and dread about that evening's meeting. Paris had become nothing more than a blue screen I was walking in front of.

CHAPTER TWENTY-TWO

SIMON AND THE ART OF TWISTING ARMS

E VENTUALLY, I RETURNED to the Brighton, took the stairs up to my room—and jumped back through the open door shouting, "Jesus Christ!"

The man sitting in the chair by the window made a downward gesture with his hand, telling me to make less noise.

"Ah, Monsieur Hough, I had nearly given up on you."

He was a powerfully built man of middle age, with a few extra pounds on him. His large mustache, slicked-back hair, and bulbous body gave him the appearance of a well-domesticated walrus.

"Who the hell are you?"

Again, he made that deprecating gesture, urging me to lower my voice. "Please, Monsieur Hough, sit down. I'm a friend, a friend who might be of some assistance, and one who might ask you to be of assistance to me. Do sit down, Monsieur Hough. And shut the door behind you."

I did as he said.

Unwilling to take the chair next to him, I sat on the edge of the bed.

From his coat pocket, he pulled out an ID card indicating his name was Jules Simon—were there still men named Jules?—and he was a police inspector.

In a flash of belated insight I thought back to Gwen quizzing me about when I planned on returning to my room. As I'd left she'd asked me not to get mad at her. Now I understood. She had called her police contact. I knew that if I asked her why she had shared with the police something that I'd assumed to be confidential, she would tell me that if I didn't have enough sense to protect myself, she needed to do it for me.

"What do you want?" I asked.

"I understand you have a meeting this evening with a network of likely drug dealers." When I didn't answer, he continued. "I believe you know we have been interested for some time in the activities of Trans-Maghreb Shipping. But we haven't had the resources to determine what they are doing. You may be ahead of us on this question."

When I didn't leap into the pause he created, he folded his hands over his stomach and waited me out.

"I'm not interested in Trans-Maghreb," I told him. Disingenuous, but not untrue. "I've been trying to find the son of an American friend."

"So I've been told. Nevertheless, through your inquiries you've discovered a great deal about this group's activities."

Still, I said nothing.

Simon made an impatient flick of the hand. "I understand. You wish to do the right thing, but you're not sure at the moment what constitutes the right thing." When I didn't reply, he tapped the arm of his chair in annoyance. "Monsieur Hough, this is no longer simply a personal matter. If you attend this meeting knowing that it concerns a drug transaction, your conduct could be considered criminal." He put up a hand to stop my protest. "I know that is not your intention. But your actions can have consequences that speak louder than your intentions, making you liable to arrest."

For an instant the thought of getting arrested struck me as an attractive option, freeing me of any need to dig myself deeper into this mess. Though the temptation to walk away in handcuffs had a certain appeal, I asked, "What is it you want from me?"

"I know you've not asked for our assistance. But this matter has gone beyond your personal wishes. You have, however inadvertently, penetrated a drug-trafficking operation. We wish to take it down. Unfortunately, we don't as yet have enough evidence to make our charges stick. As I believe you know, these men are associated—even if they are striving to break that association—with a much larger network, headed by a ruthless and powerful man named Jean Garonne. If we can use the opportunity of your meeting as a means not only to roll up this smaller network, but to get closer to this man Garonne, it would be of great benefit to us."

"Their association might go deeper than you think," I told him.

Simon cocked his head to one side, inviting me to say more.

"The members of this smaller group are scared to death that one of them is a spy for Garonne."

"Do they know whom?"

"I don't think they're even sure it's true, much less who it might be. It makes them scared of every passing shadow."

Simon thought this over before saying, "All the more reason for you to be careful." When I didn't say anything, he added, "You are going into this meeting without sufficient appreciation of its danger."

"I've thought about it."

"Think harder. I understand you wish to assist a woman and a boy associated with this gang."

Nothing in his words betrayed knowledge of Chantal's involvement in her husband's business. Still, if I assisted the police and it ended with Girard and the rest of the gang being arrested, I feared, as I had told Gwen, that Chantal, too, would wind up in prison. My efforts to help her and her boy looked increasingly clumsy, potentially leading to the ruin of both their lives.

"Putting them in danger is not what I intended," I said. Simon let my words hang in the air. "That's the difference between us. For you, this woman and her boy aren't the ones you're interested in. For me, they're the whole reason I'm doing this."

Simon sighed like a man having difficulty explaining an important issue to a child. "The police are dedicated to protecting society as a whole. We do not divorce that from the need to protect individuals within that society. We, too, wish them to come to no harm."

Simon's ability to reduce police work to an exercise in Cartesian logic struck me as so perfectly French I couldn't help but smile.

"I'm glad you find this amusing, Monsieur Hough."

"No, it's just . . . you're telling me everything except what you want me to do."

"Yes, let us speak practically. We want you to wear a listening device when you go to this meeting. A wire, you call it. In this way, as you discuss Monsieur Hansen's grievances and your desire to help this woman and her son, we can gather the evidence we need to dismantle the operation and put its principals in prison."

"Including Curt."

"Whatever obligations you feel toward Mr. Hansen have been satisfied far better than he deserves. In addition to breaking the laws of your country as well as ours, he has betrayed your trust and put you in danger. He is a criminal, Monsieur Hough. You see that."

For what seemed like several minutes, but was probably only so many seconds, I weighed Simon's proposition, searching for some principle that required me to say no. If it was there I couldn't find it.

"All right," I said. "I understand your interest in having me carry a wire. But how does this help me? It won't stop a bullet."

"We will follow you wherever you go. My officers will remain out of sight but will be very close. When we have the evidence we need, or at the first sign of danger to you, we will break into the meeting, arrest the others, and pull you out."

"It sounds dangerous."

"Less dangerous, I think, than going in without our protection."

"Won't they search me, see if I'm carrying a wire?"

"If they search you, they'll likely only be looking for weapons. But no, it's not impossible they will find the wire, in which case we will have to come in immediately. Keep in mind, they have no reason to think you've spoken to us. They will almost certainly continue to see you as an annoying but harmless amateur, your presence due entirely to the fact that you're Hansen's friend."

I looked out the window at the wide expanse of the park below and wondered at what point it was that I had so compromised myself as to put me in the hands of criminals on the one hand and the police on the other, both of them wanting to use me to their advantage. For a guy who'd always been a straight arrow I'd gotten myself into one hell of a mess.

"What if I say no?"

Simon raised his hands, palms up. "If you still intend to go to this meeting and will not help us, I suppose we could arrest you for criminal conspiracy before you even leave the hotel. We might have a difficult time getting a conviction, but it would be very troublesome for you and would likely involve you spending time in jail."

"I don't like being threatened."

He smiled and spread his hands. "No one does. But you're not a diplomat any longer, Monsieur Hough. You are a private citizen, subject to French law while you're here, like anyone else." He waved a hand to sweep away his words. "Monsieur Hough, we don't want you to assist us simply under threat of compulsion. I respect your position. You are trying to aid this woman and her son. And I think you are further constrained by a lingering fidelity to a man who doesn't deserve it."

He again waited out my silence. There was no rushing him.

"All right. What if I say yes?"

He leaned forward in his chair, his hands clasped in front of him. "I understand you are to meet Monsieur Hansen at seven o'clock this evening at a bar near the Chateau Rouge Métro stop."

I couldn't help but admire the completeness of Gwen's report on our conversation.

"A plainclothes officer will knock on your door here at six o'clock and attach the device to you. You will then proceed to your rendez-vous with Hansen at . . . What is the name of the bar?"

"Bar Good Time."

"Bar Good Time." He repeated with a tone that indicated that the name of the place sounded as silly to him as it did to me. "We will have an officer there before you arrive. He will follow you from there to your meeting. Did Hansen say where the meeting with the others would take place?"

"No, his text only said it would be a few blocks from the bar."

"All right. Get Hansen to mention the name of the meeting place before you leave the bar. The wire will pick it up. That will make it easier for us to get there ahead of you. Once they're in position, my officers will cover all the exits and can come to your aid on a moment's notice. I will be with them."

"They'll see your men, won't they?"

He smiled faintly. "No, they won't."

"What if something goes wrong? What if you're not there?"

"We will do everything we can, but I won't try to tell you this is without danger. Plans can go wrong, and some of these men are killers."

I thought it over but realized there wasn't much to think about. "I don't have much choice, do I?"

Simon's Gallic shrug was a work of art. "You have a number of other choices, Monsieur Hough. They are all worse."

I took my time penciling out the complex equations of duty and betrayal, honor and deception. I could go to prison if I refused to help. And the police might end up arresting Chantal, though it seemed unlikely she'd be present at the meeting. Maybe things would end with the police arresting only those who were there, including Curt. I told myself he had it coming. Yet, such are the ties of ancient friendship that betraying him stirred a deep shudder of guilt.

These thoughts flashed through my head in far less time than it takes to express them. I decided to cling to the hope that we could leave Chantal out of this.

I got up and opened the door. "All right. Send your man. I'll be here."

Simon rose from his chair. "Thank you, Monsieur Hough. However difficult your decision, we are truly grateful."

"Well, that's just swell."

As he started to leave, I held out a hand to stop him. "They may be keeping an eye on the hotel, watching me. Won't they spot a policeman coming to see me?"

"The officer will be in plain clothes. He will have the equipment in his pockets. He'll appear to be a man like any other, simply visiting someone in the hotel."

I nodded, but with the risk I'd be taking no longer an abstraction, I found it difficult to speak.

"Until tonight, Monsieur Hough," Simon said and disappeared down the corridor. I might have appreciated a reassuring smile, but he gave none.

After I'd shut the door I picked up my phone to give Gwen an angry blast for putting me on the spot like this, then decided against it. She'd understood better than I did that if I was in a spot, it was because I had put myself there. She had done this to protect me because I didn't have enough sense to protect myself. She'd done it for love.

As never before in my life, I felt the need to call my son. It was still early in the morning back home, but that would have to do.

After several rings Tom answered his phone, his voice thick with sleep. "Dad. It's five o'clock in the morning. Is there something wrong?"

"No, everything's fine. I just needed to say hi. It's going to be a busy day. I wanted to catch you while I could." I didn't want to tell him I'd called because a part of me was afraid I might never get another chance.

We spoke for a few minutes, long enough for him to tell me the house was fine, his studies were going well, life was good. It didn't much matter to me what he said, I just wanted to hear his voice.

I talked about the weather, about how beautiful Paris is in the fall, told him I loved him.

"Sure, Dad. Love you too."

"Go back to sleep now."

Simon's man wouldn't come for a couple more hours. At that moment, those hours seemed like so many years. And they gave me just enough time to do what I needed to do.

The color and voices of the Goutte d'Or once more lent me the illusion of home, but my mood allowed me little comfort this time. For a moment I felt the temptation to disappear, hide out here from the bind I'd gotten myself into until people stopped looking for me. But I had other things in mind.

Though Chantal had my number and could text me if she chose, the lack of any word from her over the last couple of days made me anxious. So I had decided to visit Khadija, the Vegetable Lady, to leave a message for Chantal, and to see if she had left one for me.

The woman's faceful of resentment as I approached made clear she wished she'd never met me, but she didn't try to avoid me this time.

I walked into her little shop and said, "Tell Chantal the meeting is tonight."

She shrugged as if it were none of her business.

Fine. I turned to go.

"She tells you not to go."

I stopped in her doorway. "What?"

"She tells you not to go."

I waited for more, got nothing.

"Why?" I asked.

She shrugged, letting me know she'd rather not be bothered with telling me. "Danger," she said. "Too much danger."

For a moment I couldn't draw a breath. "Tell her I'm sorry, it's too late. I have to be there."

The woman shrugged to make clear her indifference. It was my funeral.

I made my way back to the Brighton, kidding myself that with a potentially long night in front of me I might take a nap. For a time, I lay on the bed, eyes open, thinking of the one way that the meeting could go right, and the many ways it could go wrong.

The soft tap on the door startled me like a rifle shot.

The police officer, fiftyish, wearing a stained overcoat and smelling of cigarettes, nodded at my greeting without returning it and came in without waiting for an invitation.

"This will only take a few minutes," he said.

He told me to take off my shirt. From his coat pocket he pulled out a battery pack and transmitter, about the size of a pack of cigarettes. With bored detachment, he showed me how to turn the device on and off with a small switch located on the battery pack, and told me to tuck the pack into my waistband. "You'll wear your jacket and your overcoat over it," he said as he attached a wire to the pack, ran it over my shoulder and taped it down, first to my back, then to my chest. To the end of the wire he attached a tiny microphone, secured it to my chest with a double-sided bit of stickum, then told me to put my shirt back on.

"Wait until you leave the bar where you're meeting this man before you turn it on. We don't want the battery wearing down. I'm told to remind you that, after you turn it on, you need to ask him where you're meeting the others."

"What if he's already told me while we were in the bar?"

He huffed with impatience. "Then ask him again." He looked me up and down without making eye contact. "They shouldn't find it."

The remark didn't fill me with confidence.

The officer looked at his watch. "You'd better get going. I'll leave first. Wait a few minutes before coming down. I don't think anyone's watching the hotel, but still, there's no point in us coming out together."

He paused in the doorway a moment as if he had more to say, but only waggled his head unhappily and left.

CHAPTER TWENTY-THREE

TWO RIDES, ONE OKAY, THE OTHER NOT SO MUCH

T HE BAR GOOD Time was a cheery place—bright, noisy, and full of happy customers. Me? I felt gloomy, frightened, and full of dread.

Curt stood at the zinc bar. He smiled and raised his glass to me as I sidled up next to him. I asked for a white wine. Curt waved a hand at the bartender to cancel my order. "He'll have a Johnny Walker Blue. A double," he said to the bartender, then to me, "Best whiskey they have. Something a little stronger will help us both."

I thought it made more sense to go into a meeting like this stone sober but could see the advantage of a couple of drinks. If we were sober, we probably wouldn't do this.

"C'mon, Sam, don't look so glum. Y'know, it's funny. I used to hate the meetings in the foreign service. There was no end to them. But I'm looking forward to this one," he said, making me wonder how much confidence he had already drunk. "It's hot in here. For God's sake, take off your overcoat."

Keenly aware of the wire on me, but thinking he might become suspicious if I refused, I shrugged off my overcoat and slung it over my arm.

Trying to appear casual, I looked around the bar for the police officer Simon had promised would be there, but couldn't find anyone who looked like a cop. He was either very good at blending in or I was unperceptive or—God forfend—he wasn't there.

My drink arrived. Made reckless by my anxieties, I downed it quickly and ordered another, taking the second one in two eye-watering gulps. On an empty stomach, it went like a haymaker to my brain.

Curt laughed. "Attaboy. We should go in relaxed. You look nervous as hell."

"I'm fine."

"Look, I know I've put you in kind of a pickle here. I'm sorry. Didn't mean for it to work out like this. Girard says the meeting will go well and everyone will walk away happy."

"You really think you can just talk them into giving you the money?"

"Hey, like I said, it's a business deal. Girard says so. They don't want trouble." His smiled broadened. He was truly in a good mood. "Besides, they won't know how to say no. I'm a charming guy. Everyone says so."

With a sweeping gesture that knocked over his empty glass, he ordered another drink. It struck me that however often he said that everything was going to go smoothly, he'd needed to suck down several drinks to build up his courage. For all his brave talk, he too feared trouble. If a few moments earlier I'd thought I was filled with dread, I was wrong. There was room for a little more.

I looked at my watch. "Hadn't we better get going?"

"We can be a few minutes late. Don't wanna let 'em take us for granted."

It seemed to me the wrong tack to take with a bunch of gangsters, but I tried to tell myself he knew them better than I did.

As he downed his drink, I pushed away from the bar. "Okay," I said with a decisiveness I didn't feel. "Let's get going."

"You're jumpy as a flea on a frying pan. Settle down." Before I could back away, Curt put a reassuring hand on my shoulder. "Look, Sam, I—"

He stopped himself mid-sentence and his eyes turned hard. He yanked me toward him, our faces inches apart, his dark with anger. His grip on my shoulder tightened as he kneaded the wire. "What the hell is this?"

"What are you talking about?" I thought of putting my overcoat back on, but it was too late for that.

"Come with me," he said and pulled me toward the restroom.

I thought of making a scene, forcing the cop to jump in and help me, but knew, if I did, the evening would end early and badly.

I jerked away from his hand but followed him back.

Once inside, he rounded on me. "You've been talking to the police. My God, Sam, I never imagined you would do something like that to me."

"After you've been so loyal to me."

"Hey, I told you I was sorry."

"I guess I forgot."

"You want to screw this up for me?"

"The police told me I was neck deep in this and threatened to arrest me."

"I never imagined you'd go to the cops."

"I didn't. They came to me."

He shook his head in confusion. "How'd they know to talk to you?"

"I told you. I've got a friend who knows what we're doing tonight. After I spoke to her, she called a friend with the police and a detective came to my room. He insisted I wear this. I didn't have any choice. They would have arrested me if I'd refused."

"This woman's some friend," he said, chuckling. Charm can trap the charmer as well as the charmed. Even after all this, I think he still saw me as his friend, someone who wouldn't betray him.

"She's concerned about my safety."

"Yeah. Good. Fine. Touché." He patted me down, trying to find the transmitter and battery.

"Leave it alone. It could protect us both if there's real trouble."

"And if these guys with Girard find it, it could get us both killed. Besides, I can't get my money if the cops come running in. If you don't get rid of it, you're not going. And don't worry, I have my own ways of protecting us."

I dismissed his words as another drunken reference to his inexhaustible charm, but I realized later I should have asked him what he meant.

The door opened and a young guy came in. For a moment I wondered if he might be the cop Simon had promised, but he only glanced at us and stepped up to the urinal.

While he went about his business, Curt and I stood facing each other, neither of us quite sure what to do next.

When the man left, Curt found the battery pack and pulled it out, then reached in through my collar and yanked the wire off me, nearly ripping my skin off, and threw all of it into the garbage can. I couldn't help but reflect that I might get killed, but at least the police would get back a fully charged battery.

I thought as quickly as two double whiskeys allowed. Simon had said I needed to get Curt to say the name of the place we were going so he and his officers could arrive before us. Without the wire on me, it didn't matter now whether he told me or not. I took what comfort I could from the assurance that the plainclothes officer Simon planted in the bar would follow us as we left. It was riskier than I wanted, but I hoped, a little forlornly, that things might still work out.

Part of me wanted to refuse to go any farther. Seeing me as a snitch, he'd probably like it if I did. But if Curt left me behind, I couldn't do anything to help Chantal and Nassim, which, I reminded myself, was my real purpose, Simon and his men notwithstanding.

"Okay," Curt said, his earlier affability gone. "Let's get out of here."

Though Curt had told me the meeting place was only a couple of blocks from the bar, which would make it easy for the policeman to follow us, we had hardly reached the sidewalk when he threw up a hand to flag down a taxi.

"I thought you said we'd walk to the meeting."

Curt laughed. "I'm too drunk to walk anywhere."

It was a Friday night, but we got lucky. A cab pulled up almost immediately. Curt opened its door, shoved me in, and took a seat beside me.

The taxi had hardly stopped before we were underway again. Curt handed the cabbie a piece of paper and asked him if he knew where the address was. The cabbie nodded.

As we pulled away, I glanced over my shoulder and saw a man rush out of the bar and throw out his arms in vexation as we merged into traffic and drove off. He spun around on the sidewalk and waved for a taxi.

I had never felt so alone in my life.

Leaning back in his seat, Curt misread my uneasiness. "Don't worry, Sam. It'll all go fine."

Several thoughts raced through my whiskey-addled mind as we weaved through traffic. When I failed to activate the transmitter, would the police understand the wire wasn't working, or would they simply think that their idiot of a snitch had forgotten to turn it on? Either way, I was on my own. I could only hope that Curt was right and the meeting would go smoothly.

Trying to sound casual, I asked, "So, where are we going?"

"Some dump off the Place Pigalle. Just a few blocks away." He laughed, leaning forward in his seat, keen, excited, drunk. "Whole area used to be a red-light district, y'know. The GIs called it Pig Alley."

I tried to get him to focus. "Who exactly are we meeting?"

"Huh? Oh. Girard, and the head of his gang. Mr. Big. Or Monsieur Big, I guess." He laughed at his joke.

Chantal had said we were dealing with a small breakaway group—which made this guy Mr. Not-So-Big-As-Curt-Thinks, but I didn't bring it up.

"These guys know I'm only coming to this meeting to help Chantal and the boy, right?"

"Yeah, I told them. Don't worry. They've figured you for a chump all along. Your insisting that you be there is just in keeping. It might even help the optics."

I chewed on Curt's words and wanted to spit them back at him but kept my temper and told him, "I'll tell my friend where we are as soon as we get there." If I could get a moment alone, I could also tell Gwen to contact Simon and tell him Curt found the wire.

"Fine. Whatever."

A few moments later the cab stopped in front of a cheap eatery, its dim lights barely penetrating the dirty windows.

"This is it," Curt said. "Let's go."

My stomach felt like a butterfly preserve.

Curt paid off the cabbie and walked in ahead of me. Girard waited for us just inside the door. The two men shook hands, though only Curt smiled.

As I started toward the door, a squeal of tires made my head snap up. A taxi had rounded the corner and come to a stop half a block away. Within its shadowy interior I thought I caught a glimpse of the cop who had run out of the bar as Curt and I left. His presence lifted a large quantum of unease from my shoulders. I wouldn't have to ask Gwen to call Simon. He would know where we were. In a few minutes he and his men would be close at hand.

Telling myself to stay calm, I pulled out my phone and texted the address to Gwen, adding, a little forlornly, "Love."

Scowling with irritation, Curt continued to hold the door open for me. Thinking of the Vegetable Lady's warning of danger, it felt like he was holding open the lid to my coffin.

A righteous voice from within me said, "Walk away. You owe Curt nothing."

Spurred by a new determination, I took a step in the direction of the Place Pigalle. And stopped. Whatever Curt deserved, I couldn't bring myself to break faith with Chantal and Nassim. If I'd had another drink I'd have told myself I was doing this for apple pie and motherhood too.

Violating every kind of good sense, I followed Curt inside.

Even on a Friday night, the shabby bistro was nearly empty. But it was warm, and the aroma of *steak frites* made it feel pleasant and homey.

Girard eyed me coldly and made no greeting. Though I saw my presence as a means of helping his wife and Nassim and, indirectly, him too, he didn't look like the sort to appreciate it.

He gave a sign to the man behind the restaurant's tiny bar. The bartender nodded and cocked his head toward a corridor that led toward the back of the place.

Girard indicated we should follow him, saying, "We've arranged for a private room."

He led us down the poorly lit corridor and opened a door to our left. Standing in the light spilling from the room, Girard waved us in like an usher.

As we went through the door, Girard shoved me hard into Curt, sending us both staggering. We had hardly stumbled into the center of the room when the lights went out. I got out no more than, "Hey!"

before someone wrenched my arms behind my back, fastened a zip tie around my wrists, and thrust a hood over my head.

Curt shouted, "What the hell are you—"

I heard the thud of a blow, followed by a groan and a curse from Curt.

The sound of a door opening was followed by a rush of fresh air. Our captors hustled us outside and threw us into the back of some kind of van, apparently parked in an alley behind the place. Both of us landed roughly on its metal bed.

Though the cop in the taxi had by now probably told Simon we'd gone into the bistro, he couldn't have seen us being hustled out the back door. When Simon and the cavalry arrived they would assume we were still in the building.

With my hands tied behind me, it took some time to struggle into a sitting position against the side of the van as it drove slowly down the alley and then, judging by the sound of rushing cars around us, turned onto a busy street.

"Where are we going?" I asked.

"How the hell should I know?" Curt snapped.

We rode in silence after that.

CHAPTER TWENTY-FOUR

MEETING RAOUL

OVER THE NEXT ten minutes or so—it's hard to keep track of time when you're blindfolded, trussed up, and frightened—the van sped up one street and down another. I noticed we were turning predominately to the right, leaving me with the impression we were making a large circle. When the van eventually came to a stop, I guessed we weren't far from where we'd started.

The back doors of the van were thrown open and rough hands dragged us out, yanked us to our feet, and frog-marched us up some steps and through a door. Once inside, we were pushed and pulled up several flights of stairs, then down a corridor and into a room. When the door shut behind us, our hoods were taken off and the zip ties cut from our wrists.

After our enforced blindness it took a moment to adjust to the bright light, but I soon made out a young man—no more than mid-twenties—leaning back on the rear legs of a straight-backed chair. He was a peculiar-looking fellow, his head looking like it had been caught in a vise at a young age, making it unnaturally long and narrow. Under thick black eyebrows his eyes protruded oddly, carrying, I thought, a glint of madness.

Dressed in blue jeans and a cheap sports coat, he sat with his hands clasped loosely behind his head, his feet on the table in front of him, grinning up at us. He clearly wanted to appear relaxed and in control, but one leg was bouncing up and down, betraying a nervousness that belied his casual pose.

A small canvas sack lay on the table next to his feet.

"You enjoyed your ride?" he asked. "I had to make sure you weren't followed. People have been . . . sniffing around us for weeks. But you . . . don't know anything about that, do you?"

He spoke with exquisite slowness punctuated by peculiar pauses. His voice was high-pitched and delicate, which he tried to disguise with a self-consciously macho tone. No doubt this was the Raoul that Chantal had mentioned. I remembered her saying that the whole bunch of them acted as if they were in a movie.

"I said . . . you wouldn't know anything about that, would you?"

I figured he was talking about Garonne, the unseen presence that dominated everyone's thoughts, though he could have meant the police. Either way, I wasn't going to say anything.

Curt would. He snapped back at Raoul, "No, I wouldn't know anything about it. In fact, I don't know who you're talking about."

Raoul laughed and turned toward the two young thugs who had dragged us upstairs. "He doesn't know who I'm talking about."

They snickered with pleasure at his remark.

I recognized one of the two thugs as the guy who had shoved the note into my hand outside my hotel, setting up my first meeting with Chantal. The other might have been the one who followed me to the Métro near Montmartre after I'd spoken to Khadija the first time.

Girard stood near the door, apart from the others. He wasn't laughing. I had the impression that he stood apart from the other three in some significant way, perhaps only in age and judgment. At thirty-five or so, he was, by maybe a decade, the oldest among them.

Before talking to Chantal I had assumed, and I believe Curt had too, that we would be dealing with adults, mature if crooked men with whom we could strike some sort of reasonable agreement. But she'd been right.

Instead, we had a bunch of kids playing movie gangster because they had no real idea what they were doing.

Raoul regarded the cloth sack on the table and toed it aside. For several moments he simply blinked, as if trying to remember where he was. His pupils were dilated, making his eyes black as death.

Curt and I glanced at each other. We both saw it. The kid was high as a kite. And Curt was drunk, and I wasn't much better. How many ways could this go wrong?

Raoul cocked his chin at his two younger henchmen. "Pat them down," he said, then seemed to momentarily lose track of his thought before picking the conversation up again. "After you do that, go downstairs and guard the door. Maybe Garonne—" He stopped himself. "Maybe someone followed you here. Maybe the police. We have to be careful."

The two youngsters frisked us carelessly. As Simon had anticipated, they seemed to be looking only for weapons. I don't think they would have found the wire. They nodded at Raoul that we were clean and went downstairs, leaving us with Maurice Girard and the young guy at the table.

"You're Curtis Hansen," Raoul said, as if Curt might not have been clear on this point. He looked Curt up and down, shook his head and chuckled. "I was expecting someone more . . . impressive."

"Expect whatever you want," Curt said. "And whom do I have the pleasure of addressing?"

The young man snorted dismissively before turning to me. "And you are his faithful sidekick, Lucky Luke," he said, giving me a name from a French comic book series that my son used to like. "You two have come to the complaint department, yes? You want to strike some deal. Get some . . . satisfaction."

At the mention of striking a deal, Curt took a step forward, ready to pound the table and lash his tail.

Raoul stopped him with a raised hand and patted a lump under his sports coat, letting us know he was armed and would decide who spoke and when. "So, tell me what your problem is."

Assuming an aplomb he couldn't have felt, Curt glanced at Girard, then said to the young man at the table, "I gave you a hundred and fifty thousand dollars. You promised me a shipment in return, but you didn't deliver. I want my money back." Apparently thinking he hadn't made a strong enough impression, he added, "I can make plenty of trouble for you."

With a derisive laugh the boy gangster looked over his shoulder at Girard. "We've . . ." He paused, his drug-infused mind disengaging for a moment. "We've kidnapped this guy. He's our prisoner. We've got guns and the money, and we can give him plenty of whichever one we want. Yes, he's really got us over a barrel." He kicked at the sack again and said to Girard, "What do you think we should do, Maurice? You know who they're really working for, don't you?"

That put a new chill through me. It didn't make any sense that we'd be working for Garonne, but if Raoul believed it, the truth didn't matter and we might be dead any moment.

Raoul repeated himself. "You know who they're working for don't you, Maurice?"

"Whatever you think, Raoul."

Banging the front legs of his chair down on the floor, Raoul glared at Curt. "He's right! It's whatever I think. And I'll do whatever I goddamn want. You hold no cards. You don't even get out of here alive unless I decide to let you." He was pale and sweat glistened on his forehead.

When neither of us said anything, the would-be kingpin regained his composure and smirked at Curt. "You don't understand. You were never going to get anything. Nothing. We just took your money and kept the shipment." He laughed at his own duplicity. "I was working for someone big then. Like I'm going to be big soon. Me! This deal with you was just a little . . . a little transaction on the side. I needed working capital. And I got it from you. But . . ." He tilted his head to one side and gazed at us in a curious way. "But, I never thought you'd be stupid enough to try to get it back." He cocked his chin at me. "Or to get this pussy to track us down for you." A smile crossed his face as he looked at me. "You're slippery. I'll give you that. Slippery . . . and stupid. I send someone to the Gare de l'Est to . . . pay you off, make you go away. And you take a swing at him."

His revelation solved that little mystery. The guy at the station was probably reaching into his coat for the money. I wouldn't have taken it and, what the heck, I might have felt sufficiently offended to have taken a swing at him anyway. A shame Ulysses hadn't caught him. He could have used the money.

Raoul laughed at my foolishness and looked to Girard to join him. Girard didn't react. He seemed to hold Curt, Raoul, and me all in equal contempt.

Curt returned us to the matter at hand. Between clenched teeth, he said, "I want my money back." He put his fists on the edge of the table and leaned toward Raoul as if he might flip it over on him.

With surprising speed for a guy as strung out as Raoul, he reached inside his coat and drew out a large automatic pistol. He pulled back the slide to put a round in the chamber and pointed it at Curt.

Curt jumped back, though he still looked angry. If I'd been wondering how much the whiskey was affecting his judgment, I had my answer.

Raoul nodded at the cloth bag. "You think you can come in here and tell me what to do?" He snickered. "Maybe you really are that stupid. I've got twenty-five thousand euros here. I was thinking of giving them to you. It makes for less . . . cleanup than killing you. That's all you're worth to me. And now I'm not even sure you're worth that." He nodded in my direction. "What do you think, Lucky Luke? Is that good enough?"

Curt snorted. "My friend here thinks you should give the money to Chantal and my son."

Raoul twitched in confusion. "Your son? Yours?" Raoul turned toward Girard. "Is that true, Maurice? This guy is the kid's papa, not you? I thought the . . . kid was yours, that you were . . . a father. But you're not?"

Humiliation pushing his anger, Girard reddened and clenched his jaw. Raoul laughed at him, apparently uncaring, or unaware, how much this might threaten Girard's sense of manhood. "All this time I thought you were this big man with a wife and a kid. Turns out you don't have a kid at all. And . . . this guy got to your wife before you did." With a prolonged shudder, as if sloughing off one skin and putting on another, Raoul regained his former pose of menacing calm.

He turned his regard on Curt and said, "Give the money to Maurice's wife and . . . this guy's son? I like that." Without taking his eyes off Curt, he nodded at me. "Yes, I like Lucky Luke's idea. Let's give it to Maurice's wife. She'll probably handle it better than Maurice would."

"No!" Curt shouted. "The money's mine. I'll give it to her if I want. You keep out of it!"

I had to admire his guts, though I might have admired it more if he'd been sober.

"No? No?" Raoul's eyes popped in surprise that turned quickly to menace. "Don't you say no to me. Ever." To my bafflement, the rage in his eyes slowly dimmed and he released a long, relaxed sigh, more dangerous than any show of anger. "I get it. You don't think I'm really going to give it to Maurice's wife, that I'll just keep it for myself. I'll show you I'm not kidding. I'll promise it to her face. Right now." He turned to Girard. "Go get them, Maurice—your wife, and this other man's kid. Let's give them a chance to thank us."

Raoul might have done well to catch the look in Girard's eyes as he left, but he didn't, and the older man left the room without a word. And with that, I knew where we were. After all the driving around, they had brought us to the apartment building where Girard had spoken to Curt two nights earlier. I should have guessed. Chantal had told me that most of the gang lived there.

Silence thick as fog filled the room as we waited for Girard to come back with Chantal and Nassim. Raoul's head twitched involuntarily, adding to the impression that he held only the most tentative control over himself. His eyes darted at us and he knew we'd seen it. To cover, he waved his pistol at Curt, smiled, and said, "Bang!"

Curt backed up a step, but his face went stony in resentment at the young punk's manner.

Raoul's smile grew broader. He again put his feet on the table and tilted his chair on its back legs, cradling the gun against his chest.

"So, Papa, what do you think about your son being brought up by another man? That is, if he's really your son."

"Shut up about the boy."

A verbal slap can sting as much as any kind. Raoul lowered his gun on Curt and pulled back the hammer. "Say that again. I dare you. Say it again."

Curt froze. Unable to breathe, we watched Raoul's finger on the trigger. Curt's life trembled on the thin edge of a drug-addled boy's impulse.

"I said, say that one more—"

At that moment my phone rang.

Raoul stopped mid-sentence and looked around the room in confusion, gripping his gun tightly, the depth of his paranoia written in his eyes.

"What's that?"

The phone rang again.

This time he understood. Collecting himself, he labored to re-acquire his previous languid manner, but he was squeezing the pistol as if he might strangle it. His voice wavering with menace, he said, "Go ahead, Lucky Luke, answer it."

The phone rang a third time. It seemed dangerous to answer, but more dangerous to refuse. I pulled it out and looked at the screen. It was Gwen.

Curt and I hadn't had the time or wit to tell Raoul about our backup, that Gwen would know where we were. Of course, at this point she didn't.

"Answer it!" Raoul shouted, swinging his pistol around on me.

I thought of simply hanging up but feared Raoul's reaction. So I pushed the talk button, ready to tell Gwen I'd call her back later, if I was still alive.

Before I could say anything, Gwen jumped in. "Sam, are you all right? Simon called and said—"

I hung up, but it was too late.

Raoul brought his chair down onto its legs, his gun aimed squarely at my chest. "Who was that? Somebody knows you're here?"

"No one knows where I am," I answered. True enough in the literal sense, but beside the point.

"Who's Simon? He's with Garonne, isn't he? You sons of bitches!" All trace of his drug-induced haze had vanished under a surge of fear. "Give me your phone!"

"It was just a friend who—"

"Give me the phone!"

I tossed the phone onto the table in front of him. Raoul picked it up and tried to find the list of recent callers, but he didn't have the patience to figure it out. With a growl of frustration, he tossed the phone on the table and smashed it with the butt of his gun.

The act of petty violence seemed to further stoke his fury. Losing his last gram of self-control, he jumped to his feet and turned the pistol on me.

I wondered if I was living my last moment on earth. An eerie calmness settled over me as I waited.

Before Raoul could decide whether to let me live or die, the door burst open and Girard came into the room, dragging Chantal by the arm. She looked terrified. Nassim followed, holding onto his mother's skirt, looking from one of us to the other, little lines of fear and confusion crossing his young face.

Chantal was pleading with Girard, "No, it's not what you think!"

Girard pushed her against the wall, holding her there at arm's length as she struggled to get free.

"Don't move," he told her. "Don't you dare move."

Chantal's eyes darted to me, to Raoul, to Girard, before finally coming back to Curt, registering a mix of emotions I couldn't begin to decipher.

Somehow ignoring the air of violence pulsing through the room, Curt's face softened with a faint look of wonder.

Oblivious to anything else around him, he smiled and said, "Hello, Chantal."

It couldn't have been more clear. Whatever his betrayals, whatever his crimes, he loved her, just as he'd said. And the thought again struck me hard. Curt and I had both come to Paris, at least in part, to seek the women we had once loved. Though our paths had led us in different directions, we might yet end up sharing the same end.

As Girard pinned her against the wall, Nassim gripped his mother's skirt more tightly.

"Enough!" Raoul sliced the air with a downward stroke of his arm. "What the hell's going on?"

"It's her!" Girard shouted. "It was her all along. The spy for Garonne."

Chantal tried to wrench free of Girard's grip.

The young gang boss couldn't take it in. "What?"

"I caught her on the phone to Garonne."

"No!" Chantal cried and tried to step toward Raoul, but Girard held her tight. "I swear I wasn't."

Nassim began to cry, a frightened, almost silent sobbing that quickly rose to a howl.

"Shut the kid up!" Raoul yelled.

Chantal put her hand over Nassim's mouth, trying to muffle his cries.

"Be quiet, Nassim," Girard told the boy. At the words from the man he thought was his father, the boy stopped crying, though the terror in his eyes remained.

Girard turned back to Raoul. "She's the one who's been spying on us, telling Garonne who we are, what we're doing."

There was fear in Girard's eyes as he spoke, fear that Raoul would hold him responsible for Chantal's betrayals, real or imagined.

Raoul waved his hands in front of his face as if fighting through cobwebs. "Shut up! Everybody shut up!"

Desperate to clear himself, Girard ignored his boss's order. "She was calling Garonne. Started telling him about this meeting. But I cut her off before she got far."

"It's not true!" Chantal cried as if she were pleading for her life. It only took me an instant to realize she was.

"You *con!*" Raoul shouted and turned the gun on her.

It was no idle gesture. He meant to kill her.

Girard saw it and took a step away from her.

Driven by an impulse that would have made Gwen tear her hair out, I shouted, "Don't!" and started to move between Raoul and Chantal.

Instantly, Raoul turned his gun on me.

I knew I was about to die. Then Raoul would shoot Chantal, making my gallant gesture doubly futile.

What came next happened faster than I could take it in. As Raoul squeezed the trigger Curt shouted, "Sam!" and shoved me out of the line of fire, the bullet passing inches from my head.

A pistol had materialized in Curt's fist, a small automatic, hardly bigger than his hand. I'll never know where he'd hidden it, but now I understood why, back at the bar, he had said he had his own way of keeping us safe.

Gasping in shock, Raoul turned his gun on Curt. Too late. Curt stood only three feet from his target and could hardly miss. He fired, sending Raoul backward over his chair.

Girard fumbled for the gun in his shoulder holster.

Curt shouted to Chantal, "Out of the way!"

Grabbing Nassim in her arms, she dived for the floor.

Girard unholstered his pistol too late. Curt fired twice. The first shot missed and went into the wall. The second shot hit him in the forehead. With an astonished gasp, he fell against the wall, pulling the trigger in reflex, sending a shot into the floor.

The explosion of the shots in quick succession was deafening.

Nassim struggled from his mother's grasp. Shaking with fear and horror, hurtling toward hysteria, he looked at Girard, who lay against the wall like a pile of dirty clothes.

The boy turned toward Curt and shouted, "Papa! Papa!"

His face transfigured with joy, Curt opened his arms. "Yes, Nassim. Papa."

But he had misunderstood.

Nassim cried, "Papa!" once more and grabbed Girard's pistol from where it had fallen on the floor.

"Son!" Curt thrust out his hand to stop him.

As Chantal had said, Nassim had seen Girard and the others fooling around with their guns. He knew what to do. He fired before Curt could tell him to stop, hitting him in the chest.

With a groan that might have been a sob, Curt fell backward and collapsed onto the floor.

Dumbstruck, Nassim dropped the gun, unable to fully grasp what he had done.

For an endless moment Chantal and I could only look at each other, paralyzed, wishing we could somehow return to the long-ago world of ten seconds earlier.

Nassim stared at the bodies and didn't move.

Two things jolted us out of our shock. A grotesque sound coming from the back of Raoul's throat as he twisted back and forth in a sickening parody of a man trying to get to his feet. And, from below, we heard shouting and the distant sound of two men pounding up the stairs.

For an instant I thought of picking up the gun and shooting Raoul again. But I couldn't do it. I still don't know if my refusal was to my credit or not.

"Quick, come with me!" Chantal cried and grabbed Nassim by the hand. The boy balked, hypnotized with the horror around him, unwilling to move. Chantal picked him up and ran out of the room.

I started to follow, but as I reached the door I went back and grabbed the cloth sack from where it had fallen on the floor and stuck it in my coat pocket. Next to it lay Raoul's gun. For a moment I hesitated. I'd never carried a gun, never owned one. Taking it up now would force me to acknowledge I had entered a world where I might need to kill someone. I shoved the thought from my mind, picked up the gun, and put it in the other pocket.

I tried not to look at the three men lying on the floor. Raoul let out a deep groan and levered himself up onto his hands and knees. I kicked his hands out from under him and turned toward the door.

As I did, I saw Curt lying on the floor, unmoving, and couldn't help thinking he had no more corners to cut, no more regs to ignore, no more money worries. He lay at peace. When he had pulled out his gun, he had saved my life, and paid for it with his own. I said a little prayer for him and ran out of the room.

Gripping Nassim by the hand, Chantal had stopped in an open doorway at the end of the corridor.

"Hurry!" she called.

As the sound of feet running up the stairs got closer, I ran down the corridor. The doorway led to a dark stairwell. Looking down into it was like looking into the maw of a monster, knowing we had already decided to jump in. I picked up Nassim and said to Chantal, "Go. I've got him."

We scrambled down the stairs at the same moment we heard Raoul's gunmen in the corridor.

The five flights of stairs to the bottom seemed like twenty. With only the faintest of light from a bulb mounted on the wall halfway down, we bumped into the walls, banged into each other, slipped on the stairs in our hurry to get out.

After what seemed like an hour we arrived at the bottom, out of breath, and stopped by another door. Chantal fumbled at the handle. It didn't open. She stepped aside while I put Nassim down and tried the handle, first easily, then desperately as the door refused to budge.

Trapped, we looked up the dark stairwell, wondering how long it would take the two guards to piece things together and come after us. I thought of going back up one flight, finding the main staircase, and escaping through the front door. But every instinct told me not to run toward the gunmen.

I stood back and gave the door a kick. It shook in its frame but didn't give. Catching our fear, Nassim began to cry again, a weary, hopeless sobbing. I pushed Chantal aside and charged the door with my right shoulder. It gave a sharp crack. I ran at it again.

With a crash that must have echoed to the top of the building, the middle of the door splintered. I kicked at the shattered wood until I'd made a hole big enough for us to crawl out.

Fresh air never tasted so good.

CHAPTER TWENTY-FIVE

CITY OF LIGHT, CITY OF SHADOW

T HE BROKEN DOOR opened onto an alley at the side of the apartment building. Hugging the brick wall, we walked quickly toward the street. Nassim was sobbing in a frightening, rhythmic kind of way. Holding him in my arms, I put my hand over his mouth and peeked around the corner of the building.

After hearing the shots fired in the room on the fifth floor, I thought—hoped—that someone in the building must have called the police by now, though in fact it seemed like the sort of place where no one, under any circumstances, would call the police. In any case, with Raoul's gunmen running through the corridors with guns in their hands, looking for us, we couldn't wait around to see if the police might show up.

For the moment, though, the two gangsters were nowhere in sight. I motioned to Chantal to follow me. I held Nassim tightly to my chest and we ran down the street. When we'd gotten a block away, I looked back, expecting to see Raoul's two thugs coming for us. But the street was empty. It must have taken them a few minutes to figure out what had happened and a couple more before it dawned on them that Chantal and Nassim and I and the sack of euros had all gone missing.

I hoped they would try to patch up Raoul rather than come for us. My deepest fear was that, if Raoul could talk, he would tell them of Chantal's betrayal, that she was Garonne's spy. Then they would know they couldn't let us get away.

We made our way quickly down the dark, silent street, Nassim growing heavy in my arms. I looked down at the little guy, his head resting on my shoulder.

He had stopped sobbing, but his eyes were open wide, staring into nothing, deep in shock.

We reached the boulevard and I threw up a hand to flag down a taxi. My gesture might as well have been a way of making myself invisible. Friday-night traffic clogged the streets and all of the cabs were engaged.

We continued walking while I continued to turn every few yards and wave for a taxi. All the time, I watched the side street we had come from, afraid the gunmen would appear, looking for us with murder in their eyes.

Finally, a cab pulled over. I yanked open the door and we tumbled into the back seat. Nassim jumped into his mother's arms and clung to her.

"Go!" I shouted to the cabbie.

He sighed. "*Oui, monsieur,* but where?"

I leaned into Chantal and whispered. "The safest thing would be to take you to the police and tell them what happened." The fear in her eyes ramped up another notch. "I know it would make problems for you, but—"

"No. The police will know who I am. They'll throw me in prison."

"If you tell them they forced you into it—"

"You don't understand. I'm a Moroccan, an Arab. I've been involved with a drug gang. They'll have no mercy on me. And what happens to Nassim? No. I can't go to the police. Please."

Reluctantly, I nodded. "Okay."

For an instant I thought of heading for Gwen's. But just as I couldn't take Chantal to the police, I couldn't ask Gwen to get any further involved in my troubles.

Unable to think of anything better, I told the driver, "Hotel Brighton."

Friday night in Paris plays out like Friday night in any big city. The sidewalks were crowded and traffic filled the streets. For unending seconds we didn't move. Chantal kept turning around, looking behind us, knowing that at this rate Raoul's thugs could catch up to us on foot.

They wouldn't hesitate to shoot us through the windows of the cab and run off. As Ulysses had said, committing murder in a public place has its advantages.

After perhaps ten minutes in which we moved all of a hundred yards, I saw the entrance to a Métro station and told the cabbie, "Stop here."

"We're already stopped," he muttered without turning around.

I overpaid him and we ran for the Métro, dashing down the steps into the anonymity of the crowded platform. A train arrived and we squeezed on, taking seats near the doors.

Slowly, our silence filled with the weight of the question I had to ask. "Was your husband right? Were you working for Garonne?"

She turned away and gazed out the window, though I could see her reflection in the glass.

"I hate Garonne like I hate that terrible infant Raoul. And I fear them. I'm afraid every day—of Garonne, of Maurice, of Raoul, afraid of everything. And all the time I'm afraid for you because you don't have enough sense to be afraid for yourself. I feared the meeting with Raoul would end with you dead. You should have gone to Khadija. She would have told you not to come."

"I did. She tried."

She looked at me, astonished at the depth of my folly. "Why didn't you listen?"

"I wanted to help you. Coming to the meeting was the only way I could do that. But tell me, why were you on the phone to Garonne when your husband came to get you?"

"I did it for you. I needed to call someone, get Garonne's men there, stop the meeting. Do something to . . ." Still unable to face me, she sighed, her breath clouding the window, obscuring her reflection. "I should have known they would never have gotten there in time." She snorted ironically. "At least Raoul's dead."

"Don't count on it. The last I saw him, he was still alive." I saw the dismay in her face. "Only the good die young."

"*Zut!*"

"Why did you do it, agree to work for Garonne?"

"Garonne's people understood something was wrong. Clients were saying their drugs were cut. That's bad for business. They narrowed their suspicions to Trans-Maghreb, to Momo's garage, to Raoul. They were sure I must know something, and they knew I wouldn't have much choice but to help them. Garonne and his bunch could turn me in to the police. Or they might kill me if I refused to help. Then what would happen to my boy? And I was afraid for Maurice if Garonne found out he was with Raoul and those other children."

"So you told Garonne about the others, but not of your husband?"

"I told Garonne's men about Raoul and this pathetic little gang. I never spoke to Garonne directly. For Nassim's sake I couldn't tell them about Maurice, that he was one of them." She glanced down at the little boy. He had retreated deep into himself and wasn't listening. Still, Chantal dropped her voice. "He liked Maurice. Called him Papa. I needed to protect him."

I didn't know if she meant she wanted to protect Girard or Nassim. But it came down to the same thing.

"And you were afraid they'd kill Curt?"

"I don't know. I was afraid of everything." She spoke in a groan, shaking her head, weary, helpless. "But, yes, Curt too. I wanted to slap him in the face for what did to me, to Nassim. But I didn't want him dead." The saddest smile I'd ever seen crossed her face. "But I never get what I want, do I?"

We got off the train at the Place de la Concorde, only a couple hundred yards from the hotel. A quick walk, and then refuge. I would try again to persuade her we needed to call the police. I hoped that the matter would be taken out of my hands—that once he had lost track of me, Simon might have sent someone to my room to see if I'd come back.

Anyway, all the whos and whats and whys didn't matter much now. If Raoul's men found us they would kill me, thinking I had shot Maurice and Raoul. And they would kill Chantal for betraying them and to shut her up for good. They might even shoot Nassim too, just to keep things tidy.

Like every boulevard in Paris that night, the rue de Rivoli was backed up for blocks. After coming up from the Métro, we threaded our way through a line of idling cars and pushed into the crowd on the other side of the street. Within a few moments we had come in sight of the hotel. I felt a surge of relief—a surge that died as quickly as it was born.

Two men stood near the hotel entrance. One of them, short and wiry with a buzz cut, looked like the guy who had come out of the shadowy doorway near Gwen's place and slugged me. The other, taller and thinner, also familiar-looking, stood with a phone to his ear, his head bent, nodding. I didn't need to hear the conversation to know he was talking to one of the gang members we had left behind when we ran from the apartment building.

Sensing my sudden tension, Chantal, who had been cooing quietly in Nassim's ear, stopped in the middle of the crowded sidewalk and looked toward the hotel.

"Migod! It's Bernard and Putin."

"Who?"

"Bernard, the one who sat near us at the café the first time we met. The short one, I don't know his real name. He's a Russian. Everyone calls him Putin."

They hadn't seen us yet. Putting a hand on Chantal's shoulder, I turned her around and said, "Stay calm. Don't run." We would walk away quietly and blend into the Friday-night crowd on the sidewalk without being noticed.

Or so I hoped.

Neither of us had thought that the sight of a familiar face would bring Nassim out of his shock.

Beaming with relief, he called, "Bernard!"

Chantal put a hand over his mouth. Shaking his head, the boy twisted away. "Bernard!"

Puzzled, Bernard lowered the phone and looked around. When he didn't find us he shook his head in a dismissive way, put a finger in one ear to block the noise around him, and brought the phone back up. Before he spoke, he took one more glance around. This time he saw us.

He shouted something into the phone, slapped the man Chantal called Putin on the shoulder, and pointed at us.

Putin reached into his pocket. I was sure he wasn't reaching for a stack of money like the guy at the Gare de l'Est. I saw the butt of a pistol in his hand. Bernard gripped him by the arm and spoke sharply to him, probably telling him it's one thing to walk up to a man in a crowded street and shoot, and another thing to fire wildly into a crowded sidewalk. Putin made a face but let go of the gun and pulled his hand out of his pocket.

They began to walk toward us, determined, not hurrying. For an instant I thought of pulling Raoul's pistol from my pocket but, like Bernard, understood the madness of a gunfight in the middle of a Friday-night crowd.

Taking Chantal by the arm, I turned her around and started walking back toward the Place de la Concorde and the Métro.

They were pros. Leaving Putin to follow us, Bernard started across the street to block us from running for the Métro entrance on that side.

Yes, they were pros. But, thank God, not very good ones. Single-mindedly keeping his eyes on us instead of where he was going, Bernard managed to step in front of a car just as it lurched forward. It hit him at the knees and knocked him over. Forgetting about us in his fury, he jumped up and turned on the driver, shouting obscenities and pounding on the car's hood. I recalled what Chantal had said about most gangsters being idiots.

We had come even with the narrow side entrance to the Tuileries gardens on the other side of the street. The Métro entrance lay fifty yards beyond it.

With Bernard still indulging in a hissy fit in the middle of the street, Chantal grabbed my hand. "Come on!"

We dodged the barely moving traffic and headed for the Métro entrance on the other side of the street. A car braked to keep from hitting us. Another driver leaned on his horn as we ran in front of him. A motorcycle speeding next to the curb nearly knocked us down, but we reached the sidewalk before Bernard, who was still shouting at the driver of the car that had knocked him over. We had an open path to the Métro entrance. But in the very moment I saw it, it closed. Putin had finally realized his partner, rather than chasing us down, was shouting at traffic in the middle of the street and we had gotten past him. He ran into the street just as the light turned green. I had never in my life so hoped to see someone get run over. But, if his head was a veritable rock quarry, his feet were surprisingly light, and he scampered through the traffic to get between us and the Métro.

It was time to come up with a plan B. With Putin blocking our escape, we dashed for the side entrance to the Tuileries, hoping to disappear into the darkness of the park.

A gray-haired guard with a walrus mustache, ready to lock the gate for the night, was shooing a young couple out of the park. He looked at us quizzically as we ran toward him. Chantal gave the old guy a heart-melting smile and said coyly, "Pardon me, my love," and squeezed past him. I gave the guard a jaunty salute and followed her, took the cloth bag out of my pocket, and called to Chantal, "Madam, you've forgotten your sack!"

The old guy wasn't as dim as we gave him credit for. He quickly shouted, "*Arret!*" Stop.

As he started to shut the gate and come after us, Bernard ran up and also tried to get past him. At the end of his patience, the guard shoved him back. Bernard hit him in the jaw, knocking the old guy against the gate.

Even with Chantal towing Nassim by the hand, we had gained some ground as Bernard and the guard struggled. We were maybe a hundred yards ahead of him. Unfortunately, that wasn't good enough. Bernard spotted us and came on the run. On the fortunate side, his altercation with the car had left him limping.

Instinctively, I looked around for Ulysses. He'd told me that if I needed him he'd be there, and he had always been as good as his word. But now he was nowhere in sight. If I lived long enough to see him again I'd have to give him a piece of my mind.

In the distance, we could hear the guard frantically blowing his whistle.

Though hurt, Bernard, unhindered by children or middle age, was gaining on us. Figuring I could run faster than Chantal, even with a child in my arms, I picked up Nassim. Maternal instincts engaged, Chantal cried, "No!" and grabbed for him, but I was already pulling away.

The little carnival was closing up for the night, the workers clearing off their counters and bringing down their awnings. The remaining light from the booths and the rides glowed with a kaleidoscope of bright colors—and made for stark shadows. Inane carnival tunes played from a couple of the rides, taking on a weirdly sinister tone as we ran to escape the killer behind us.

We ducked into one of the lanes between the game booths, the only path we could see clearly. The problem: if we could see it clearly, Bernard could just as clearly see us.

The workers looked at us curiously as we ran past them. Behind us, Bernard, limping badly now but only a few yards away. Misjudging his audience, he shouted to the workers, "Police! Stop them!"

He should have known better. A bunch of carny workers aren't the sort of people to help a cop chasing down a mother and child.

Bernard was near enough that I could hear him panting, almost feel his breath on my neck. Against every sensible instinct, I looked over my shoulder.

He was right behind us, reaching out, ready to grab Chantal by the shoulder and pull her down. If he did that, I knew I'd have to stop and fight. And I would lose.

But in the same instant I turned, he disappeared.

One of the carny workers had stuck out his foot, sending Bernard sprawling. With overplayed apologies, the man grabbed Bernard by the shoulders, yanked him to his feet, spun him around and, with further expressions of regret, started to brush him off.

Nearly as stunned as Bernard, it took me a moment to see that, in fact, this was no carny worker.

"Ulysses!" I cried.

Holding the battered Bernard by the shoulders, Ulysses looked at me with an expression of wounded pride. "Didn't I tell you I'd be here?"

After one more swipe to clean up the bruised and baffled Bernard, Ulysses smiled, then gave him a headbutt that sent him back to the ground.

With a roar of anger, Bernard jumped to his feet, shoved Ulysses away, and pulled a pistol from his pocket, murder in his eyes.

Given a moment's breather by Ulysses' intervention, we ran into the shadows thrown by the lights of the rides.

For an instant I thought we'd gotten away, but Nassim, perhaps sensing our danger, maybe confused to see us fleeing from his friend, Bernard, picked this moment to start crying again.

Bernard fired blindly, the bullet clanging off the metal façade of the roller coaster and smashing a bank of lights. The music from the ride's loudspeaker played merrily on, adding its bizarre note to our attempt to escape. I was sure I'd hear that music in my head till my last dying breath, which might come at any moment.

Running as hard as I could with Nassim still in my arms, we came out of shadows and into the light of the Ferris wheel, silhouetting us perfectly.

Bernard fired again. The bullet clanged off the wheel's metal skeleton and whined into the darkness. Again, I thought of pulling Raoul's gun from my pocket and firing back, but feared I would hit one of the carnival workers.

Nassim's crying turned into a howl of fear and outrage at his upended world. We needed to stop, sit him down, and try to comfort the little guy. But we had no time. If we remained lighted from behind even a moment longer, Bernard would likely hit one of us. Frantic, we ran into the darkness, putting the carnival's lights behind us.

A few yards ahead of us, a gap in the park's iron fence appeared through the gloom, a gate apparently left open when we interrupted the guard's rounds.

We had run into the park to escape Bernard. Now it was time to run out of the park before he noticed we were gone.

Panting like a steam engine, my heart beating two hundred to the minute, I wondered how much longer I could keep this up. Chantal saw me struggling and stopped, breathing hard, her head down. She handed me the cloth sack, took Nassim from my arms, and set him on the ground. Looking into his eyes, she touched her forehead to his. "We need you to run some more. Can you be a good boy and run?"

Nassim managed to nod.

The three of us dashed through the open gate, coming out on the sidewalk of the rue de Rivoli.

I looked behind us but didn't see Bernard yet, but I knew he couldn't be far behind. If we continued running through the well-lit streets, he would catch us. His blood up, his judgment unpredictable, he wouldn't hesitate to shoot us.

Yet, in the ticktock of good fortune and bad, the pendulum swung our way once more. Only few yards away, we saw the possibility of escape in the glow of a Métro entrance. With luck, a train might pull into the station as we reached the platform. We could jump on and be gone in seconds. I didn't want to think of the possibility that if there was no train we'd be trapped, with Bernard between us and any way out.

While I worked through this quick and perhaps flawed calculation, I glanced up the street. What I saw banished any hesitation I had.

Walking toward us along the sidewalk, peering through the railings of the iron fence, was the short, weaselly form of Putin. He spotted me at the same moment I spotted him.

With a shout, he came running at us.

We ran for the Métro and dashed down the stairs, praying for a train.

Halfway down the steps, Chantal stumbled, pitching head first toward the concrete steps. I grabbed her by the arm, stopping her mid-fall. Somehow, through the strength of a mother's love, she had hung onto Nassim.

Our little dance, however, had given Putin time to catch up. He ran down the steps and grabbed Chantal by the neck. I swung at him and missed. Chantal, though, had regained her balance and ground her heel into the arch of his foot. With a strangled cry, he tried to jump back. I pushed him hard and, his foot still pinned by Chantal's shoe, he fell, hitting his head on the steps, his arms splayed out like a rag doll's.

We staggered down the stairs.

There was no train.

I looked over my shoulder and saw that Putin had gotten to his feet, his head down, hands on his knees, trying to pull himself together.

In the same instant, I saw that Chantal was limping badly.

"You've hurt your ankle," I said.

"No, the heel of my shoe broke off when I stepped on Putin's foot."

By now, Putin had gotten to his feet.

Chantal muttered, "That bastard."

Before I could stop her, she handed Nassim to me, took off her broken shoe, rushed at the still-disoriented Putin, and started hitting him over the head with it. With a cry of astonishment, he fell to the ground and curled into a fetal position as she pummeled him.

I ran over and took her by the arm. "We've got to get out of here."

"I'll kill him!"

"You can't kill him with a shoe."

"I can try!"

"Come on."

She threw the shoe at him and reluctantly allowed me to pull her away. For good measure, she wrenched herself from my grip, took off her other shoe and threw that at him too.

Though we were running for our lives, pursued by killers, the absurdity of the scene made me laugh. Chantal whipped her head around and looked at me as if she wished she had another shoe left so she could kill me as well. Then she laughed too and we took off, Chantal making good speed barefoot.

As we left Putin behind, the distinctive rumble of an approaching train echoed off the station walls.

We bulled our way through the crowd, running along the platform as best we could while the train slowed.

Though I'd hoped to get on the lead car of the four-car train, we'd only managed to catch up to the second-to-last when the doors opened. Chantal and I each grabbed Nassim by a hand and muscled our way onto the train through the opposing tide of passengers trying to get off. The warning tone sounded and the doors started to close behind us. For a moment I thought we'd gotten away.

Before the train could move, though, Putin, apparently recovered from his beating, jumped onto the car in back of us, and jammed his arm between the doors to keep them from closing. For a moment, I didn't understand. Then it came clear.

Bernard must have seen us go down to the Métro, or maybe Putin had given him a shout before chasing us down the steps. In any case, Bernard was running pretty well for a guy with a banged-up leg, and jumped onto the car beside Putin, who let the doors close, trapping us on the same train as our pursuers.

The train lurched from the station and gathered speed.

From where we stood in the aisle, I had a clear view through the emergency doors into the car behind us. And the two thugs had a clear view of us, or at least Bernard, taller than Putin, did. He tapped

Putin on the shoulder and nodded in our direction, saying some-thing I was sure meant us no good.

Already, the train was slowing for the next stop. Bernard nudged Putin, cocked his chin toward the door. The two of them got ready to shove their way out the moment we stopped.

I said to Chantal, "We'll have to jump onto the platform as soon as the doors open."

She nodded and smiled down at Nassim. "Are you ready to run some more?"

Nassim nodded. "*Oui, Maman.*" She gripped his hand. I took his other hand, ready to swing him off the car and dash for the exit from the station.

"You can run in bare feet?" I asked her.

"Why not?"

As if mocking our desperation to get out, the train eased into the station with maddening slowness. After an eternity of maybe three seconds the doors popped open. We jumped through the mob of passengers waiting to get on as Chantal and I looked toward the front of the train, trying to find the way out of the station.

Chantal hissed, "*Merde!*"

The only exit from the station lay in back of us. Bernard and Putin had already reached the platform, blocking our way out.

If we tried to get by them, they'd have us. Our only chance was to run ahead to the next car, knowing they would have to fight against the same press of passengers we did to reach us.

Faking a bright smile, Chantal said to Nassim, "Let's run this way," as if our need to escape the two gunmen were a game. It struck me how much easier it is to be brave when you have someone to be brave for.

We pushed our way through the mass of boarding and depart-ing passengers. A man in a suit backed into Chantal and she fell hard. Full of apologies, he helped her to her feet.

Grabbing his arm, I told him, "If you want to help her, stop those two men. They're bothering her."

The man pulled his head back in surprise, but he looked at the boy and at Chantal, saw the fear in their eyes and decided he was on her side. Game as they come, he turned toward the two men and held up his hands like a traffic cop.

With a stiff-arm a football running back would admire, Putin knocked him out of the way. Angry now, the man jumped up and grabbed at Putin. Bernard hit him hard in the chest, knocking him down again. But he'd bought us the time we needed. Putin and Bernard were forced to jump onto the car we had just vacated or get left on the platform.

The doors shut and the train pulled away. Chantal and I gasped with relief at our reprieve, though we knew it wouldn't last long. It had been a neat trick, but with only one car ahead of us, our next chance to run ahead would be our last. Unless one of the next two stations had an exit toward the front of the train, things would end badly.

I considered throwing the sack full of money at our pursuers when we stopped, but feared they would only grab it and keep coming. They'd no doubt been told by the two guards back in the Goutte d'Or of Chantal's betrayal and our theft of the money. Equally without doubt, they had told Bernard that I'd been the last man standing in a roomful of dead and wounded. They needed no further proof to assume I'd killed Girard and shot Raoul. They wouldn't care who killed Curt. And if they thought we might go to the police, they would also be protecting their own skins.

The train began to slow for the next stop. We'd arrived at Chatelet, where five Métro lines come together in a labyrinth of intersecting rail lines and pedestrian passageways.

I pulled a pen and paper from my pocket.

Chantal squinted at me. "What are you doing?"

"I've got the money. Maybe if we split, they'll follow me, not you."
She looked at me skeptically.

I handed her the slip of paper. "This is the address of a friend on the Île Saint-Louis. Go straight there as fast as you can. Push the buzzer for d'Alembert. The owner's name is Gwen. Explain who you are. She'll let you in. Tell her I'll get there as soon as I can." I didn't add, "If I'm still alive."

"What if they follow me instead?"

"I'm sure at least one of them will stay with me. If the other goes with you and Nassim, you'll just have to find a way to lose him. Whatever you do, don't let them see you go to that address. That's clear?"

"Yes."

"I'm sorry I can't do better than that. Maybe we'll get lucky." Her face darkened with uncertainty. "Look, if you stay with me they'll catch us both. If you run now and I stay on the train, they'll probably hesitate a few moments while they decide what to do. You'll at least have a chance."

She thought it over for a moment. "I don't think this is a very good plan."

"Neither do I." I tried to smile. "Sorry to make you do this barefoot."

The train slowed for Chatelet. Chantal told Nassim to get ready to run again. He nodded, though he seemed to have gone to some place in his head we couldn't reach.

Fear sweat broke out on my hands.

As we rolled into another crowded platform, I prayed Chantal and the boy could get through the wall of waiting faces before they were caught.

"Chantal, when you get there, tell Gwen." I tried to sound normal, but my throat squeezed shut and for a moment couldn't speak. I pushed my fear down and said, "Tell Gwen I . . ."

Chantal looked in my face and saw everything she needed to see. "I will tell her you were thinking of her."

The doors opened. She kissed me lightly on the cheek. I pushed her and Nassim through the door and followed them out, ready to stand between them and the gunmen.

Chantal cried, "Look!"

I nearly laughed with relief to see an exit sign at the front end of the platform. Chantal took off running, Nassim in tow.

Trying to make a path for them to escape, I pushed a young guy and his girlfriend out of their way. The guy gave me a look that let me know he didn't like it. I couldn't afford a fight and nodded an apology. He accepted it with bad grace as Chantal and Nassim made for the stairs.

Bernard and Putin had shoved their way onto the platform. When he saw me standing alone, Bernard looked around, searching for Chantal. I hoped she had gotten out of sight by now. But Bernard spotted her. He grabbed Putin by the arm and pointed toward the exit. "There she is!"

For a crucial moment of indecision the two men froze, uncertain what to do. Go for me? Go for her? Split up? To focus their thoughts, I grabbed the sack of cash from my coat and raised it above my head while giving the two thugs my best taunting smile, hoping to make them mad enough that they would both come for me. But no. Bernard slapped Putin on the back and sent him after Chantal. I could only hope the few seconds they'd stood there trying to figure out what to do would be enough for her to get away.

I tried to take comfort in the thought that Chatelet's crisscrossing Métro lines and its spaghetti-like maze of passageways and staircases gave Chantal an advantage. She knew where she was going. Putin did not. The shorter gangster took off after them, on the run. With a spasm of despair, I felt certain he would catch her and the boy before she could lose him in the labyrinth of the Métro network.

She'd been right. This wasn't a very good plan.

But even as I kicked myself, Fate put her thumb on the scale. Putin hadn't made more than a few strides when he ran into the same young man I'd shoved out of the way a moment earlier. The collision sent both of them to the pavement.

The young guy'd had enough. He popped up, grabbed Putin by the collar, and gave him a short, sharp jab to the nose. Putin howled in pain and twisted out of the guy's grip. He started to take a swing at him, but the young man hit him again before he could connect.

Grunting in pain and rage, Putin pulled his gun. People scattered like startled pigeons. Someone screamed. The young guy raised his hands, either in self-defense or to show he had no weapon. I think Putin might have shot him anyway, but Bernard put two fingers in his mouth and gave a piercing whistle. Startled, Putin looked at his partner.

French is not a language that lends itself to cursing, but Bernard did his best to ream Putin out and remind him of his priorities.

Coming to his limited senses, Putin headed for the steps, going after Chantal. I was nearly certain now he was the one who had gut-punched me after I'd walked Gwen home. My greatest fear was that the little thug, having seen me in front of Gwen's apartment building a few nights earlier, might guess where Chantal was headed.

In the meantime, Bernard was my more immediate concern. His eyes like icepicks, he came at me as the doors began to close. Barely squeezing through before they shut, I jumped back onto the lead car, leaving him on the platform. Delighted with my luck, I allowed myself a smile and a wave. Too soon.

At the last instant, he jammed his hands between the doors as Putin had done earlier. With a stutter of protest, the doors reopened. He jumped on. We were separated only by the length of the car. I'd either have to outrun him when the train stopped or outfight him. Bad leg or not, I didn't like the odds on outrunning him. And the thought of outfighting him would have made me laugh if I'd been in a laughing mood.

The train accelerated. We faced each other along the length of the car. Our tableau didn't last long. He began pushing his way through the passengers standing in the aisle, making for me like a torpedo.

I tried to tell myself that Bernard knew enough not to shoot me on a Métro car full of witnesses, with no escape before the train stopped again. No, much smarter to wait a moment, shoot me, and take the sack of money when we'd stopped and he could jump off and disappear into the crowd.

Like a recurring nightmare, the train began to slow. I eased toward the doors at the front of the car. Bernard had shoved his way halfway up the aisle and stood by the middle doors, his eyes burning into mine. I felt I was looking at my own death.

We pulled to a stop. Passengers got up from their seats, further clogging the aisle. I took a deep breath and braced to run.

The doors opened. I feinted toward the platform, hoping to draw Bernard into jumping off while I stayed on the train. He gave me a pitying smile and waited for me to commit.

Since our flight from Raoul's place, I had been aware of the weight of Curt's gun in my pocket. By now it felt like an anvil. Rather than reassuring me, it only kicked my anxiety higher. Could I shoot a man, even in self-defense?

I bolted through the open doors. Bernard shoved his way through the middle, both of us raising curses from the throng on the platform as we pushed our way out.

Running past the front of the train, I could only hope there would be an exit in front of me. I allowed myself one glance over my shoulder and found Bernard, shoving people out of the way, coming for me like a feral dog chasing down a deer. A set of stairs appeared ahead of me. Though only a few yards away, it felt like as many miles. After getting shoved into the van back at Pigalle, followed by the deadly mayhem with Raoul, fleeing the apartment building, then running through the Tuileries with Bernard chasing us, my stores of adrenaline had nearly run out. Exhausted, despairing, I felt the air growing thick with the weight of a night full of bad decisions.

Bernard—younger, more ruthless—was only a few feet in back of me. It seemed like I'd spent the whole night running from him.

Too leg weary to run, I took the stairs one at a time. After only a few steps I was out of breath.

From the commotion behind me, I could tell Bernard was bulldozing his way up the steps behind me. In a moment he would catch me.

At the top, the stairs took a right angle into a pedestrian passageway. Panting, I ducked around its corner, drew the gun, and stopped.

Bernard came around the corner an instant later, eyes full of homicide.

I hit him full in the face with the gun butt.

He roared in shock and pain and fell against the stair rail.

I hit him again, hard.

People scattered, shouting in shock and outrage. In a moment someone would play hero and tackle me. I had to keep moving.

First, though, I hit Bernard one more time, feeling a surge of animal satisfaction as his eyes rolled up into his head. At that instant I could have happily killed him. The impulse frightened me.

Blood running down his face, he dropped to one knee. With his free hand, he fumbled for his gun. I kicked it from his grip.

I thought of hitting him again, but decided no, I'd done enough. I staggered along the passageway and into the night.

CHAPTER TWENTY-SIX

16 QUAI D'ANJOU

FEARING SOME GOOD citizen might yet chase me down and call the police, I reeled away from the station as quickly as I could. After I'd gone three blocks with no one in pursuit I stopped and leaned against the window of a shuttered store. At the end of my strength, I doubled over, my hands on my knees, and tried to catch my breath, my bearings, and my nerve.

Ten minutes passed, maybe more. The night had come on cool and smelled of rain. Part of me wanted to stay pressed against the window and do nothing but take in the fresh air until all my troubles went away. But there was too much I still needed to do.

With the immediate danger gone, I thought again of Chantal and Nassim, hoping they had gotten away and that Putin had not yet guessed they were heading toward Gwen's. If—when—he put it together, he would likely call the others for backup. Then Gwen, too, would be in danger. I took a cleansing breath, stood up, and tried to orient myself. Nothing around me looked familiar. Then, in the distance, I saw the spires of Notre Dame rising above the rooftops, and I knew where I was.

Though I'd hit him hard, I feared Bernard might have recovered enough to come looking for me. My moral qualms exhausted along with my strength, I vowed that if he came for me again I would shoot him.

I headed for the river and the Île Saint-Louis.

Rather than crossing the bridge leading to the middle of the island, I walked along the right bank for a couple hundred yards, looking across the river toward Gwen's place, searching for anyone waiting outside. Satisfied it was clear, I crossed the bridge at the eastern end of the island and headed for her door.

Though I'd seen no one near the place, I walked up cautiously, keeping to the shadows until I could lurch up the steps and press the buzzer.

"Sam?"

The anxiety in her voice touched my heart more than any kiss could have.

"Yeah."

"Thank God."

The door clicked open.

Too weary to walk up the stairs, I got onto the birdcage elevator and rode it up to the third floor. Her door opened before I could knock. Gwen didn't rush into my arms, didn't cover me with kisses, only held out her hand. But the look in her eyes was all I needed or ever would. I took her hand in both of mine and let her draw me inside.

"Is Chantal here?" I asked.

"Yes, and the boy."

"Has she told you what happened tonight?"

"She's pretty shaken. She didn't say much—except to beg me not to call the police."

"Yeah. They'll probably arrest her if they find her. And she's half sick worrying what happens to the boy if she's in prison. In the meantime, we have half the gangsters in Paris after us."

Gwen gave me a look that showed what she thought of my continuing display of poor judgment.

She looked over my shoulder. "Where's your friend, Hansen?"

"He's dead."

Most people would have hyperventilated at the news. Gwen only grew more calm. "And Chantal's husband?"

"Dead. And his boss shot, wounded, maybe dying."

"Good God. Where were the police that were supposed to be with you?"

"Who knows?" It was too much to think about, too much to explain. "Where are Chantal and Nassim?"

"They're in the kitchen. I gave the boy some hot chocolate. He's badly shaken. Did he see all this?"

"He's the one who shot Curt."

Gwen gasped.

"He didn't know what he was doing."

I hoped Chantal would never tell him that in avenging the man he thought of as his father, he'd killed the man who was.

"Gwen, I'm sorry I sent them here and got you mixed up in this. I didn't know what else to do."

"It's all right. I'm glad you did."

"We have to get out of here—Chantal and the boy and me. One of the men coming after us knows where you live. I'm afraid he'll figure out we're here. He'll call for reinforcements. Then . . ."

"We'll deal with that if it happens."

"No. I can't put you in danger too."

"Where would you go?"

"I don't know. A hotel somewhere."

The vagueness of my reply shook me.

In the rush of our escape from Bernard and Putin I hadn't had time to figure out what came next. In the foreign service I'd been well regarded for my ability to think ahead, plan for the unexpected. Since I'd landed in Paris it seemed I'd spent every moment playing catch-up with reality.

I told Gwen, "I need to see them."

They sat at the kitchen table. Nassim, staring sightlessly in front of him, held a cup of hot chocolate in his hands. Chantal stroked his forehead, speaking softly to him in Arabic.

She looked up as we came in and smiled to see me safe. Nassim, though, cringed at the sight of me and buried his face in his mother's shoulder. I felt awful for the kid.

Chantal whispered in his ear, just loud enough for me to hear, "He's our friend, Nassim. He's helping you and your mama."

The boy was having none of it.

I set the cloth sack on the table and sat down.

"You got away from Bernard," she said.

"Yes." I didn't want to say more in front of the boy.

"Then we're safe."

She so wanted to believe it that I had a hard time spoiling her sense of relief. "No, we're not. We have to get out of here. Do you know a place we could go? Somewhere we'd be safe?"

Nassim started to whimper. Chantal squeezed him tight and told him, "I'm sure you could ask Madame Gwen for another cup of chocolate."

Like a sleepwalker, he got up from the table and crossed to where Gwen stood by the stove. She put on a smile and poured him more chocolate. "I'll bet you'd like to see my husband's army uniforms," she told him.

Overwhelmed with shock and fear, I'm not sure he could track what she was saying, but he nodded and allowed her to lead him away.

Chantal's eyes followed them as they left, then turned on me, probably trying to piece together who Gwen and I were to each other. I wanted to tell her that if she figured it out she should explain it to me.

"Chantal, do you have any friends we could stay with, even for one night?"

She expelled a bitter breath. "You've met my 'friends.' They're all criminals." She threw her head back, tears in her eyes. "Though Maurice . . . Maurice could sometimes be all right, and he was kind to Nassim."

It was the only eulogy he would get.

Not knowing what to say, I put my hand over hers. She squeezed it briefly, then pulled away.

"What do we do? Where do we go?" She said it without despair or self-pity.

"Maybe it's time for you to go home."

She looked at me as if I, too, might join the list of those who would betray her.

"Back to Morocco," I said and put the cloth sack on the table. "You've got the money to do it now."

She closed her eyes and shook her head.

"Chantal, Curt told me your father wants to see you again, wants to see Nassim, but has too much pride to admit it. It's been a long time. People get over things. Go to him. He can take care of you."

"No."

I let it go. "What about your friend with the grocery?" I asked.

"Khadija?" She considered it for a moment. "No, I can't do that to her. Staying with her and her husband could only lead them into trouble. And you can't stay here." She shook her head. "We've both become a danger to our friends. There is no safe place for us in Paris."

"Maybe the best thing would be to get a train out of Paris and find a hotel in some little town while we figure out what to do next."

Seized by the chimera of an actual plan, I stood up from the table. "The Gare de Lyon isn't far. We could call a taxi and be there in a few minutes."

My enthusiasm lit a tiny glow of hope in Chantal's eyes.

It didn't last long. Gwen came back into the kitchen. Her voice flat, she said, "You'd better look out the window."

Chantal and I followed her into the drawing room. Three stories below us, two men stood on the other side of the street. Even at this distance they looked tired and discouraged, and far too familiar. Putin and Bernard had caught up with us.

I muttered a combination of oaths I hadn't realized I was capable of, though I took some satisfaction in seeing that Bernard looked dazed and had to lean against the river wall.

Gwen motioned to us. "You'd better get back or they'll see you."

As we stepped away from the window a taxi stopped below us and two men got out. Raoul's ineffectual guards had apparently patched him up, or he had died, and they'd come to make up for their earlier failure to stop us.

At the sight of the two men Chantal gasped and looked around the room. "Where's Nassim?"

"He's fine," Gwen said. "He fell asleep on my bed."

Below us, the four men crossed the street and disappeared from sight as they mounted the steps to the entrance of the building.

Though we expected to hear them immediately buzz us on the intercom, nothing happened.

"What are they doing?" Chantal asked, unable to disguise the fear in her voice.

"They're pretty sure we're in here somewhere," I said, "but they don't know Gwen's name, and don't know which button to push. It's kind of funny if you think about it."

The look the two women gave me made clear that the humor of our situation escaped them.

I asked Gwen, "Is there a back way out of here?"

She shook her head.

Finally, the intercom buzzer sounded.

None of us moved.

The buzzer sounded again.

Some well-meaning resident of another apartment had no doubt mentioned to them the name of the American who lived in the building.

Now they knew where we were.

For a moment we stood frozen. Gwen was the one to break our paralysis. She walked over to the intercom and pressed the button to speak. Using her harshest Parisian accent she asked, "What do you want?"

A voice I didn't know came back at her. "The woman and the man and the money."

"I have no idea what you're talking about."

"We know who you are," the voice said. "Send them down or we're breaking in, and everyone gets hurt."

Gwen stepped away from the intercom. With a quick, determined step she went into the kitchen and came back carrying the sack of euros.

"Gwen . . ."

She raised a hand to keep me quiet.

The buzzer sounded again. Angry voices came over the tinny speaker. One rose above the others. "Listen, we're going to come up there and—"

"Be quiet!" Gwen barked at them.

To our surprise, and probably theirs too, they shut up.

"I'm coming down," she told them. "I want you away from the door and on the other side of the street."

"And why should we do that?" the voice demanded, playing tough guy for his companions.

"Because I don't want you rushing up the stairs the moment I open the door. Do it, or I'm not coming down. You want the money or not?"

Muttered protests came from the speaker. "We want the woman too."

I noticed that I had already dropped from their demands. I wasn't really important to them.

Gwen gave them a simple, "No."

"She's a spy."

"I don't care what she is. If you get to the other side of the street, you can have the money. We'll talk about the rest. That's it."

The muttering grew louder, but the voice finally said, "All right."

For all their menace, they were, after all, boys who liked to be told what to do.

Gwen started for the door.

I tried to cut her off. "Gwen, no. Let me do this."

She shook her head. "They'd probably kill you, take the money, and call it a night. They're not necessarily angry at me."

"'Not necessarily.' Sounds pretty weak."

"I'll take my chances."

"Then at least take this too," I said and pulled Curt's gun from my pocket.

She considered it for a moment and shook her head. "I've negotiated with much tougher people than these idiots. Never needed a pistol—though there were times I might have enjoyed using one." She put her hand on my arm. "Don't worry. I'll be all right. Stay here. I'll be back in a few minutes."

Sack in hand, she went out the door.

Chantal and I edged toward the window.

As Gwen had insisted, the four punks had backed across the street. A couple of them rocked nervously on their feet, like miscreant schoolboys waiting to see the principal.

For several baffling minutes nothing happened. The men on the street fell into some sort of argument, gesturing wildly, their words visible as puffs of steam on the chilly night air.

"Where is she?" Chantal whispered.

"She'll be there in a moment," I said, though I was as puzzled as Chantal that Gwen hadn't arrived at the front door.

"Maybe she lost her nerve."

"No, that's not something she does."

The words were hardly out of my mouth when Gwen appeared at the bottom of the steps.

One of the young men strutted forward. Gwen held up her hand and he stopped.

It wasn't a happy conversation. Several times the guy waved his arms in exasperation. The others added their voices, the puffs of steam coming off like a circus calliope. Though I feared they might take her and use her as a hostage to force us to come down, they might have realized she was much closer to the door than they were and could get back inside before they grabbed her. More likely, she had simply cowed them into paralysis.

Gwen held her ground and waited for them to talk themselves out.

When the puffs of steam had subsided, Gwen said something to the one who stood in the middle of the street. We didn't need to hear her words to know she had gone downstairs with a weak hand but was playing it to win against a bunch of amateurs. God, I was proud of her.

Whatever it was she'd said, the young guy eventually lowered his head and nodded his agreement.

Gwen tossed the sack into the street.

The young thug dashed forward, picked up the sack, looked inside, then raised his chin defiantly to cover his retreat. He said something to the others that caused them to throw their hands in the air or point menacingly at Gwen, all of it to another chorus of steam, thick as smoke.

But when the young guy with the sack ran off down the street, they followed him.

Chantal clutched my arm, weak with relief.

A moment later Gwen came through the door.

"I got them to go away," she said.

"You really are the consummate diplomat."

"Thank you, sir," she said with a brightness that couldn't conceal the shaking in her hands. She collapsed into a chair. "Pour me a drink. Something stiffer than a Kir Royale."

I gave her a scotch. She took a long pull.

"How'd you do it?" I asked.

"It wasn't easy."

"You just gave them the money and they walked away?"

She threw her head back and blew a long breath toward the ceiling. "That was never going to be enough. I told them I'd called the police. They could forget about you two, take the money and go, or they could stay and wait for the police to show up. They took the money and ran."

Awed, I laughed out loud. "And they bought the bluff."

She glanced at Chantal before telling me, "I wasn't bluffing, Sam. The police are on their way."

Chantal gasped.

Now I knew why she had taken so long to appear on the street. She had stopped to call the police before stepping outside.

"It was the only way to get them to leave, the only way to keep us safe."

"But you could have waited for the police," I said. "Kept the money."

"I didn't know how long it would take them to show up. And these jerks might have panicked when they heard the sirens. Who knows what they would have done then? No, I had to make them go away right now."

She said it quietly, no hint of defensiveness, only a statement of fact. But I could see what it had cost her to do it.

Chantal started toward Gwen's room to wake Nassim, saying, "We have to leave before the police come."

"No, Chantal," Gwen said, stopping her. "I'm sorry, but you said it yourself. You have no place to go. Even if you got away before the police arrived, those boys I chased off might be hiding a block away, waiting for you and your son to come out."

Chantal made no reply. The stricken look on her face said everything that needed saying.

"I wish I could have done better for you," Gwen said. "But there was no better."

"You don't understand. I'm a Moroccan. They will never deal fairly with me."

"Whatever the police do, it will be better for you and your boy than whatever these creeps will do if you leave here."

Chantal sank into a chair, staring wide-eyed into the empty space that was her future.

I said to Gwen, "When the police get here, they'll arrest her."

She couldn't look at me. "I know."

"What happens to her boy?"

With a bare shake of her head she said, "I don't know." She looked at me, her eyes glistening with tears. "At least they'll still be alive, Sam."

The sound of the intercom buzzer made us all jump.

I went to the window. Two police cars had pulled up in front of the building. I nodded to Gwen. She rose and pressed the button on the intercom.

"Yes?"

"This is Chief Inspector Simon. I would like to come up."

She buzzed the door open.

Like a painted still life, we stood motionless, waiting.

We heard the sound of the elevator rising toward us, followed by the clack of its stop at the landing.

The knock on the door echoed through the silent room.

Gwen let them in, Simon and two plainclothes men.

Simon nodded in my direction. "It is good to see you, Monsieur Hough."

He waited a moment for me to express similar sentiments. Let him wait, I figured.

With a cock of his head that might have indicated embarrassment, he said, "Not everything went according to plan."

"No, it didn't."

"I'm sorry. Once they rushed you out the back of that restaurant we lost contact. You didn't turn on your wire."

"Hansen found it and ripped it off before we left."

Simon raised his eyebrows. "It turned into quite a mess, eh?"

"Three men shot. Two of them dead, maybe three."

He'd had difficulty looking at me as we spoke, but now he raised his head in surprise. "Where?"

"An apartment building near the Goutte d'Or." I described its location as best I could while one of Simon's men punched the information into his phone.

"Your friend Hansen?" Simon asked.

"Dead. And a man named Raoul, shot. Maybe still alive, maybe not."

Simon glanced significantly at his men. Clearly, the name was familiar to them.

"And Maurice Girard?" he asked.

"Dead."

Again, Simon raised his eyebrows, apparently his only means of showing emotion. "How did you escape this . . ."

"Massacre? Curt saved my life."

The policeman looked at us all in turn before coming back to me. "Many things went wrong tonight. I'm sorry for it. We will need to speak at some length." He turned to Chantal. "You are Madame Girard?"

She nodded.

"I'm going to have to ask you to come with us."

She rose to her feet, her hands clasped tightly in front of her. "What about my son?"

"Your son?"

Gwen said, "He's asleep in my room, Inspector."

Though she had opened the door for them, Simon only now seemed to register Gwen's presence.

"Madame la Marquise," he said with a small bow.

His use of her title took me by surprise, as if he were talking to a woman I had mistaken for someone I knew.

"Thank you for your call," he said. "Can I ask, Madame, where these men have gone?"

His deference to her jolted me into realizing that I was once again in a foreign country, under foreign customs, foreign laws, speaking in a language not my own.

"I don't know, Inspector," Gwen said. "I wasn't sure how long it would take you to arrive, and I feared they would break into my apartment. So I let them know you were on the way and they ran. I decided that was good enough."

"That was wise," Simon replied, though the momentary twist of his mouth betrayed his disappointment. "We'll get them in the end." He turned to Chantal. "And we'll be able to apprehend them more quickly if we have cooperation from those who know them."

She turned away to keep his words from touching her.

He beckoned to the two men with him and turned to Chantal. "Madame Girard." He held out his hand to her.

She took a step backward. "What about my boy?"

"He can come with us."

"No! I don't want him to see me taken away from him at a police station."

"Madame Girard . . ."

Anguish in her eyes, she turned to me. "Please, Monsieur Hough, will you take him to Khadija?"

I looked at Simon, who shook his head and again motioned to his men.

Chantal took a step backward. "Don't!"

With a huff of displeasure, Simon said, "Please, Madame Girard . . ."

She looked at Gwen and me with such accusation that neither of us could hold her gaze. It would help nothing to tell her that this wasn't what either of us wanted.

Simon bowed his head under the weight of Chantal's despair. "Madame Girard, if you and the boy will come with us quietly, I'll arrange to have him taken to your friend tonight. Will that be all right?"

Chantal hesitated, then understood that this was the best they could do. She struggled to keep from sobbing with both shame and relief.

At Simon's instruction, one of his men started toward the bedroom to get the boy. Chantal put up her hands, ready to push him away. The officer stopped. Chantal went back to get Nassim.

When she had walked out of the room, I asked Simon, "What will happen to her?"

"That will be up to the judge."

"Inspector, whatever she did, she was coerced into it. They had her under their control through her son."

My plea made Simon uncomfortable. "Her husband would have protected her if she didn't want to participate."

"No, he was first and foremost a member of the gang. She was his wife only unwillingly."

Simon blew out a weary breath. "I'll speak to the judge. If what you say is true and if she can help us catch these men, it will be taken into account. Likely she won't be in custody long."

"A few weeks? A few months?"

"Yes, I suppose."

"And what happens to her then?"

He shrugged at the obvious. "She and her son will be deported to Morocco."

"But she—"

I fell silent as Chantal came back into the room, holding Nassim's hand. Even half asleep, the little boy still looked frightened, though his confusion and shock were tilting now toward anger.

His mother knelt and said, "You and Mama are going with these men now. Then, I'll be going on a trip. You'll go to Khadija's. I'm not sure when I'll be back, but I'll see you as soon as I can and I'll hug you and kiss you and . . ." Her voice failed her.

I had come to Paris to help the boy, give him a better life. Instead, I had made it far worse.

I felt the need to say goodbye to the little fellow, tell him how sorry I was. "Nassim . . ." I said and knelt down to him.

With all the strength he could put into his little fist, he struck me in the face.

Chantal threw her arms around him. "Oh, darling, no."

Wrapped in his mother's arms, the boy threw back his head as if to cry or scream or simply shout out the horror of the last few hours, but no sound emerged from his open mouth. In its way, it was the most terrifying moment of the night.

Chantal picked him up and started toward the door.

"Madame Girard," one of the detectives said, stopping her. He pulled out a pair of handcuffs.

Simon coughed to get the man's attention, shook his head and nodded toward the boy.

The detective understood. He put his handcuffs away and took her by the arm. She bowed her head but would not weep in front of her son.

As the two police officers led her and Nassim out, Chantal stopped and turned in the doorway. I noticed patches of blood on the floor where she walked and only now realized she was still barefoot and had torn her feet in her effort to escape. She looked at me, her eyes desolate. "Thank you, Monsieur Hough. I know you did the best you could."

Her decency cut deeper than any curse, underscoring all my failures that night. I tried to speak but couldn't and only nodded.

None of them thought to shut the door as they left. Nassim and his mother got into the tiny elevator and turned to face us. While one of the two departing cops took the stairs, the other squeezed into the elevator with Chantal and Nassim, pulled the birdcage door shut, and pressed the button for street level. Chantal looked at us steadily as she descended from sight.

None of us—Simon, Gwen, me—could speak as we heard the elevator reach the bottom and its door open. The sound of footsteps on the tiled foyer, then of the building's front door clicking shut behind them broke the agony, allowing us to breathe again.

Simon thrust his hands in the pockets of his overcoat and once more assumed his official pose. "Monsieur Hough, as I say, we will need to have a long talk. I still have work to do tonight. I can trust you to come by my office tomorrow to make a deposition."

It wasn't a question.

"Will I need to serve as a witness at the trial?" I asked.

"I don't believe so. Your deposition should be enough. If you need to testify after you've returned to America, we can arrange to do it electronically."

"I'll come by your office after lunch tomorrow."

"Good." He pulled his hand from his pocket to shake mine, then thought better of it. "Again, I'm sorry for tonight's events. We had no wish for it to end like this. On the positive side of the ledger, our intention was to bring down this gang, and we have made important progress. We are grateful for your help. We have your description of the building to which you and Monsieur Hansen were taken. If we hurry, we may be able to arrest them all."

"You think they'll go back there tonight?" I asked.

"It's very possible. First, they really have nowhere else to go. Second, they're a bunch of cretins. I think it will end satisfactorily."

"Except for the dead men."

His indulgence toward me had run out. "These men chose their course, Monsieur Hough. Their lives would likely have ended like this at some point with you or without you. For them, it was tonight. Even your friend, Monsieur Hansen, behaved very foolishly. They might very well have killed him in any case, and you with him. It was his insistence on demanding something he should have understood they had no intention of giving him that precipitated tonight's events. When he first saw they had betrayed him he should have cut his losses and got on with his life. He was swimming in waters far too deep for him." Simon had given this little speech while digging some imaginary dirt from under his thumbnail, but now raised his eyes and regarded me. "And he should never have asked you to come here, should never have put you in the middle of this situation." He scowled. "There's something funny about this, Monsieur Hough?"

"No," I told him, but I couldn't get past the irony that, throughout his charade, Curt had repeatedly told me he was a dying man. And so he'd been, though he hadn't known it.

"He didn't intend to put me at such risk, Inspector. I believe he was sincere in telling me that."

The inspector grunted. "Intended. Meant to. Empty words, Monsieur Hough. He betrayed your trust. You're very fortunate to be alive."

"He saved my life when one of the gang was going to shoot me."

"Well, it was the least he could do, wasn't it?"

While his cynicism left me speechless, he gave Gwen a respectful nod and murmured, "Madame la Marquise," and showed himself out, shutting the door behind him.

The silence he left behind grew until it filled the room. The trials of the night—physical and emotional—hit me like a rogue wave. I sat down, rested my head in my hands. I realized I was weeping. I hadn't cried since the day Janet died.

Wiping my face with my hands, I smiled at Gwen in embarrassment. Her smile in return warmed me as nothing else could have.

Neither of us was capable of finding the words that could give meaning to what had passed that night. Though alone in her apartment, as we had been before, we could only regard each other like unmoored islands receding from each other.

Gwen went into the kitchen to clean up the cups and saucers left behind by Chantal and Nassim. I wandered in behind her.

"What happens now?" I asked.

Busying herself with the dishes to avoid looking at me, she said, "As Simon said, she and the boy will be sent home to Morocco, and this man, Raoul—"

"You know that's not what I mean."

She stopped what she was doing and leaned over the sink. "You have to go home too, Sam. I guess I've been saying that since you got here." She allowed me a sidelong glance and a fleeting smile. "You've kept your promise to Curt. Tough luck on him that it didn't have anything to do with what he really wanted."

We had tried to retrieve the past—Curt, Gwen, me—tried to undo things we'd done, reclaim what was gone. Gwen and I had tried to reclaim young love, while Curt had wanted to reconcile with Chantal. We can spend our lives trying to recapture the thrill of the first time. But the first time only comes once. Thinking you can recreate it is a vain and dangerous game. Curt had paid with his life.

Gwen and I were lucky. After a certain age you expect sadness. Like second love, it doesn't throw you so far off-center.

"Everything I've touched has ended in death or heartbreak."

"No, Sam. Simon was right. Their whole scheme was ready to collapse. It was only waiting for the tap that would bring it down. If it hadn't been you, it would have been someone else."

"But it was me."

She put her arms around me and held me tight, her hands still wet, the dampness sinking into me like a part of her soul. Slowly, unsure of what came next, I put mine around her.

Her head against my chest, she said, "I thought I had left this all behind years ago. Falling in love. The yearning, the excitement, the confusion. And I figured good riddance. This sort of love is for people young enough to bear it." I could sense the sadness in her smile. "They say youth is wasted on the young. Maybe. But it wouldn't do the rest of us much good either. We'd burn ourselves out, you and me. There's no going back to Badger Cottage." She said it with a little laugh and pulled away from me. "I have a comfortable, no fuss love with Georgie. It's good and it's real and it's just right for us. No great passion, but great affection. He's a good man and I'm lucky to have him." She waited for me to reply, but the truth of what she said left me with nothing to say. "You know, Sam, when we're young we want happiness. As we get older we'll settle for peace of mind. I have that. I want you to have it too. You're not the sort of man to break up a marriage. And I would hate myself for making you something you're not."

"I'll bet you're wishing I had never come and upended everything." I tried to say it lightly.

The lines of care and age on her brow faded, and with her smile I again saw the young woman I had loved so many years ago.

"Oh, Sammy, my Sammy, I'm so glad you came."

With that, it was time to leave.

At the door, we kissed lightly, neither of us trusting ourselves to do more.

As I pressed the button for the elevator I turned and looked back at her, still standing in the doorway. We waved goodbye, as we had that long-ago morning in Copenhagen, but this time we knew it was for good, and that it was all right.

I would talk to Simon the next day, try to reconcile my responsibility for what had happened by thinking of my noble and utterly foolish intentions. The staff at the Brighton would book a flight for me, would make sure I was home in Oregon by the following day. They have always been good to me.

For now, I went downstairs and out onto the street and walked through the light and the shadows back to the hotel.

ABOUT THE AUTHOR

S TEPHEN HOLGATE IS the author of four published works of fiction. *Tangier* won the Silver Medal in Fiction from the Independent Publishers Association and made Bookreaders ten-best list in the Indie Mystery/Suspense category. *Madagascar* met with similar critical success, receiving a coveted starred review from *Publishers Weekly*, a nomination from *Forward Reviews* as Best Book of the Year in the fiction category, and another listing from Bookreaders among the ten best Mystery/Suspense novels of the year. His most recent works, *Sri Lanka* and *To Live and Die in the Floating World* have received similar acclaim.

A fifth-generation Oregonian, Holgate has served as a diplomat for American embassies overseas, worked as a congressional staffer, twice toured the United States with an improvisational theater group, been a crew member of a barge on the canals of France, and lived in a tent while working as a gardener in Malibu, California.

He lives in Portland, Oregon with his wife, Felicia.

You can reach him at stephenholgatewrite.com

ACKNOWLEDGMENTS

T HOUGH ONLY ONE name appears on the cover, every book is a team effort. I want to thank Kent and Ruth Obee for their friendship and their valuable comments on the passages set in Pakistan. Thanks, too, to Marlin Goebela and Mireille Luc-Keith for a close read of an early draft and their helpful suggestions. I am deeply grateful to my editor, Helga Schier, and copyeditor, Ellen Leach, and all the good people at CamCat Publishing. And, as ever, my thanks to my agent, Kimberley Cameron, for her boundless support and encouragement.

If you enjoyed
Stephen Holgate's *A Promise to Die For*,
please consider leaving us a review
to help our authors.

And check out
Benjamin Bradley's *What He Left Behind*.

CHAPTER

1

——◦◦◦◦◦——

G RAY DRIZZLE CLUNG to my raincoat as I pressed myself
against the centuries-old door to Oak Hill Grocery and said
a silent prayer to no one. The scripture on the dimly lit sign
out front opined about the valley of death—a threat or a promise,
I wasn't sure. Pushing inside, I navigated the cramped aisles and
let raindrops tumble from my shoulders onto the scuffed linoleum
floor. When I'd assembled enough for a hearty dinner, I moved
toward the counter where Margo Locklear, the biggest gossip in all
of Oak Hill, North Carolina, waited with a frown.

"Jacob Sawyer is back in town," she said.

The name hit me like buckshot, even though I knew it was
coming.

"You hear me, Grace?"

"I heard you, Margo."

Silence hummed as rain trickled down gutters and gurgled into
the drain. I didn't take my eyes off the box of noodles in my hand,

instead lifting it to the counter to lie next to the massive jar of marinara. If I combined all the rumors I'd heard sneak out of Margo's lips, there stood a good chance that it was every combination of words and letters possible.

"Hell," Margo said. She lifted my handful of groceries from the counter and swiped them across the register. "He doesn't look half bad for an outsider."

"Just because he left town doesn't mean he's an outsider," I said, half-hearted.

"He came in searching for some medicine." She let out a throaty laugh. "As if he doesn't know that's not something I shelve. Like that big ole pharmacy sign three blocks down ain't lit."

"Medicine?"

Parmesan cheese took two swipes and then toppled onto the rest of my dinner ingredients.

"I guess he came back to take care of his ma. Willa's sick, didn't you hear?"

My throat went dry. I did my best to force a smile. "I heard. Everybody heard."

"Beats hospice care. Those bills. Unimaginable."

"Right," I said. "Hope she recovers quickly."

"That's not how cancer works, dear."

I rarely stopped to listen to the talk that swirled around town like hawks overhead. Not that I was above swapping stories about the failures of other residents. We all have that instinct. But I could never risk the idea of hearing a whisper with my name attached.

"Sometimes it does."

"Once death gets its grubby little fingers on you, it's over."

I didn't need to ask why she knew that. There were no secrets in Oak Hill. I had firsthand witness accounts of her late husband Henry's diagnosis, downfall, and death. He stood in the background of stories and memories like a leaf on a tree.

"That's some lullaby, Margo. I hope you tell that to the grand-kids."

"Sawyer's been gone since the accident. I remember when your daddy came in here and told me the news like it was yesterday."

"Nat's always had a big mouth," I said.

"Even so. That's a long time. Fifteen years since you folks grad-uated high school and went into the woods. Fifteen years, Grace."

My body tensed, pushing away memories that were nudging their way into my mind. I said nothing. I simply laid my cash on the counter and fixed my eyes on Margo's until she broke the stare.

"Why don't you seem interested, Grace?" She picked up the bills and held them between her fingers like a cigarette. Her hand fell to the countertop.

"I'm only interested in getting my dinner started. Nat's probably waiting for me back at home and wondering what the holdup is."

"Isn't that part of your job? Protect us from the outsiders? From the trouble that creeps in and takes root in a small town?"

"Who says he's trouble? It's been a while. Maybe he—"

"Fifteen years. He's had more time outside the city limits than inside. That makes him as good as gone. He doesn't know this town from Adam."

I kept my eyes on the counter, willing Margo to punch the keys on the register and collect my money so I could run home. She stared at the cash as if checking the serial numbers against some mental database. I heard the cheese growing warm. My stomach growled.

"Heard you had a big interview today," she said, palms flat on the counter.

"Just the first round," I lied. "Mind if we—"

"Right," she said. "Hope it went well." She ripped the receipt off the printer and handed it my way. I stuffed it in my bag and hurried out the door. It would be a matter of days, hours even, until word spread that I'd fumbled my words and botched the opportunity to become chief of police. But that was tomorrow's problem. And Jacob Sawyer's arrival in Oak Hill seemed like fate doubling down on my misery.

No matter how hard I shut my eyes and willed myself to forget, memories of the last time I'd seen Jacob Sawyer raced through my frontal lobe like floodwater. To be honest, I thought he was gone forever. But nothing truly lasted forever. The grief of losing a second parent, this time to a vile disease that no saintly woman such as Willa deserved, must've been enough to beckon him home. And now, sneaking up on fifteen years to the day, I walked through downtown and lingered on the silhouettes in the distance, wondering if I'd recognize his shadow among a crowd.

I made it to my car without glimpsing the ghost from my past and raced home, taking the long way to skirt around Sawyer's street and avoid pushing my luck. I worried that if my gaze strayed from the road for a second, I'd see the contours of my youthful stride as I scrambled out to meet Sawyer in some shoddy, rough-hewn structure we'd built with fallen timber. Those ghosts were best left alone in the forest.

Nat's house, and by default mine, was an unspectacular slab-on-grade with a wraparound porch and windows in the bedrooms that leaked when it rained. Weeds had overgrown the walk. Crabgrass crept beyond the borders and onto the well-trodden path that led to our front door. Unless I found the time, Nat would be down on his knees, picking the roots of each dandelion by the weekend. Come Monday, he'd be bedridden and aching, lamenting about a younger version of himself with dreams and hopes and a working spine.

My loyal tabby, Agatha, watched me enter from the armchair, too comfortable to greet me, until I entered the kitchen where her food waited. Water boiled. Noodles softened. Sauce gurgled. I tugged at my hair, neat in a topknot, and let it fall to my shoulders like curtains at the end of a play. In the fridge, I spotted the unmistakable logo of Mickey's Bar and Grill, a clue about Nat's night. No doubt his supper had included red meat and deep-fried somethings, two food groups his cardiologist requested he avoid. It was always those who took tremendous care of others who couldn't take care of themselves.

I flipped on the TV and let the hazy flicker wash over me like a balm. I uncorked a bottle, poured a glass of red, and drained it faster than planned. Agatha sniffed at my plate but opted for the warmth of my lap over the scraps of my pasta, enthused by the familiarity of our routine and the banality of my life.

Nat squirmed in his bed, blankets coiled around his legs. I tiptoed over and shut the door to let him rest. Hinges howled, an ailment Nat had maintained he'd fix by the next weekend for thirty-something years now. By the time tiredness crept in and replaced worry, I had relived that humid June day sixteen more times with no inkling of what was to come. I'd warned my younger self that feelings and instincts are two different things, and you can't listen to both at the same time.

I carried Agatha, purring all the while, into the bedroom and dragged the door shut. She leaped onto the comforter and nestled into the corner as I changed out of work clothes and smiled at faded photographs tucked into the edges of my mirror. Nat and I looked younger than possible in the top shot, adoption certificate in my hand and a wide-eyed smile on his face. In another, I stood stubborn and surly on the front steps as Nat snapped a photo of my first day of work with Susan Orr and the Dockery Center. In the corner rested one that I'd avoided for some time. Cliff, Sawyer, and I stood against a background of sprawling pines. Our lanky limbs fell onto one another's shoulders and our smiles were wider than the Murphy Road drag. I let myself linger for a moment. Just long enough to wonder what he looked like now. Then I tucked the memories back into their spot and fought Agatha for room on the bed.

I plugged headphones in and let my head fall onto the pillow. The wine helped usher sleep in with crimson waves that calmed my mind long enough to crash. When sleep arrived, it was fitful and discomforting—like ants crawled in my bedsheets and tickled my bare skin. Maybe it was a warning. A nudge from the world to keep me half awake. Whatever it was, it worked. I jumped to my feet when the phone rang.

I heard the words on the other end but struggled to comprehend. There was seldom an event in Oak Hill that required the emergency response team to wake the ranking officer and beckon them into the darkness. But like that June evening, things changed in a millisecond.

"Grace?" Patty Glassmire's voice came through, hushed and immediate.

"I'm here," I said.

"We need you out on Ray Cove Road. Lionel Sutton's place."

"Break-in?" I asked.

"No," Patty said.

A long pause followed.

"There's a body."

2

O AK HILL LOOMED deserted and dim, my headlights the only flash of color in the night. Murphy Road cut through downtown like a river, but my foot hovered over the brake, expecting nature's nightly takeover. Coyotes and foxes slunk around under the moonlight and scavenged for scraps that humanity left behind.

I sped through the stop sign and veered onto Ray Cove Road, thankful the rain had quit. A flicker of red stung my eyes through the sycamore and oaks, some interstellar hue that stained the stars above and clouded everything with panic. Even after ten years of service, my heart still galloped when I heard a siren. It meant something was wrong. And by the sound of Patty's voice on the other end, I knew I was walking into a mess.

I eased onto the shoulder behind a cruiser and dug my flashlight out of the glove box. Crisp winds pushed through stands of loblolly and caressed my bare neck as I walked, a rare occasion for North Carolina in late May. Officer Miguel Munoz stood in the brush, alone, staring down into an illuminated stretch of knee-high corn-stalks. He held a handkerchief over his mouth with one hand and a flashlight trembled in the other.

"Munoz?" I called out from the roadside.

He turned to me, pale as a shut-in. "Over here."

"You all right?"

"I'll be fine."

"Where'd you vomit? I don't want to step in it."

He pointed off to the side. "Out of the way. Didn't want to disturb the scene."

"Wise of you," I said, high-stepping toward him. The thick air hung on my shoulders like an overcoat.

As I approached, the first thing that came into view was the worn sole of a boot. Then a second. I set my feet and crept close enough to get a full glimpse. Munoz stepped back.

"Who is it?" I asked.

He shifted the light toward the head where blood streaked the forehead and matted in the untamed brown hair. I swallowed the sick in my throat. "Don't know."

"Huh," I said. "Me either."

The smell hit me like a wave and wretched something awful in-side me. It was only then that I realized I'd never seen a dead body, let alone a murder victim. I kept a brave face and directed my eyes to the patchy weeds around the lifeless limbs.

"I stopped by the store for coffee before my shift. Margo said there was an outsider in Oak Hill," Munoz added. "Maybe she's the one."

"No," I said. "She's just starting a commotion about Jacob Saw-yer being back in town."

"No shit?"

Those two words summed up Munoz's philosophy on life. He was a no nonsense or bullshit kind of person. And I couldn't blame him. Juggling a budding family and a full-time job was inconceivable from my vantage point. Hell, I couldn't keep up with Nat's appointments and medication, let alone tussle with the sleep schedules of toddlers.

"No shit indeed," I said.

"You seen him?"

I glared at him.

He raised his hands in surrender. "Point taken."

"Who called this in?"

"Lionel Sutton heard a car door slam and tires squeal as he was getting ready for bed. Sent his dog out to shoo away the threat and found the pup by the body."

"Lucy okay?"

"She's fine. I gave her a belly rub when I pulled up. Sutton is inside settling down. He agreed to keep the news under wraps. I asked if it was one of his workers, but he shrugged it off and changed the subject."

"Smart of him to look out for their best interests, although we're not ICE."

Munoz stared down at the body. "I don't know if she's illegal. Could be. Lionel outsources sometimes."

I snapped on a pair of gloves. "You check the pulse?"

"Yeah. Sutton said he didn't see the point, but I confirmed his notion."

"Gloved up first?"

"Of course."

"Good work, Munoz. If you need a minute, go catch your breath. She isn't going anywhere." I studied her face once more, hoping for a sense of recognition or a trace of family resemblance.

"Thanks, Grace," he said. "Want me to call Macon?"

"Might as well," I said. "But it'll take some effort to get the coroner out this way."

Munoz looked up and down the road. "Might need directions."

"Nobody has reason to come out this way. Let alone somebody from the county."

"We'll see." Munoz stepped away, and I held my breath as I knelt next to the chest of our victim. In the commingling of hazy moonlight and powerful fluorescent bulbs, I jotted down a few rudimentary observations in my notebook. She didn't look older than fifty, maybe younger, but I couldn't say for sure. She wore faded blue jeans with tears on the knees and a long-sleeve checkered flannel, red and black. No undershirt or bra. I gently turned her body with one hand and reached into her back pocket. No wallet.

"Munoz, did you take the wallet?" I shouted.

"No wallet," he said. "No ID."

I cursed under my breath and dug around anyway. With tender hands, I raised her skull and examined the wounds. Something big and heavy had come down on the back of her skull. Another blow had hit the crown of her head. Blood had oozed out of both wounds and pooled in the surrounding soil. The crimson color looked blacker than the sky. Maybe that was normal. Maybe not. I had no sense of what was normal in a murder scene. I'd never been to one.

I stood and snapped a photo of the woman's face. Lord knows that nobody wants to stare into the lifeless eyes of a dead body, but somebody in Oak Hill would recognize that face. The flash from my phone's camera lit her in an ugly, unnatural light. I felt for her. She wasn't just a woman. She was somebody's daughter or mother or cousin or aunt. That much was certain. Somebody would cause a fuss, right?

Munoz tramped back with a bottle of water before I could finish my thought. "County is on the way."

"ETA?"

He looked at me blankly.

"Lovely," I said, kneeling back down beside the body.

"What's the procedure here?"

I shrugged. "First murder we've had here in my lifetime."

"Wonderful."

"I took a photo of her face. I'd like to show Susan Orr."

Munoz tensed in the corner of my eye. "You think she's a vagrant?"

"She prefers the term unhoused."

"You think she's unhoused?"

"She's got ratty hair and a film of dirt on her skin. Add in the grime under the fingernails and the faint scent of urine—it's clear she'd fallen on hard times. And when you fall hard in Oak Hill, Susan finds you."

"What's the female version of a saint?" he asked.

"I should ask you. I haven't darkened the doorstep of a church on a Sunday morning in years."

"I know." He paused for a moment. "If you want to go... after seeing this, they'd welcome you back with open arms. We all would."

"Thanks, Miguel."

"Anything else you need me to do?"

I crinkled my lips. "Once Macon County gets out here with their team, they'll push us to the sidelines. Odds are you'll never see another murder victim before you quit the force, so if you were ever curious or anything—"

He chuckled, but it was half-hearted. "No, thanks."

"You'd drink for free at Mickey's. Probably for life."

"Sadie would love that," he said. "You planning to tell the tale?"

I stared into the woman's lifeless eyes. "You know me better than that."

"You never know."

Dawn spread through the sky like lavender and lilacs blooming in springtime. Munoz and I gawked at the watercolor painting above us, juxtaposed with the grisly scene on the ground.

I kept my eyes set skyward, at a loss for words.

Munoz prayed.

———∞×∞———

SUN PAINTED THE field and chased the fog away. I planted myself beside the body, with enough distance to avert my eyes out
of some mix of respect and fear. After fifteen minutes, Munoz
flagged me down from the road and jogged over. Sweat slunk down
his tanned neck and painted a full picture of his emotional state,
seeing that it was borderline frigid out. The sun hadn't yet gotten to
work to dry the morning dew.

"Mayor Rice is here," he said, the words careful and slow.

"Shit," I said. "Thanks."

Munoz smiled at the mayor and disappeared from view. Cliff
stepped down from the jacked-up frame of his oversized silver truck
and within seconds of his boots hitting the ground, he fussed with
a toothpick in the corner of his mouth. "Some mess we've got here."

"You look like a cartoon cowboy, Cliff."

He transferred the toothpick to the other side. "Now isn't the
time to be hitting on me, Grace."

That running joke had grown stagnant somewhere in high school, but he still dredged it up whenever possible. Male egos, I guess. Carlos Clifford Lee had gone nine rounds with Father Time and wobbled from the ring, having sustained more damage than most. Stress collected in bags beneath his eyes that, even in the hazy morning, seemed purple and puffy. A horseshoe of hair remained around the sides of his head, although he always hid it with a cap. Despite his heritage and Hispanic roots, he'd insisted on going by his middle name, Clifford. I never thought he was much of a Carlos anyhow.

I tapped the badge affixed to my belt. "That's Detective Bingham to you, sir."

"Right, and I should expect you to call me Mayor Rice, too? Pigs can fly, Grace."

"How'd you hear?"

"Patty rang."

"There some kind of secret arrangement you have with her?"

"No secret."

Despite warnings otherwise, Cliff had made a pile of promises during his inaugural campaign, and keeping a pulse on happenings around town had risen above the rest. You couldn't sneeze in Oak Hill without somebody hearing it and Cliff showing up to whisper, "God bless you."

"Right," I said.

"A man needs to be aware of what's happening in his town, Grace."

A man. His town. Like somebody handed him the deed to the city when he won the vote by a peck. Give a man an inch, right?

"What about the women? We're left for the buzzards?"

"You can park that feminist crap on the sidelines. You know damn well what I meant. Now, are we going to square dance or are you going to guide me to the body?"

"We're preserving it for Macon County."

"Who's our victim?"

"No clue."

Surprise sparkled in his eyes. I recognized the look from years back. Years when the world still could surprise us, more often in severe, cruel ways than the pleasant delights that youthful splendor brought. Like when your best friend sneaks out of town without a whisper of a goodbye or explanation. "And here I thought you could name every soul within city limits."

"I'd wager I could," I said, meaning every word. If Oak Hill was a Guess Who board, I'd clean up. One of the pitfalls of the job. Dirty laundry wasn't a secret, nor was it all that dirty.

"Then what's the issue?"

"An outsider, maybe." I hated myself for letting Margo's words sneak into my mouth. The very act of calling anybody an outsider validated the idea that insiders also existed. The world wasn't that simple. Neither was Oak Hill.

"From where?"

"Keep asking questions you know I can't answer, Cliff."

"Got ID?"

"I'm warning you."

He raised his hands in surrender. "I give. I give." He turned and stared down Munoz from a distance. "You advise him not to say a word to Margo or anybody in town?"

"Don't need to. He knows."

"It's murder?"

I nodded.

"Then be sure and remind him anyway."

"I'll consider it."

"How'd the interview go?"

I grimaced. "You already know the answer to that."

"Thought I'd hear it from you instead of the crows."

"It could have been better."

"Well then, this case is your best shot to earn the job."

My eyes widened. "I assumed they were going with somebody else."

"Your fellow applicants sputtered out when they learned the starting salary."

"Gold diggers."

"A quick win would go a long way to warming over some icy hearts, Grace. I did go to bat for you though."

"Figured you might. Thanks."

"Old friends. Can't make new ones."

"Speaking of, have you heard?"

"Yeah, I—"

"Reyna tell you?"

He turned cherry red. "No, we don't . . . uh." His voice trailed off.

"Have you seen him?"

"No," Cliff said. "And I don't plan to."

"Can't be that bad. You've had fifteen years to let your grudge crumble."

"I'd say it's hardened more than crumbled. Heard anything about Willa?"

"Haven't been over since I heard the diagnosis. I was prepping for the interview, then Margo told me about Sawyer."

"And you didn't book a trip to Miami?"

"Look at my skin, Cliff. If I set foot in Miami, I'd come back a lobster."

"There's such a thing as sunscreen, you know. Hannah reminds me of that every time the sun peeks its head out. Think he'll stick around?" Cliff asked, shifting the toothpick to the other end.

"If you're asking the likelihood of you having to face him, it's high."

"Why?" he asked.

"I don't know. You've got words you've left unsaid for the better part of your life. Questions you want answered. Fate will give you that window."

He studied my face. "You don't have questions?"

"I did," I said. "Until I didn't."

"What changed?"

"That grudge got heavy. And Nat talked some sense into me after a while. Kept on about Sawyer's character and how that doesn't disappear overnight."

"But he did."

"Right," I said. "But Nat's point is that if the Sawyer we loved left without a warning, he must have had a good reason."

"Doesn't take a detective to link it to the accident."

Munoz hollered from afar. In the faint dawn light, I saw the county vehicles steering down the road toward us. Tires crunched on gravel. Cliff pasted on his best mayoral smile and tossed in a new toothpick. Two tired faces frowned at us from inside the van. From the driver's side, a slender woman in her late forties stepped out and stretched toward the sky. She had sharp features with darkened eyes that seemed blacker than night. Shoulder-length black hair framed her face. Once she was limber, she tucked a hand into mine and shook firmly as she smiled. "Tessa Brown, sorry for the long wait."

"Detective Grace Bingham," I said. "And this is Mayor Clifford Rice."

"Mayor," Tessa said. She pointed to her teammate, who had disappeared behind the vehicle. "The worker bee over there is Blake Tucker. He's all business at this hour. Wait until he's two cups deep before you introduce yourself."

"Noted," I said. "Can I lead you to the scene?"

"Please. Later on, we'll need your boot prints for elimination," she said. "And the guy by the road too."

It took everything in my power not to blurt that I'd never seen a dead body before and this was my first murder scene. Our first as a town as far as I knew. But I held it in check.

"Owner of the land lives few hundred yards north," I said. "He heard something on the property. The kind old gent discharged his hound on the supposed intruder, but Lucy didn't return. When Sutton walked out to find her, the pup was sitting next to the body."

Tessa stared down at the body. "And this is no dog bite."

"No, ma'am. I don't think so."

Tessa smiled. "No need to ma'am me. My sore back already reminds me of my age plenty."

"Head wound," Cliff said, the color drained from his face. The toothpick was gone.

"Two," I said. "One in the rear of the skull and one at the top. Blood streaks from both."

"Any ID?" Tessa asked, kneeling closer to the body.

I shook my head.

"That's okay," she said. "We'll find something to identify her. But for now, she's a Jane Doe."

CamCat
Books

VISIT US ONLINE FOR MORE BOOKS TO LIVE IN:
CAMCATBOOKS.COM

SIGN UP FOR CAMCAT'S FICTION NEWSLETTER FOR
COVER REVEALS, EBOOK DEALS, AND MORE EXCLUSIVE CONTENT.

CamCatBooks   @CamCatBooks   @CamCat_Books   @CamCatBooks